The Good Women of Fudi

The
GOOD
WOMEN
of
FUDI

Liu Hong

SCRIBE

Melbourne | London | Minneapolis

Scribe Publications
18–20 Edward St, Brunswick, Victoria 3056, Australia
2 John St, Clerkenwell, London, WC1N 2ES, United Kingdom
3754 Pleasant Ave, Suite 100, Minneapolis, Minnesota 55409, USA

Published by Scribe 2024

Copyright © Liu Hong 2024

All rights reserved. Without limiting the rights under copyright
reserved above, no part of this publication may be reproduced,
stored in or introduced into a retrieval system, or transmitted,
in any form or by any means (electronic, mechanical,
photocopying, recording or otherwise) without the prior
written permission of the publishers of this book.

The moral rights of the author have been asserted.

Typeset in Fournier by the publishers

Printed and bound in the UK by CPI Group (UK) Ltd,
Croydon CR0 4YY

Scribe is committed to the sustainable use of natural resources
and the use of paper products made responsibly from those
resources.

978 1 915590 57 2 (UK edition)
978 1 957363 78 3 (US edition)
978 1 761385 55 1 (ebook)

Catalogue records for this book are available from the
National Library of Australia and the British Library.

scribepublications.com.au
scribepublications.co.uk
scribepublications.com

To Ann, May, and Lily
And to Dade, all my love

Chinese Names

Most Chinese names have a maximum of three syllables. The surname, usually one syllable, comes first. Given names can be either one or two syllables. Those with one syllable in their given name are addressed using their full name, i.e. surname followed by given name — for example, Wu Fang (Wu, surname; Fang, given name) and Li Jian (Li, surname; Jian, given name) — while those with more than one syllable in their given name can be addressed by their given name only — for example, Jiali (Shen being her surname) — especially in an informal setting.

1

'You again,' whispers the lean, muscular East Asian man dressed in Western clothes as the ship approaches the ancient pagoda perched on top of the looming hill.

'Elegant, no?' admires the passenger standing next to him, a tall, blonde European. 'I'm Charles,' he leans over and introduces himself in Chinese, the language the young man had spoken, though Charles has also heard him conversing with the ship's captain in Japanese.

'Elegant, maybe,' says the first man without giving his own name. 'But what does it do for the country? China is filled to the brim with such useless piles of elegance, which foreigners admire, while its people sleepwalk into oblivion. Serves it right to be ruled by the merciless Manchu. Long live Emperor Guangxu!' he mock bows.

The European, affronted, turns his face away. He should have known: another arrogant Japanese man who thinks anything Chinese is inferior. Ever a keen critic of his own culture, Charles does not mind the Japanese's pointed comment about foreigners, but to further dishonour the Chinese, already so humiliated after the Opium War? Charles' own sympathy is, as always, with the underdog — yet the dapper Japanese man speaking enviable Chinese in his Western suit intrigues him: though the man spoke contemptuously of the pagoda and what it stood for, the gaze he gave it was fond.

'Fudi, Fudi!' the hands on deck shout the name again and Charles, knowing its meaning in Chinese, 'The Land of Happiness', gives the approaching land closer scrutiny. Beyond the busy harbour his eyes trace the outline of this pretty Chinese town. It has good feng shui: the green hill with the pagoda on top; the clear open water to the south. The grey, sweeping texture of the rooves that climb the hill; the occasional flash of red, blue, and gold from banners, lanterns, and flags. A picturesque sight, what folks back home imagine China to be like, but can he really make a home here?

The Japanese man, too, leans over the railings of the ship, studying the pagoda with intent; a slight frown creases his otherwise smooth face into a more sympathetic expression and the corners of his long eyes curve a little downwards, softening the earlier impression of sharpness given by his distinctive, well-defined jawline. It is an intriguing face, Charles realises, and he feels compelled to give the man a second chance.

'You know this town well?' he asks.

The Japanese man nods. The hands that grip the railing firmly, Charles notes, are unusually small and delicate, for a man.

'How old is it?' Charles points at the pagoda.

'Late Song Dynasty.'

'So around 800 years.'

'The pagoda itself is not interesting,' the Japanese man dismisses him. 'But the story about the pagoda, that you should hear.'

Charles smiles encouragingly.

The Japanese man continues, 'Once there were two friends:

2

women, who were devoted to each other. Then one fell in love with a scholar, an undeserving, weak man.'

'In what way weak?'

'You will hear. When his lover became pregnant with their child, the scholar met a monk who told him that she was a snake who had deceived him.'

'How shocking!' exclaims Charles. 'A snake …'

'… who had taken on a human form. But why does it matter? Love is love, whatever we are! She had made great sacrifices for him. She traded her shape-shifting magic to stay human. She gave up all her powers.'

Charles is amused, both by the story, and by the young man's emphatic defence of the snake. 'Did he believe the monk, this scholar?'

'He went home, and tricked his lover with sweet words, and got her to drink yellow chrysanthemum wine, just as the monk had told him to, and her true form came out.'

'So there lies on the bridal bed a drunken serpent …'

'… pregnant, and in love.'

Charles conjures up a rather beautiful image of a coiled serpent with glistening silky green skin, exuding serenity. How odd, he thinks: he has always had a morbid fear of snakes. It must be the commanding voice of the Japanese man, which carries such conviction that one can't help but follow him. It is just a story, Charles reminds himself; a foreign story in a foreign country.

'So what did the deceived scholar do?' he asks with good humour.

'When she was sober and had returned to her human form, the scholar begged his lover to release him from their union — I

3

told you, he was weak and did not deserve her.'

'But his was only a very human reaction,' Charles protests. 'You and I would do the same, I'm sure.'

The Japanese man regards him with cool contempt, then moves his eyes away, continuing the story: 'She persuaded him to stay, promised him she would remain his human wife, that her true form would not come out again. But the monk, who was also a shape-shifter, and was jealous of the couple's happiness, would not let that stand.'

'The snake and the monk fought, and the monk won,' Charles nods. The story is beginning to sound familiar: he is sure he's read it, or some version of it, in one of the many Far Eastern journals he had gathered in preparation for his trip. He glances at the pagoda.

The sharp eyes of the Japanese man catch him: 'You know how it ends then.'

'After she gave birth, the monk trapped her in an urn, and buried it …'

'… right underneath the pagoda.'

'What, this exact one?'

The Japanese man becomes vague: 'Might well be. There is a troublesome spirit trapped underneath every Chinese pagoda.' Then he grins, eyes glistening. 'Wouldn't it be the thing to do, to set them all free?'

Charles remembers the rest of the story now: 'It doesn't end there though, does it? Years later, she was set free by none other than her best friend, who had helped deliver the child and had raised him and taught him all the skills necessary to defeat the monk. Isn't there a saying in Chinese: "For a gentleman to revenge a wrong, ten years is not at all late"? She made sure

4

the boy never forgot his mother. Think of the years of practice, patience, and determination.'

'The Black Snake, that was the friend,' the Japanese man murmurs, 'a true friend.'

'And the one that fell in love with a human was the White Snake ... I remember it all now — it is the story of a Peking opera.'

'The only story worth knowing.'

'Why do you say that?'

'Do you know of any other that tells of how women are capable of devotion and faithfulness, not to a man, but to each other?'

Charles swallows. He sees that he was wrong: the Japanese man, far from being arrogant and cold, as he had first thought, is passionate and just — and yet something about the young man still puzzles him.

*

The shore is temptingly close now, but they are delayed in landing due to a sudden, freak local storm — not uncommon in this subtropical part of China. The violence of the storm has driven all below deck, except Charles.

Alone, at the front of the ship, he breathes in deeply: the gust of wind refreshes, welcome, the storm calming the storm within him. He reflects on his earlier conversation with the Japanese man. It had been the first time in three days that he'd ventured out of his cabin, shunning the other westerners on the ship, presenting as an aloof, solitary figure. Grief, still so raw, held him in a comforting tight embrace, into which no one can intrude, and from which Charles did not have the will, nor indeed strength, to unclasp. But something about the young man's manner had aroused Charles' curiosity; perhaps, also, the fact that he spoke such enviable Chinese, for someone from Japan.

Charles cannot explain it, his love for the language and culture of this ancient country, an obsession that started with a trip to a bookshop, aged twelve, where he refused to leave unless his aunt bought him that worn copy of a Chinese astronomy book. 'You won't understand a word of it,' she had said. 'I will learn,' he'd declared.

And he did.

'Blossoms in the mirror, moon in the lake.' His ancient Chinese teacher had given him these enigmatic words as his parting gift before Charles set sail from the other side of the world. When Charles told him what he thought it meant, Teacher Ning pronounced him accomplished in the essence of Chinese language and culture. He had toiled over its notorious tones and unfathomable strokes for so long that now he sing-songs his own tongue while those around him complain that his eyes slant and his smile has become inscrutable. But how can they understand the joys of deciphering yet another elegantly shaped character, ascertaining the meaning of one more pleasing sound? Years of study had led to this job working in the country of his dreams. And yet even as he waved his teary goodbye to his teacher, he still could not comprehend that the words and stories he'd pored over for so long would truly come alive for him now.

So engrossed in his thoughts, Charles almost resents it when another figure slips out onto the deck and comes to stand next to him, though he smiles when he discovers it is the young Japanese man, staring ahead at the darkened sky, cursing softly, still in

Chinese. Now he has warmed to the Japanese man, Charles no longer thinks it odd that the man uses Chinese so much. Charles often catches himself whispering in Chinese, he reflects. He hears the word 'wedding'.

'What's this about a wedding?' Charles shouts over the wind at the crestfallen young man.

'It's today; now, in fact.' The young man wipes the rain from his face. 'I fear I shall miss it.'

'Perhaps they will wait for you.'

'They won't. They had no idea I was coming. I had written to say that I couldn't make it.'

'And then you changed your mind.'

The young man lowers his head. 'I was hoping to surprise her.'

'Who?'

'Her, the bride.'

'What is her name?'

'Shen Jiali.' The Japanese man murmurs the Chinese name softly, then his face breaks into a smile. 'You won't meet the like of her anywhere. Though all of Fudi knows of her beauty and wit, of course, they have no idea how special she truly is.'

'I see,' murmurs Charles. He fears asking the obvious: the Japanese man is most certainly in love with this bride, though how curious that she is a Chinese woman. Unlucky fellow. Arranged marriage is the custom in China, Charles knows from his reading. The young man probably never had a chance. Perhaps this was why he had seemed so grumpy earlier, feeling sorry for himself; Charles quite understands.

'She is a poet and master swordsman.' The man's pride is evident.

'Swordsman?' Charles raises an eyebrow: well-bred Chinese women are often accomplished poets, that much he knows, but a swordsman?

'Yes, a fantastic swordsman, the best!'

'What, with bound feet?'

'She is a Hakka — Hakka women do not bind their feet. But even if she weren't,' the man is adamant, 'she is not the sort of person who would meekly agree to bind her feet — she would have put up a good fight.'

'I see.'

The wind has died down a little. The light shines on the earnest face of the Japanese man, which Charles now finds appealing.

'So, the bride is remarkable,' Charles looks thoughtfully at the Japanese man. 'What of the groom, to match the best of women in China.'

'I can't tell you, for I don't know him well, but I have heard he is a teacher.'

'Oh?' Charles blinks.

'At the naval college. The one with ocean-man style buildings, on the other side of the harbour. It's a new joint venture set up by the Chinese and ...'

'I know about the college.' Charles chuckles, impressed by the man's use of the words 'ocean man' — a term used by the Chinese to refer to foreigners, people from across the ocean. 'In fact ...' He hesitates and then thinks better of it. 'What is he a teacher of?'

'Stars and planets. She has written to me about how clever he is: for each couplet she composes about the moon, he gives a most exact scientific explanation, apparently.' The young man speaks with a hint of sarcasm.

'Isn't science important though? I would imagine this is exactly what China needs right now.'

'You are not Chinese,' the young man dismisses him.

'Neither are you. I must say, for a Japanese …'

'… Japanese, me?'

'Aren't you?' Charles is taken aback: 'I heard you speaking Japanese to the ship's captain in Shanghai, and you are dressed in …'

The youth grins, baring his white teeth like a mischievous child. 'You are not the first to be mistaken. All the way from Tokyo to Shanghai, people assumed I was Japanese, and I enjoyed correcting them. After a while, I did think of putting a label on my chest declaring my true nationality, but I ask you: are the Japanese the only people allowed to wear European-style clothes?'

'Indeed not, indeed not,' Charles nods heartily, caught out, but not at all offended. 'How long have you been away from Fudi for?'

'Two years. I was studying medicine in Japan. I would have become a surgeon if I had stayed, China's first.'

'And now you've missed the wedding, too. So you have interrupted your medical study for nothing. What a shame.'

'But it is worth it,' insists the man. 'I want to see my friend again. And there is now a Western-style hospital in Fudi, run by missionaries. My aim is to get a job there, where I can continue to train.'

Their conversation is interrupted as the sleek ocean liner cruises majestically into the busy harbour, boiling with movement. The traffic goes two ways: crawling up the jetty towards the cavernous opening of the bustling town are those beasts of burdens — coolies weighed down by the heavy cases of opium on their backs — while white-sailed tea clippers are loaded with tightly packed cases of oolong to speed back across the ocean.

'We ruin the Chinese by forcing them to legalise trade in opium,' says one westerner who has emerged on deck; another counters light-heartedly, 'Then they sell us tea, equally addictive.' Charles turns, wanting to see the reaction of the man he now knows to be Chinese to these comments, but can find him nowhere.

In the rush to disembark, he momentarily forgets the Chinese youth, though after he climbs into the carriage, sent by his consul to fetch him from the harbour, Charles sees the man, whose name he still doesn't know, a slight figure leaning over the railings, the last person left on the ship. How desolate he seems, to have missed the wedding.

Charles' carriage trundles up the hill, leaving the harbour behind.

'I have been instructed to take you to the International Club,' the driver explains. Charles nods and leans back. The vivid tropical colours and scents stir his heart. A beautiful and special place, this, the land withholding a secret, he feels. Charles means to discover it, because, for the first time in a long time, he senses peace, hidden somewhere among the damp, indescribable smell.

Peace, Anne, peace, he appeals to the woman the memory of whom evokes both pain and pleasure in equal measures. Anne means peace in Chinese, an apt name given the tremendous feeling of calm he always felt in her presence — surely proof that theirs was a true love, which he has now lost, forever. There has been no peace for him since Anne's gone.

Later, deeper in the hills, his mind drifts back to the Chinese youth. He has a feeling their paths will cross again, not least because the object of the young man's desire is almost certainly married to Charles' new Chinese colleague at the naval college.

*

Alone now, the youth murmurs: 'Jiali, oh Jiali, why wouldn't you wait?'

How exquisite she would have looked in red satin, the traditional dress of a bride, her skin softer than the fabric; now the groom would be leaning gingerly to unveil her, catching sight of the face whose beauty 'obscures the moon and shames the prettiest blossoms'. Oh, how they used to laugh at the crudeness of such cliched lines, and yet, how appropriate they were to describe Jiali. Does she smile and meet his eyes, or is she coy, glancing away? At any rate, what happens between them from now on is theirs only. They are alone, for the wedding guests will have all left by this hour, leaving the two to experience the pleasure that, the youth, eyes closed, murmurs to himself, '"I will never forget, even when I am a toothless old woman."'

The last two lines from the Tang dynasty poem *Wedding Night*. The bride knows these lines well, as does the young man. Sending each other poetry — both ancient, and their own couplets — used to be one of their favourite pasttimes. He lowers his head and hugs himself.

He casts a forlorn figure.

'Wu Fang! Young Mistress — no, I beg your pardon, Young Master! Little Fang.' A chorus of voices makes the youth glance up.

A fine entourage waits eagerly at the shore: a purple silk-covered sedan with carvings of prunus blossom; faithful servants and maids with cushions and fans; friends young and old; and, last but not least, leaning on their sticks, elderly parents, welcoming home their rebellious only child; Wu Fang leans back a little, trying to ascertain from the distance how much they have aged. A sudden feeling of loneliness hits home.

'My little Fang,' murmurs Wu Fang's mother when her child stands in front of her at last.

'Ma, hold me as if I were a girl again!' They embrace, and as the daughter smells the familiar scent of her mother — *oh, home* — she drops a tear.

'We did as you asked and did not tell Jiali that you were returning, so you could surprise her,' her mother smooths the back of Wu Fang's head, 'but I fear you have arrived too late ...'

'I know, I know. The wedding is over.'

'Never mind, my child. You two will soon catch up, old friends that you are.'

Of course she and Jiali will be friends again, but friends as the world knows it, not how they used to be. She should never have gone away.

As the sedan sways along familiar lanes, Wu Fang leans out and greedily takes in the street scenes she has missed so much. Then, leaning back, eyes closed, she sees herself and Jiali as thirteen-year-old girls, kneeling on the stone boat in her father's lake. Poetess and swordmaster. Would-be doctor and herbalist. The world is unjust, and they have a special hatred for marriage: an institution that oppresses women, the pagoda that traps passionate, rebellious snakes.

'I solemnly swear, never to marry, so long as I live,' her own

loud and determined voice announces vehemently.

'I, too, swear, never to marry, for as long as I shall live,' Jiali's softer voice affirms.

2

The moss-covered steps of the pagoda are still wet with morning dew as Wu Fang races to the top, each familiar sensation triggering past memories: the sudden flight of the roosting pheasant — whose hurried feet is it disturbed by? The soft stroke of the moist air tinged with hints of wild garlic, pungent at this time of the year. The sleepy voices of early market people setting up their stalls in the distant harbour … now she is here, Wu Fang can't think why she was so dismissive of the old tower to the European on the ship; so much of her and Jiali's childhood was spent on it. She hears the echoes of her own breathless laughter, not at anything in particular, perhaps merely for the fun of the chase. Wrapped up in their own world, one needed only to say the first half of a sentence before the other finished it.

'*Yanbu is a modernist.*' The name of Jiali's future husband rings from her lips again, to Wu Fang's dismay. '*He is …*'

'*… different.*' Wu Fang's own voice, lower, deeper; she hears the resentment in it now.

'*He is studying at the new naval college, is about to finish actually. He is so good that they will make him a teacher, he wrote. It's … refreshing that he doesn't send in a matchmaker, like the others. Don't you think?*'

'*He doesn't need to, you two have been engaged since you were babies. The others were just trying their luck.*' Her voice is guarded,

14

though Wu Fang remembers trying to sound casual.

'It was a drunken arrangement made between our fathers at a banquet. It wasn't serious.'

'But the Yans are keen now, right?'

'His mother visited us, and brought gifts. But I haven't agreed to meet him properly yet.'

'When was the last time you saw each other?'

'At the funeral of his great uncle, but it was hardly a proper meeting, we just exchanged pleasantries, and all under the watchful eyes of a roomful of ancient relatives. You know how it is at such occasions ...'

'What about his couplets?' Wu Fang interrupts.

Jiali laughs.

'Don't pretend he hasn't written you any. Well, are they any good?' Wu Fang insists.

'Quite, but not good enough. That's why I never bothered to show you.'

Wu Fang relaxes; they still have this between them at least.

That was two years ago, almost to the day. Funny how she remembers this conversation now; at the time it hardly registered.

Jiali's letter, informing her of the formal engagement and the forthcoming wedding, had arrived while Wu Fang was taking her exams in Japan. Though her teachers and fellow students thought her mad, she didn't hesitate: she missed her last exam and made straight for home.

She should have waited for me, Wu Fang thinks bitterly, forgetting for a moment that it was she who has written, deliberately, saying that she would not be back in time for the wedding; she had wanted to surprise Jiali. But then came the storm.

Even if she had made it to the wedding, what then? Nothing can be changed, it all happened. Her best friend is now someone's wife.

She hears the faint sound of a horse's hooves, and hurries back down the hill. The stony steps are harder to navigate than when she climbed up them; the cumbersome ladies' tunic — which her parents had insisted on her wearing — is of course to blame for all these unfamiliar feminine weaknesses: wobbly feet, quickened heartbeat, sweat on her forehead. Damn, she can't stride. As she passes Jiali's old family home, the rumbling red-brick house right next to the pagoda, she hesitates, but all is quiet, and Wu Fang will not disturb its residents: the Shens have a big day ahead. Impatient, she turns onto the path, where the young couple will be certain to appear soon.

*

The awkwardly dressed woman, deep in thought, is first spotted by the groom, inside a sedan, who remarks to his bride, riding a horse alongside him: 'Look, Jiali, a lone woman. She is out early in the morning.'

'She walks funny, Young Mistress,' observes Lanlan, the maid, who rides beside Jiali.

'She has a limp,' determines the bride, narrowing her eyes. 'Let's see what we can do to help.' She tightens her grip on the reins, then pauses, puzzling, 'but how familiar she looks.' Shaking off the feeling, she kicks the mare and they gallop on.

As the sedan catches up, the groom and the rest of the servants hear Jiali let out a muffled cry — alarmingly, as if in pain — then exclaim: 'Oh Buddha! ... It is ... But it can't be!'

They watch Jiali jump off the horse and collapse in front of the woman. Then the two are clasped in a wordless, tight embrace, the only sound the heavy puffing of the two horses and Lanlan's excited voice repeating: 'Miss Wu, Miss Wu. This is unbelievable, unbelievable.'

The hesitant, gentle voice of the groom tears the two apart: 'So it is Miss Wu, after all.'

Wu Fang sighs and steps back: apart from the spectacles on his keen face, the handsome, well-mannered young man standing in front of her is exactly as she had imagined him. At first, she feels relieved — he seems nothing special — then disappointed — surely Jiali's husband should be exceptional.

'My ears have practically grown rusty from hearing your name from Jiali,' Yanbu teases. 'Such an unexpected pleasure.'

'My plans changed; I didn't have time to tell anyone.'

'The surprise is all the sweeter.' He turns to his wife. 'Look how happy you have made Jiali.'

Still clasping Wu Fang, Jiali merely grins.

'But come, let's go in, don't keep your parents waiting,' Yanbu urges, leading the way ahead. The two women follow, eyeing each other with a mix of excitement, curiosity, and affection.

'So funny to see you wearing a tunic!' Jiali laughs, looking Wu Fang up and down. 'In all the time I have missed you, I never imagined you looking like this. Even as you set off for Japan ... I remember it so vividly: you, standing in the rain in a man's gown, crying buckets on my shoulder — like a girl!'

'My parents asked me to wear this, to show respect to your parents. I should not have listened to them, for I know Father and Mother Shen would welcome me as I am, but you,' Wu Fang pushes Jiali away a little to examine her very feminine outfit. 'I guess your days of wearing men's clothes are long gone, now that you are married.'

'Not at all.' Yanbu glances back. 'Jiali shall wear whatever she likes.' He smiles. 'Her eccentricity is what's so special about her.'

'I am not sure my mother-in-law agrees,' whispers Jiali to Wu Fang as soon as Yanbu's back is turned.

*

The generous welcome, typical of the Shens and bestowed equally onto Wu Fang and Yanbu, produces the curious effect of making Wu Fang feel incensed; she sees in every speech and gesture clear signs of Yanbu's provocation and triumph. How dare he look at Jiali in that way? How maddening that he refers to her as 'mine'? What a shock to hear him calling the Shens 'Father' and 'Mother', bowing, producing gifts of fruit and cakes that are heartily accepted by the two she had always considered additional parents!

The family dog stands up for justice. Ignoring Yanbu's solicitous hands, Zhuzi makes straight for Wu Fang, an offering of someone's shoe between his teeth, tail erect, head seeking her hands, responding to her keen rub by circling around her, making loud, joyful whines that draw everyone's attention.

Jiali, laughing, wrestles the shoe off the dog. Leaning down to rub its back, she whispers to Wu Fang: 'Zhuzi remembers you! He never took to Yanbu, I have no idea why.'

'Really?' Wu Fang beams.

'Father said it was because of Yanbu's spectacles, but I think it's just because Zhuzi is getting on and set in his ways.'

'Silly old thing.'

The exchange, though brief and seemingly trivial, lifts Wu Fang's mood and she remains in good spirits until the time comes for the newlyweds to say goodbye. Zhuzi, by now Wu Fang's steadfast guardian, sits up; alert to Jiali and Yanbu's movements, the dog turns his face to Wu Fang inquiringly. It occurs to Wu Fang that she has not had a moment alone with Jiali, something she had previously taken for granted. To request one now seems wildly inappropriate. She rises also and follows the couple out of the Shens' front door, feeling like an actor in a play. Whatever the others say, she nods and repeats, a wooden smile on her face, a stiff and sore pair of sticks for legs, moving of their own accord.

They wave until the entourage is out of sight. Only then does Wu Fang notice their transport arrangement. Nothing else had registered upon their first meeting besides the excitement of seeing Jiali after so long.

'I'm glad to see her in-laws let her return home on horseback,' she remarks, 'Naturally, Jiali rode a sedan at their wedding?'

Her eyes still on the empty path, Mother Shen smiles. 'Yes, she did, to be mindful of her mother-in-law's feelings. But this morning, they swapped as soon as they left his home. It was Yanbu's idea, Jiali told me. A very considerate young man, not at all like his … more traditionally minded mother. Will you stay for supper?'

*

When she is finally home, Wu Fang is a sight to behold. Dismissing the concerns of the old, faithful door man, who at first takes her for a beggar, she rushes to change out of her tunic before going to see her parents, who are anxiously waiting.

LIU HONG

Two separate carriages had been sent to fetch her, and both had returned empty. Where had she been all this time, in the rain, in the dark? Had she been robbed? Her long-suffering mother and father are full of questions.

She laughs, feeling her buoyant self return now that she is back in a man's attire.

'What a ridiculous idea. A man who would dare to rob me has not yet been born!'

'What took you so long then? You left first thing in the morning. Were you lost?' questions her mother.

'Me, lost in Fudi? Do you forget I've crossed oceans?'

'Fudi has changed so much in the last few years. China itself is no longer the country you left!' warns her father.

'China is never the country we want it to be, and we know who to blame.'

'Wu Fang, hush! You should not talk so loudly of such things.' Her father's voice grows weary. 'You are no longer a child. We were the talk of the neighbourhood with you riding about town dressed as a man and going abroad on your own; we have indulged you, but now you must ...'

'Settle and get married?'

'Why not?' says her mother. 'Jiali has, though of course she and Yanbu were engaged since they were children, so it was not a surprise.'

'She wasn't going to marry him.'

'Oh?'

'Father Shen fell while gathering herbs; Yanbu happened to be passing by and saved him, so they told me tonight. Jiali felt that she owed him for her father's life.'

Wu Fang's mother nods her approval at such filial devotion,

20

though Wu Fang herself is convinced that the Shens, of a generous nature, must have exaggerated the part Yanbu played in the rescue of Father Shen.

'She went ahead, even though her parents told her not to rush into a marriage, not for their sake!'

'You must admit they are a perfect match,' smiles Mother Shen.

'I see why the Shens felt grateful to Yanbu, but I just don't understand why she had to marry him.'

'Nobody forced her,' her mother says.

'He did! Ever since the accident he pressured her, visiting day and night, sending pages and pages of couplets ...'

'Couplets?'

'Oh, she has this rule about her suitors having to match her couplets.'

'Then he must be a clever and persuasive young man, for we all know the Shens have high standards, their literary reputation ...' approves her father.

'Why should it be Yanbu that happened to pass by?' Wu Fang groans.

'You don't sound very happy about the marriage,' chides Mother Shen.

'I feel sad for any woman who has to marry. It's a prison.'

'There you go again,' her mother muses. 'How you two used to talk! Such childish ideas — swearing never to marry, as if you can be spared the fate of all women.'

'The fate of all women does not have to be ours.'

'You just saw Jiali. Did she seem happy?'

'Well ...'

'Well then.' Wu Fang's parents exchange looks.

*

The night brings two notes for Wu Fang. The first, delivered by a servant from the Yan household, is written in Jiali's familiar elegant handwriting: *Yanbu will return to college the day after next, come.* The second note arrives much later, nobody having seen the messenger, and is written in a way that would confuse any other reader.

All are fast asleep as the young mistress turns on the lamp and writes her replies in earnest. Time alone with Jiali is something she feels entitled to, and yet she is also a little nervous of the prospect. Wu Fang leans back and closes her eyes. Now, finally, she allows herself the luxury of remembering the delicious moment on the path when Jiali had first recognised her: the catch in her voice, the joyous scream, the rosy cheeks. It always surprises Wu Fang that the world does not stop the moment Jiali does or says anything. She is even more heartbreakingly brilliant than Wu Fang remembered, and her obvious delight in seeing her old friend cheers Wu Fang, bringing a grin to her face.

Having sealed her letter to Jiali, she glances over to the second note: the seemingly harmless words 'gathering' and 'harvesting', she knows, are codes for more daring activities; words whose true meaning it would never do for her parents to discover. In Japan, the prospect of these activities had filled her heart with excitement, but now, she feels dread, not for herself, but of what the implications could be for those that she loves. Is she making a mistake involving herself in this?

3

Leaning against the doorway to his study, empty now he is back at the naval college, Wu Fang imagines Yanbu the scholar: dignified, content, sitting with his back to the world, the table in front of him adorned with astronomical maps and books with ruled columns headed 'Object', 'Right Ascension', 'Declination' — a strictly ordered, meticulously catalogued world of stars. The room smells of old oak furniture and is dark. She only has their brief meeting two days ago to go on, and yet she thinks she knows the type of man he is: dependable, clever, easy going, the sort of young man her parents want for her, too. Her going away to Japan for two years did not at all dampen their enthusiasm for matchmaking, and Jiali's marriage has added fuel to their fervour. Her visit to the Yans today was very much encouraged by them: 'Go and see for yourself,' they said, 'how happy Jiali is being married, if you don't believe us.'

'… and so I sleep here, and him there,' Jiali was saying.

Wu Fang swings back into the bedroom, where Jiali stands. 'What?'

'As I said, he in the study and I on this bed.'

'I don't understand.'

'Have you not been listening?' Jiali laughs. 'He didn't match my couplets.'

'But you are married.'

'He knows that's out of gratitude for saving Pa's life. We've agreed that we would take our time. He mustn't rush me.'

Wu Fang, fists uncurling, sinks down on the bed.

'Where is your wedding outfit?' she whispers.

'Why?'

'Put it on.'

'What, now?'

'Why not? I have a picture of you wearing it in my mind, from when I was on the ship, and since I missed the wedding, you owe it to me.'

'All right,' Jiali says cheerfully. Still chatting, she strips off her blue day-gown, steps out of it, standing in her white undergarments.

'How fit you look,' Wu Fang admires; there is indeed something different about Jiali's figure, something she can't quite put her fingers on. Or is it her mind playing tricks on her? Jiali is married, she must be different somehow, Wu Fang thinks vaguely. Things haven't felt real for a while, not since she came back.

Still Jiali stands, holding the bridal gown.

'What are you waiting for?'

'The top,' Jiali murmurs, 'It's not here.' She potters about the room in bare feet, opening and shutting drawers. Wu Fang's eyes follow her. Even half dressed, Jiali possesses a natural ease that draws one's eyes, and Wu Fang can no more resist watching her closely than a stranger in the street could. Jiali remains unaware, speaking half to herself, puzzling. Bedding and clothes are strewn about as she searches half-heartedly. Then, at her appeal, Wu Fang joins in the hunt, and discovers many curious items of clothing she has no name for and has to be educated on, but the wedding top is nowhere to be found. Lanlan is called for and consulted, and, after the briefest pause, locates the item in Yanbu's study.

'What on earth is it doing there?' Jiali asks.

Lanlan blinks: 'The young master had it in his hand last night, sitting by his desk. He seemed to be studying the peony pattern quite diligently, as he brought the top up close to his face and …'

Jiali blushes and snatches the top from Lanlan. 'Enough, thank you Lanlan. Now go and make us tea!'

'So he is keen,' Wu Fang speaks in an ordinary voice. 'Has he never tried anything, at all?' She adjusts the collar for Jiali, and buttons the top from the waist upwards.

'Well,' Jiali's eyes are down, following Wu Fang's fingers on the buttons, 'the wedding night was certainly strange.'

'Tell.'

'To start off, he called me "Elder sister". It was how he used to address me, but somehow, on the night, it sounded all wrong. His voice, too, was thin and pinched, I guess he was nervous, as was I.'

'Go on.'

'At first he was really shocked that I asked him to match my couplet.'

'That was silly of him. I am sure he was just pretending to have forgotten.'

'Then I asked him if he was curious to know more about me.'

'What did he say?'

She pinches her nose and assumes a stiff voice: '"Of course. But we will get to know each other by and by. Elder sister, we

25

match, that is the most important thing. Your wit and beauty, my ... position in the New Learning."' She bursts into a giggle.

'What pompous words! I wonder if you didn't throw him out then?'

Fully attired now in her wedding clothes, Jiali sits cross-legged on the bed. Wu Fang stares at her, lost for words. On the ship, she'd had a thousand thoughts of how Jiali would look as a bride, but now Jiali is in front of her, Wu Fang finds it unsettling: for though she smiles broadly and looks the picture of contentment, Jiali has not transformed into another person. It feels as though Jiali had simply changed into another set of clothes. *I guess I should be pleased about this,* Wu Fang tells herself, but then, begrudgingly: *why marry, if you don't seem any happier?*

'What is it?' Jiali laughs.

Wu Fang collects herself, 'Well? Did you throw him out then?'

'He saved himself by showing me the night sky. Wu Fang, he knows so much about the stars!' Jiali plays with the strips of the veil's red tassels and beams. 'His voice changed when he talked about them — the voice of Yanbu the teacher — and it was as if the stars he showed me had been picked from an immense trunk of treasure and laid in front of me as jewels. He had transformed; he was forgiven.'

'I suppose he does know his stuff.' Though she is agreeing, Wu Fang's voice is dismissive. *If it's an astronomy lesson you need,* she wishes to say, *I could have taught you! You did not need to marry the teacher.*

Jiali continues: 'You know, you can view the stars more closely through something called a telescope, which he says he will show me one day, and ...'

'But as to the couplets, he did nothing.'

'As a matter of fact, he quoted Zhang Heng.'

'Not "The Wedding Night"?'

Jiali nods.

The words echo in the minds of both women, though neither speak them aloud: *I wish to be the straw mat, covering the bed you sleep on, or the soft silk quilt, on top of you, sheltering you from wind and frost; No man alive has ever seen a sight such as this, No pleasure can ever match this one of ours tonight …*

'What if he never matches your couplet?' Wu Fang eventually asks.

'Then we never consummate the marriage — he has given me his word of honour.'

'And you trust him?'

'I do.'

'Really?'

They lock eyes. Then, slowly Wu Fang takes the red veil from Jiali's hand and drapes it over her friend's head.

'This will complete the look,' she whispers.

'Come on, you are him. Remove my veil,' Jiali urges.

Though Jiali keeps still, her breath causes the veil to stir ever so softly. Wu Fang feels light-headed: the red-veiled Jiali in her red wedding outfit is a ball of fire that draws Wu Fang in and frightens her a little. As she reaches out a hand gingerly, she hears their girlish giggles:

'Go on,' young Jiali's soft voice, suppressing laughter.

'I'm coming, darling!' Wu Fang's own, deliberately rougher, as she stretches out a hand to the quivering being in front of her, a scarf stolen from Wu Fang's mother playing the part of Jiali's wedding veil.

'Darling? You call me darling?' Feigned shock.

Then Wu Fang's hand starts shaking, as she begins to laugh uncontrollably …

How many times, as young girls, the two had played this game of 'getting married': herself, the groom, pulling the veil off Jiali, the bride. They stopped, of course, when they came to understand what marriage might actually mean for them, vehemently pledging against it, but now … With mixed feelings Wu Fang reaches out a hand to touch the veil, just as Jiali, laughing loudly, flips it off herself, grasps hold of Wu Fang's hand, and pulls her forcibly onto the bed. 'Oh, I miss this; I missed you; I missed us!'

She wrestles Wu Fang and pins her to the bed. Like children again, they tickle each other, laughing breathlessly.

*

For … how long? Neither of them have any idea of the time, but a gust of cold air rushes in bringing with it a voice that cuts like a knife: 'Get up, you two.'

A tall, thin woman, shrouded in black, with a stiff back, stands in front of them, with Wang Ma, a wrinkled-faced maid, next to her.

'Mother,' Jiali rises, catching her breath, traces of a smile still on her face.

'Barely five days married, how can you face your husband?' the stern voice of Jiali's mother-in-law thunders.

'Yanbu? He won't mind, he's met Wu Fang …'

'How dare you?' The older woman strides towards the bed, her pale face frozen in shock and anger. 'Entertaining a man in your bedroom, letting him touch you.' Ignoring Wu Fang, who is now standing with her arms crossed in front of her chest, the woman keeps her gaze on Jiali. 'I can hardly believe my eyes, and indeed when Wang Ma told me, I did not believe her. I had to see for myself. I've always known there is something not quite right! Now, what have you got to say for yourself?'

'Mrs Yan,' sighs Wu Fang, stepping forward, 'perhaps I am the one you should interrogate.'

'Who are you? And what's stopping me from calling the yamen to have you whipped?'

'I beg you not to do anything hasty, Mrs Yan.' Wu Fang bows, deep, slow, and close enough for the woman to see the heaving, ample bosom underneath her man's gown. 'I am Wu Fang, the daughter of Wu Guangzu of Fudi, glad to be making your acquaintance. I assure you my visit to your daughter-in-law's boudoir does not warrant such an extreme reaction.'

Lanlan, hovering by the door, speaks in a loud voice to the other maid. 'I did announce Miss Wu's arrival ...'

Wang Ma, annoyed, leans over to her mistress and whispers something in her ear.

Mrs Yan's rigid face goes through several transformations: she frowns, she snarls, then comes the tightening of her jaw, and the shutting of her eyes. When her eyes open again, her muscles soften, and a smile is wrinkled out: 'Well, well, a flood has washed away the temple of the River Dragon! A most unfortunate misunderstanding. We are of course honoured to have you here, Miss Wu, I apologise profoundly for the stupid blunders of my servants.'

She sighs heavily, and reaches out a slender, long-nailed hand — slowly, as if she has all the time in the world — to smooth back her tightly held-up hair, which is tied in a bun at the back of her head. A seemingly casual gesture, but somehow, the contrast between the sharpness of her nail and her slow, deliberate action impresses Jiali deeply, and makes her shudder.

*

After this, they are left alone, and Wu Fang takes her time showering Jiali with presents from Japan: cards, prints, books, new and curious men's clothes, which draw exclamations from both Jiali and Lanlan. Certain that her mother-in-law will not be back today, Jiali changes into a set of the latest Western fashion, complete with a stiff black top hat, and is greatly admired by the other two.

They go out into the now-dim courtyard, where Jiali draws her sword from its leather case. Almost playfully, she pierces the night air with the tip, then, stepping back, twisting her wrist just a little, she slices open the darkness in a perfect arch with one sweep of the sharp blade.

Wu Fang puts her teacup down, her muscles tingling in anticipation of Jiali's moves.

Holding the sword in her left hand and leaning on her left leg, Jiali arches her right foot, straining it in front of her, her breathing long and deliberate as her toes tighten into the familiar shape. The sword changes hand and she stretches the other foot. Sparkles of satisfying pain shoot over her, and Wu Fang sighs; the courtyard holds its breath, listening, watching its new mistress stamp her square Hakka feet, doing her round of its four corners, thorough as a territorial beast. Sweep, slice, swoop, the downward thrust and the upward flight of the sword in her hand, the rhythm of two fast-beating hearts.

'Fetch me another sword,' Wu Fang whispers, unable to resist.

A little out of practice, she circles around Jiali, before stepping within striking distance of her sword, and the two start sparring.

Fine, pearly beads of sweat form on Jiali's forehead. It's harder for her now that Wu Fang has joined, as, having the same sword master, whatever step Jiali takes, the two have practised hundreds of times together. Every move can be anticipated, but what fun to spar together again! As the swords warm in their hands, there emerges that familiar, spontaneous joy between them; the sensation that everything around them connects somehow. A cry of satisfaction bursts forth from one chest, and the fast dance of one sword brings about another in the second — an exclamation of admiration: 'I did not think it possible, but you are even better than before!' cries Wu Fang, stepping aside.

'The mistress never stops practising,' says Lanlan, bringing out more tea.

'And it shows,' nods Wu Fang. Though she is tired, she is happy: here they both are, just like in the old days. 'Do you remember our first lesson, with Master Gu?' she asks, wiping sweat from her brow.

'How can I forget?' Jiali smiles. 'To my eternal shame, I did not think much of him when father first introduced him, for he dressed shabbily, like a beggar.'

The air is still with expectation and there is a look of reverence in Father Shen's eyes, which, even at the age of twelve, having only just outgrown marriage games, impresses Wu Fang.

The young man spends what seems like forever holding the

31

sword, with his eyes closed. But then, suddenly, as if carried by a sweep of wind from nowhere, both man and sword are up in the air. They become one twirling, swirling, fast-moving ball. It is also a kind of dance, the most beautiful dance the girls have ever seen. The man's poor attire is instantly forgotten.

'I want to learn,' cries out Jiali, while Wu Fang stands in silent awe. Then, shyly, she also steps forward: 'Me, too.'

'Good,' the young master responds. 'First lesson, breathe.'

'We know how to breathe,' Jiali whispers.

'Not properly. Nobody knows how to at first. I didn't,' the young man says, 'For the first three years of my apprenticeship with my own master in Lao Mountain, I did nothing but chop wood for the monastery, and learn how to breathe.'

Morning, then, becomes the time when they practise breathing, for that is the best time of the day, those precious hours before the world begins, when yang energy is on the rise. The two girls sit side by side on a mat placed on the stone boat in Wu Fang's garden, inhaling and exhaling deliberately: in time their shallow, random, childish breaths deepen into long, deliberate ones; their rhythms match, and they breathe as one.

Sighing deeply, Wu Fang opens her eyes as Jiali's hand touches her arm, bringing her back from the past.

'I've always wondered,' Wu Fang says, 'why Father Shen brought Master Gu to us.'

'Master Gu was one of Dad's patients. When Dad learned he was a kung-fu master, he couldn't resist asking him to teach us.' Jiali puts on a rougher voice: '"Since you girls will not take husbands, you better know how to fend for yourselves!"'

Wu Fang laughs: 'Did he really say that? I forgot.'

'Well, we were always climbing trees and fighting with

boys, giving our parents headaches. I think father was looking for a way to rein us in; perhaps to test us. He said he wasn't sure that we would have persevered with it, and was rather surprised that we did.'

'That is very much due to our teacher — what an extraordinary man he was, Master Gu,' Wu Fang sighs again.

'Oh, I miss him so much,' says Jiali.

'I still find it unbearable, the way he died. When you wrote to tell me, I wanted to race back across the sea to tear right into those fat Manchu Mandarins, to avenge him.'

'Father was worried about me, too. For a long time, he would not let me go and pay respect at Master Gu's tomb, even though he himself tended to it often.'

'Father Shen was right to protect you. You can't be too careful.'

'But one cannot live with all this ugliness and turn a blind eye!'

'Jiali!' Wu Fang is overcome: even though Jiali has broken their pact, her old friend is still the just and passionate girl Wu Fang has known her whole life. There are so many more things she wants to say to her friend, adventures to share, secrets to unburden, but where to begin?

'Stay the night, Mistress Wu,' Lanlan beseeches, as if reading her thoughts.

Wu Fang laughs, 'I wasn't going to, but after that visit from your old mistress, I just might.'

Lanlan steals a glance at Jiali.

'On the first night, she made my mistress cook the same dish three times!'

'I got it right the fourth time though, didn't I?' Jiali responds.

'Now I know she likes very salty food.'

'How dare she!' Wu Fang is incredulous. 'And how could you put up with this?'

'It's not as if I have to cook every day,' Jiali hurries to soothe her friend, 'It's just a tradition: a new bride is meant to cook for the family on her first day in her new home.'

'To give them all the satisfaction of picking on her? That's exactly what I hate about these so-called traditions, putting women down, pressing our heads low, and not just from men, but other women, too!'

'Nonsense! My sisters-in-law are sweet to me.'

Lanlan evidently disagrees.

'I forgot to tell you, mistress, the younger Miss Yan came again today to borrow your hairpin, while you were with the old mistress.'

'You know I don't need that many hair pins. Give Mochou as many as she wants.'

'I said I would find them for her, but she insisted on rummaging through your jewellery box herself!'

'She was just curious.'

'No, mistress. Her elder sister sent her, and they …'

'Lanlan, stop! Do not be so mean. You know the girls need all the understanding we can give them.' Turning to Wu Fang, she says: 'My two little sisters are both orphans. My mother-in-law was kind enough to adopt them.'

'Kind?' Lanlan rolls her eyes. 'She was lonely and needed company. She uses them as playthings when she is bored and maids when she needs things done.'

'Lanlan!' Jiali is outraged.

'It's what Wang Ma told us.'

'Don't believe everything Wang Ma says. Now, we are both hungry, please bring food,' Jiali instructs the maid.

'Good girl!' Wu Fang nods as Lanlan retreats into the house. 'With her by your side, at least I will know if things are worse than you say. She will not keep silent.'

'Don't fuss. I know how to look after myself. They are not bad people, just old-fashioned.'

'That's just like you, always too generous.'

'Wu Fang, let's not talk about my new family any more. Tell me more about that funny professor who never guessed you were a woman.'

How many times has she dreamt of this, Wu Fang wonders, telling Jiali about her life in Japan, properly, thoroughly, the good and bad of it all, holding her hands and looking into her eyes. And now here she is, holding Jiali's hands, looking into her eyes, yet somehow, something is amiss. The wrong words come out. *When I climbed Mount Fuji, you were with me,* she wants to say, but instead she says, 'I wished you were there.' It sounds so much less than what she truly felt. Jiali's look of disgust and concern when she hears about the time Wu Fang had to run with a dead man's arm to the freezer in the basement of the teaching hospital is the opposite of the giggle Wu Fang imagined sharing with her friend. Time has wedged them apart, just a little, but apart nonetheless.

For you I have given up my dream of being a surgeon. There are things she can never say.

The night growing colder, they move inside.

'A shame that you did not complete the course,' sighs Jiali.

'Ma's health matters, and Pa is not getting any younger.' The lie comes easily enough.

'I so wanted you to be our first female surgeon.'

Wu Fang's heart melts. 'I might still be one. I won't stop learning.' Then, a worrying thought casts a shadow over her happiness: 'How long is Yanbu going to be away?'

'Two months. As a teacher at the naval college, he is obliged to stay there during term time. His next home leave is the Mid-Autumn Festival.'

Wu Fang breathes a long sigh of relief: two months is long enough for now, to catch up properly with Jiali.

4

The country inn is filling up fast, and it being warm, Wu Fang chooses a table outside. A few people give her curious looks and she glances down at herself. Has a sash strayed from underneath her man's gown? Is her hair combed the right way to disguise her feminine fringe? The checks are half-hearted though; she is used to being stared at. She far prefers that this eccentric habit is what draws the town's attention to her and not other things.

Her wine cup nearly empty, Wu Fang cranes her head, straining to see down the path; knowing that Jiali and Lanlan will come dressed as men, she has mistaken a few on horseback for the pair already. It is not like Jiali to be late.

Wu Fang has not returned to the Yans' since that first night, despite promising her friend she would. She claimed to be undertaking medical training in Shanghai, though she has mainly been riding around the county meeting people and making plans of the sort best kept discreet. Jiali will find out eventually, but Wu Fang wishes to spare her the worry for as long as possible.

They had talked well into the small hours that night, and yet for Wu Fang, much had remained unsaid, or unsayable. Alone outside the inn now, Wu Fang feels her frustration acutely: true, she had been the one to leave China, but Jiali had abandoned their ideals and married a man, surely a bigger betrayal. And yet there hadn't been any intimacy between the two newlyweds.

37

But how long can a marriage remain unconsummated? Despite Jiali's reassurances, Wu Fang has doubts: Yanbu might never match Jiali's couplets, but he could gain her heart through other means — Jiali's face lit up when she told Wu Fang about the stars Yanbu had shown her.

Wu Fang shakes her head, the better to banish this image, but now another picture comes to her, also of Jiali, smiling again, on the eve of Wu Fang's departure for Japan, as the two sat drinking late into the night.

'And anyway, even if he is the modern-day Li Bai and has the riches of the Dragon King, I will not marry him.' Fixing her eyes on Wu Fang, Jiali nods. 'No man is worth the trouble!'

How proud and determined Jiali had looked then.

Wu Fang laughs bitterly now, to think that they were both naïve enough to believe sincerely that Jiali especially, could remain unmarried forever.

A commotion alerts her to Lanlan's lone presence on horseback.

'Women these days!' slurps a drunk man at the next table. 'Out riding in broad daylight, no sense of propriety! Look at her, not even bothering to cover her head!'

Wu Fang now sees that that though Lanlan is wearing a man's gown, her head is indeed bare, showing her womanly hair. Spotting Wu Fang, Lanlan waves frantically with her hat in her hand.

'See there,' the man continues, scandalised, 'she even dares to call for attention, a real slut.'

'Say that again.' Wu Fang speaks sharply.

'A woman's place is in bed and by the fireplace,' the man sneers. 'If she was mine ...'

Wu Fang rises, her hand reaching habitually to her sword. But Lanlan waves again, more urgently. Something is up. Wu Fang glares at the man, 'Lucky for you, I am in a rush.'

*

They ride the steep way up the hill at Lanlan's suggestion, to approach the Shens' house from the back. Shouts can already be heard as they near the garden that backs on to the pagoda. Wu Fang turns to Lanlan: 'Go in and tell your mistress I am here, and stay with her.'

'But where are you going?'

'To reason with those men over there of course.' She nods in the direction of the house and passes Lanlan the reins to her horse.

'Old Master has tried, but they wouldn't budge. Old Mistress wanted to send for the yamen, but Young Mistress stopped her. She didn't want these people arrested.'

'That is wise.'

'But will they listen to you?'

'I happen to know some of them. Now go.'

Only half convinced, Lanlan nonetheless obeys. Experience has told her to always listen to Miss Wu.

*

The sudden appearance of the blue-gowned figure does not cause a stir at first, but soon a hush falls across the restless crowd, as if a cool breeze is blowing; eyes are drawn to the lean, upright figure, whose steady steps and quiet demeanour command attention. A low whisper can be heard, an attentive ring forming around Wu Fang, who nods and speaks in an almost inaudible voice to the group of rough-looking men who but a minute ago had bayed for blood.

*

Father Shen has treated men and women, young and old, and is used to the sight of wounds and suffering. The most violent men become subdued in his presence, and he in turn is oblivious to threats. He heals and that's that. The man laid in front of him, just coming to, brought in by his daughter on her way to meet Wu Fang, is an ocean man, a foreigner, Father Shen's first, though in his mind there is no difference. The face behind the yellow beard is young, and the eyes now opening slowly speak of gratitude, a universal language Father Shen understands well.

Outside, the crowd is dispersing. Father Shen observes the odd way Wu Fang bids goodbye to some of the men, putting her right arm over the left and bowing. The men return the same gesture, perhaps some new fashion she's picked up in Japan, Father Shen muses absent-mindedly, as he glances up from the jars of herbs he is mixing.

When Wu Fang enters the house through the front door, her eyes still getting used to the darkness within, she hears a voice exclaim, 'It's you! The surgeon, China's first!'

The ocean man Jiali has rescued is Charles, Wu Fang's fellow passenger on board the ship from Shanghai, who had mistaken her for a Japanese man. Against the advice of fellow Fudi Europeans, he explains, he has been straying into 'no-go' areas and today paid the price for his curiosity: a crowd followed him when he lingered in the market, tempted by the sweet scent of ripe mangos, and by the time he got to the pagoda they gave chase; stones were thrown, and he was hit in the head and fell. 'Worse would have occurred had not this kind gentleman,' he says, pointing at Jiali, 'and his servant,' pointing at Lanlan, 'happened to be passing by, and dragged me here for shelter.'

Wu Fang nods, telling herself that the European, who struck her on the ship as more sympathetic to the Chinese than his kin usually are, must have unwittingly said or done something to provoke the crowds. Such things do happen. She leans to check his injuries, batting away Zhuzi who is circling around her. Finally, she nods: as she expected, Father Shen's bitter herbs have done wonders and there is nothing else she needs to do.

'So, you two have met before?' asks Jiali curiously.

'On the ship from Shanghai,' Wu Fangs smiles. 'I told him a story and he thought me Japanese.'

Feeling perkier, Charles is full of questions: 'Were you accepted by the hospital?' he asks eagerly.

'I had my interview, and I start work there next week.' Turning to Jiali, she beams. 'I haven't had time to tell you this …'

'And … did you make it to the wedding, after all?' Charles interrupts almost impatiently.

'No.'

'But you have met up with the bride again?'

'Oh yes, many times.' Wu Fang winks at Jiali.

'And everything is all right between you?'

'I believe so.'

'The groom is … happy to see you, too?'

'So he said,' Wu Fang giggles. 'Here, ask the bride yourself.'

She places her arms around Jiali, astonishing Charles, who sees two men hug. It is the kindly Father Shen who rescues Charles with the words, 'Now then girls, enough. Do explain this strange habit of yours, always dressing as men, to the foreign gentleman.'

*

The afternoon flies by. Charles' face is darker since he was on the ship, and his Chinese, Wu Fang notices, has taken on a Fudi twang. The revelation of the two women's true identities seems to unsettle him at first, but Jiali is able to draw him out, of course, as she is apt to do even with her father's most nervous patients. Before long they learn, to their astonishment, that the European knows Yanbu, quite well in fact, for the two teach the same subject — astronomy — at the naval college.

'On the ship,' Charles, now used to the sight of the two women dressed as men — indeed liking it, to his own surprise — reminds Wu Fang, 'when you mentioned the wedding and the groom being a teacher at the college ...'

'Oh yes,' Wu Fang nods, laughing. 'I thought you looked a bit odd ...'

'The way you talked about the marriage, I thought it best that I keep quiet the fact that I was going to teach at the college.'

'Why, what did you say about my marriage?' Jiali becomes interested, as are her parents.

'Well ...' Suddenly Charles is tongue-tied. He can't very well say that Wu Fang had been disparaging about Yanbu. Indeed, the reason he had kept quiet about his encounter with Wu Fang on the ship to Yanbu, with whom he has increasingly got on, was the odd tone of voice Wu Fang had adopted when talking about Jiali's groom.

'What about my marriage?' Jiali insists, looking first at Wu Fang, then at Charles. Wu Fang blushes, also tongue-tied, an unusual state of being for her.

Even as he still puzzles, Charles realises he has to rescue the good woman: 'Nothing at all about there being anything wrong with your marriage,' he reassures. 'It was simply that Wu Fang seemed very upset to be missing the wedding and was praising you so much that I was worried she might be in love with you herself.'

'Of course, you thought her a man!' Mother Shen laughs innocently.

'Exactly.' Charles nods, grateful for her words. 'She made such a dashing figure I considered her a real threat to the groom!'

Wu Fang blushes again, but the others laugh, thinking nothing of it.

'So, what's he like, Yanbu, at work?' Jiali asks eagerly.

'He's a knowledgeable, patient teacher, and a most considerate colleague,' Charles smiles, 'well liked by pupils and well respected by us all. I think he will get a promotion soon.' Charles does indeed have a soft spot for Yanbu, even though he thinks all the Chinese staff excellent; that is, despite the huge discrepancy in pay and condition between Chinese and ocean employees. No one seems to mind that ocean staff like him are allowed to roam around Fudi, whereas the Chinese are all supposed to stay at the college during term times, except in special circumstances such as festivals and family events.

'In fact, I am sure he will. He well deserves it,' emphasises Charles, with a slight feeling of guilt.

'Well, well.' Wu Fang nods to Jiali, who smiles briefly, then lowers her head down to examine Charles' wounded forehead, still smeared with a dark-brown paste of herbs, and asks: 'Does it hurt much?'

'Hardly!' beams Charles, then: 'I owe my life to you all.' He looks in turn to each of them, then settles his eyes back on Jiali. 'I still can't quite believe the speed you rode off with me. What a heavy sack I must have been!'

Jiali murmurs, 'It's nothing.'

'It is quite something to write home about, me being rescued by a Chinese woman.'

'Do they expect us to be helpless maidens?' Jiali blinks.

Charles shakes his head. 'You would not believe what Europeans think of Chinese women if I told you.'

'You would not believe what they think of anyone Chinese if I told you!' cuts in Wu Fang curtly.

'I am quite ashamed,' says Charles, in a serious tone of voice, 'at the arrogance of some of my countrymen.'

'But it's still wrong for our people to pick on you,' sighs Mother Shen. 'You were only browsing in the market.'

'I do understand that the wars have not earned us Europeans any favours in China. I am not proud of that, and I was naïve, if not downright foolish, to mention the conflict to the man selling the mangos. I had wanted to start a conversation, but he took it the wrong way. I don't blame him at all for being offended, but I hadn't reckoned with the anger of the crowd.'

'Ah, I did wonder.' Wu Fang sighs. 'You see, for many of the Chinese, even the presence of ocean people here is an insult,' she says in a low voice. 'You must have heard of the incident in Yuandong?'

'The five Western missionaries who were killed?' Charles whispers, 'Yes, of course.'

'Twenty Chinese villagers were beheaded afterwards by the local yamen, to placate the foreigners; some were mere boys.'

'That was terrible.' Charles sighs. 'Considering the injustice being done, I really should have been more sensitive. It could have been much worse. I came off lightly.'

'The more the Manchus side with them, the less popular ocean people are.' Father Shen gestures to his pigtails in disgust. 'And the Manchus force us Hans to wear this ...'

Mother Shen rises, interrupting him, exclaiming that the rice must by now be overcooked.

As the pleasant scent of the food wafts into the room, Charles turns to Wu Fang, changing the subject: 'Don't the townspeople talk, the way you two are dressed? What do your parents think?'

'Mine have given up minding, as you can see.' Jiali laughs. 'As for hers,' she points at Wu Fang, 'she was practically raised as a boy — at her own insistence. Oh, how they indulged her. The servants were instructed to address her as "Young Master", never "Young Mistress"; a trip to Japan was granted when America was considered too far; and there,' she turns to Wu Fang, 'in the name of science, you were often in a room full of naked men!'

'Dissecting corpses was part of my medical study, you ignorant ... Oh, you mean the live ones, that's ... their custom. They bathe in public, men and women. Truly, they are so different from us.'

In the dimming light, Charles studies the two women with a look of wonder in his eyes. That first impression he had of Fudi being an exceptional place had been so true: these two are

45

nothing like what he had expected of Chinese women, and he feels exhilarated, despite his injury.

Though dinner is the humblest of dishes — rice and cabbage — the conversation is intimate and delightful, interrupted only by a loud knock on the door late at night. A servant from the Yans' arrives with the message that the young master has returned home unexpectedly from the college and is asking to see his wife. 'The old mistress is quite anxious for you to come home as soon as possible.'

'How did she know I was here?'

'Someone who was at the market told us.' The servant peers furtively at Charles.

*

Well fed and both a little drunk, Wu Fang and Charles finally leave the Shens' house, hours after Jiali departed for her husband. In the still moonlight, the pagoda is mysterious and inviting; Charles is moved to say aloud, 'I wonder what's it like up there.'

'You mean you haven't climbed it yet?'

Charles shakes his head. 'I'm waiting for a guide.'

'Hasn't Yanbu offered?'

'He wasn't that interested.'

Wu Fang hesitates a little, then says simply, 'Let's go, now.' She'd prefer to be in the company of Jiali, of course, but that is not an option tonight, and she finds the ocean man a keen enough companion. They climb the steps together.

Many a time Charles leans to touch and marvel at the reptile-like roughness of the surface of the pagoda; many a time he exclaims, in a low but emphatic whisper, how beautiful and mysterious it looks against the moonlight. Wu Fang nods in agreement and tells him that when she was a child it often reminded her of a hibernating tortoise, or the giant whale of old legend, so ancient and still that its broad back grows vegetation and birds are fooled into resting on it.

'So you are really quite fond of the pagoda,' smiles Charles, 'despite what you said to me on the ship.'

'I tolerate it,' she admits, then concedes, 'I did miss it, when I was away.'

They reach the top.

A man and a woman, alone on a pagoda, under the moonlight; Charles' heart is stirred, despite Wu Fang's men's clothes. Surprised by the sudden emotion, he steps a little apart from her, leaning over the rampart. It must be loneliness, he tells himself.

But no romance is forthcoming from Wu Fang. Sharp-mouthed, quick-witted, not a conventional beauty with her wide forehead and prominent cheek bones, she is aware that she is one of those women who men trust and confide in, but do not generally feel attracted to; it serves her just fine. But she likes the ocean man, feels a sisterly fondness towards him. There is something melancholic about him, as if he is in need of protection, so she smiles unguardedly, and her open, honest face in the moonlight causes him to swallow and say, 'My wife died at sea, on the way here.'

'I thought you looked a bit lost, on the ship.'

He keeps his eyes on the far side of the ground below, where the pagoda casts a large and sombre shadow. 'Fever, for three days, and there was nothing they could do. I shut myself in my cabin without seeing a soul. If you had met me then I would not have talked to you. I couldn't face all the condolences.'

'It must have been so hard.'

'We were on our honeymoon. I thought I could not be any happier.' His voice trembles.

Wu Fang holds a sympathetic silence. In truth, her heart is also stirred; not romantically, but beyond the sisterly fondness there now rises a feeling akin to awe: young though the ocean man seems, he has loved.

And is grieving.

'There was so much we still had to find out about each other, and now she's lying at the bottom of the Pacific Ocean and here I am, on top of an ancient pagoda, talking to you ...' Charles trails off, a little embarrassed. 'I don't know what's come over me, I haven't told a soul about this.' He glances away.

'Grief is a heavy burden to carry alone,' she murmurs kindly, 'I am honoured you have chosen me to confide in.' Then she smiles: 'But I am a doctor — well, a would-be doctor. You can tell me anything.'

Her smile disarms him and his mood shifts. 'You know, that remark you made on the ship, about Yanbu.'

'What did I say? I have quite forgotten,' she pretends.

'I don't recall your exact words, but something about him being very exact and scientific. I can't help feeling there was something odd in that remark. Forgive me if I am wrong, but it seemed there was a sense of dislike, not so much in your words, but in your tone of voice.' The woman in front of him inspires confidence and trust, and he doesn't feel odd saying what is on his mind.

'Was that why you ...' she hesitates and seems to withdraw

to the darkness a little, then, her face re-emerges, with a look of gratefulness: 'you covered for me at the Shens.'

Charles grows serious. 'Was I right then? You really do dislike him?'

She looks at him full in the eyes with her own large, frank ones. 'I cannot lie. I don't think they are an equal match.'

He shakes his head. 'But you haven't even met him!'

She gives a wry smile. 'Not then, but I have, since.'

'When?'

'The second day I was back in Fudi, they came home to visit her parents. I made his acquaintance there.'

'And?'

'He seemed pleasant enough, but ...' she trails off. She can't very well say what she truly feels: that Jiali is so very brilliant that no man can be her equal.

'Wu Fang!' he becomes animated. 'You are her best friend, of course you would think no man would be good enough for her. But believe me, in Yanbu she's found a true gentleman!'

'Is that so?' she whispers the question. She seems relieved, rather than angered by his words, as he has feared.

'I am certain.' Encouraged, he carries on: 'You only met him once. You don't know him, but I do. I work with him.'

'He sounds popular.'

'Yes, well liked and respected.'

'He is a lucky man.'

'Twice lucky, to have earned a home leave, so soon after his last.'

'Really, do you believe that's why Yanbu has returned suddenly?' Wu Fang's voice becomes alert, 'You don't think there is anything the matter?'

'Well, that's my guess. Director Zuo has a reputation for being an eccentric but kind official; apparently he often sends staff home to tend to family business, at the shortest notice, especially the newlyweds.' Charles smiles, certain that this will reassure, even entertain, Wu Fang.

But Wu Fang merely nods, then claims a sudden headache: 'I need to go home and rest,' she says hastily.

Wu Fang is uncharacteristically silent on the way down, which, on a high after his rescue and the moonlight climb, Charles does not notice. Pleased as he is with Yanbu's special home leave, it never occurs to him that the woman next to him might feel differently.

5

Jiali hesitates at the door to the study.

'Elder Sister,' Yanbu calls out to her.

'Why have you come back so soon?'

'Are you displeased?'

'Don't be silly! Of course I am pleased. It's just ... a little unexpected.'

She strides inside the room now: a large, graceful cat that he both admires and is a little afraid of.

'Has everything been all right since I left?'

'Yes.'

'Mother treating you well?'

She tells him about Wu Fang's visit, how his mother mistook her for a man. He laughs heartily with her, and eases back onto his chair. When Charles' rescue is recounted, Yanbu leans forward, and is all attention; Charles' words of praise are generously returned.

'Surely nobody is so perfect as the two of you,' Jiali teases.

'True,' he nods, pleased and emboldened by her show of interest.

'So what is Charles' weakness?'

Yanbu frowns, thinking carefully, and with an earnest air. Now he leans back, reclining in the chair, hands crossed, eyes closed, a faint smile spreading around the corners of his mouth, his face framed perfectly by the maps, star charts and diagrams pasted on the wall behind him. His relaxed pose inspires a rush of fondness in her: she always likes him a little more when he is in his study — he is more himself somehow.

Yanbu opens his eyes and catches the look Jiali gives him. Not always a sensitive man, he is nonetheless sensitive enough to be encouraged by the look, and to know that he should pretend to be ignorant of it. Glancing away, he concedes loudly that the ocean man 'does smell a little, you know, that peculiar rotten milk scent that all ocean people have', and that he finds Charles' beard 'messy'.

'So: smelly and untidy,' she laughs. What a surprise, Yanbu can be funny! She pads over to the desk by his chair, drawn by his expression of the apparent ease between the two men.

Their smiling eyes finally meet, and this time, he doesn't move his. They are both aware that this is the most intimate and pleasant shared moment, so far, of their marriage. Will they go further?

He tries.

'It's getting late. Come,' he gestures with his outreached hand.

She follows him out of the study, into their bedroom, and her heart starts to beat fast. They have slept in separate rooms since the wedding.

He heads straight for the bed, but she hangs back at the door, hesitant. He looks at her, then grows mysterious.

'What is it?' she asks, trying to sound casual.

He stirs awkwardly. 'You will never believe how I got sent home.'

'I'm all ears.'

'Director Zuo has been away, and upon his return, earlier today,' he hesitates, then speaks shyly, avoiding her eyes, 'he sent for me. He congratulated me on my marriage and,' he pauses and smiles, 'said nice things about you and your family — how much he had always admired your father's scholarship and personality and,' he lifts up his face, 'then he warned me about marrying a Hakka woman. His words were: "Hakka women are tough as iron, and they do not have unbound feet for nothing."'

Jiali blushes. 'Was that it? You talked about my feet?'

Yanbu's voice becomes even more mysterious. 'I thought nothing of the meeting but then in the afternoon, in the middle of my lesson, I got this from him ...' He jumps off the bed, where he has been sitting, reaches for his satchel, and draws something out: 'Read for yourself.'

It is a short note, written in fancy freestyle calligraphy: *I see in your face unfulfilled desire and clear indications that yin and yang are not reconciled. Physical conjugation of a marriage is vital to both the health and future harmony of both of you. It is your sacred duty to pass on the family line by producing an heir. I'm giving you five days further leave to go home to sort things out. Do so without delay!*

Watching her face change, he starts to regret showing it to her. It had seemed a good idea, earlier, to prove his point.

'Interfering old fool,' she exclaims, then, glancing up, 'how on earth did he know?' There is a tone of impatience in her voice: What a shame, she had thought they were getting closer, but this broke the spell.

'Extraordinary, isn't it?' He avoids her eyes.

'You must have said something.'

'Nothing of the sort!' he raises his voice, incensed. 'If

anything, I painted a picture of domestic bliss, and he wished me many sons and grandsons ...' He stops, as if pained, then, keeping his head down, speaks in a subdued voice. 'The director does have a reputation for being an eccentric. They say he can read fortunes. That generation of people, you know, having children really matters to them.'

'Those busybodies, how dare they tell us what to do?' she says vehemently, the better to hide her embarrassment.

'They are our seniors and mean well,' he murmurs, also preferring to focus on 'them'.

'But it's nothing to do with them!'

'It's not my fault. I didn't say a word.' His voice is sad, not at all resentful, but she feels his bitterness keenly.

They look at each other.

'Anyway, for all I know, nothing will ever happen between us.' He whispers softly, resigned.

Dropping her eyes, Jiali says quickly, 'Nothing will ever happen if you don't try.'

'I did try,' he swallows, 'but you were not ready.'

'You didn't match the couplet, the line I wrote on our wedding night.' she protests, but her voice is weaker now.

*

Later, as the two sleep in separate rooms — she in their marital bed, he on the long bench in his study — Jiali stares at the wood carvings on the side of her bed, which depict Mandarin ducks with necks entwined, traditional symbols of conjugal love, and recalls the couple's earlier conversation. She is puzzled as to why Yanbu has been so stubborn about refusing to match her couplets since the wedding night. He could easily do it, judging from their past correspondence. True, he is not as good as her, but she never minded that before, always giving him encouragement. So why not now? Is he trying to make a point?

Her breath quickens as she hears what seems to be sighing from the next room. But silence reigns once more after the briefest pause. She breathes out slowly and carefully. Turning over, she faces the Mandarin ducks again. How lonely she had been since Wu Fang had left for Japan: no one to talk to, to dress as men and go out riding with. Then came her father's accident and rescue by Yanbu, and ... to this day she can't quite believe how quickly she agreed to the marriage. Gratitude played a big part, that was true, though, she admits to herself, boredom and loneliness also influenced her decision. Wu Fang's absence had left a big hole.

Jiali sighs and closes her eyes, but now she hears her mother's voice, talking to her father, thinking she was asleep, on the night of her engagement:

'I am relieved that Jiali has finally seen sense,' Mother Shen chuckles. *'Do you remember the pledge she made, with Wu Fang?'*

'As if I could ever *forget!'* laughs her father. *'She would not marry a man ... then, as a concession to us, she would not marry a man — unless he could match her couplets.'*

'She was quite sure that such a man did not exist! It was Wu Fang's idea, I am sure.'

'Ah those two, they are not at all like other girls.'

'She is your child, you raised her!' she said in a tone only half teasing.

'Well, why should she settle for just anybody?'

Oh, Ma and Pa! Jiali falls to sleep with the voices of her doting parents ringing in her ears, though her dreams are filled with unmatched couplets.

*

Yanbu spends the whole of the next day out of the house seeing old friends, and in his mother's company in the evening, only returning to their quarters after dinner. Claiming thirst, he asks for tea. But when he picks up the cup, he exclaims, draws in a sharp breath, and drops it.

'What is the matter?' Jiali asks, and he shows her a sore-looking thumb. 'How? When?' He blushes and tells her: the morning after their wedding, he'd cut his thumb with a knife until it bled then soaked a handkerchief with it. He'd thought nothing of it, and the wound seemed to have healed, but earlier today he'd caught the thumb on a piece of broken wood, and it had started bleeding again.

'Why would you cut your thumb with a knife?'

'Don't you know?' His voice becomes tender. 'It is what young couples do these days. Quite a few of my colleagues did the same on their wedding night when their wives were not ready to … consummate the marriage. You soak your handkerchief with the blood, then …' he stops, lowering his eyes.

'Then what?' she demands mercilessly and, it seems to him, unreasonably, while not at all acknowledging his gallantry.

'Come on, Jiali, you must know!'

Jiali blushes, of course she knows: On the morning after the wedding, a blood-stained handkerchief is to be produced, as cast iron proof both of a bride's virginity, and of it being taken.

By showing her the cut on his thumb, Yanbu had meant to earn himself praise from her, but, feeling too righteous herself, she is having none of it — practices such as these are exactly the sort that she and Wu Fang have always been so vehemently against. Why should only a woman's purity before marriage be tested? And in such a humiliating way!

They are both silent, which she breaks with: 'So did you?'

'W ... what?' her voice is so indignant that he stutters.

'Show it to your mother?'

'Well ...'

She waves a hand impatiently. Of course he did. 'What did you do with it after?'

'The handkerchief?' He rubs the thumb slowly with his other hand, not looking at her. 'I was so ashamed I threw it away.'

'Oh.' She sounds surprised, and seems less angry all of a sudden. 'You should have shown me,' she says kindly. 'The cut, I mean. I could have treated it then.'

Their eyes meet.

'Wait here,' she orders.

In the small ante room, Jiali's assortment of dry herbs has been arranged neatly by Lanlan. Her father is a famed herbalist as well as a poet, and his only daughter, so the townspeople say, is a healer herself. Though not married for long, she's already treated several maids in the Yans' house. She takes her time choosing the herbs. The image of Yanbu standing with his head bent stays with her. A part of her is stirred by his thoughtfulness and show of humility. Though the suffering of a cut thumb is not great, it is for her sake. The warm feeling of affection grows stronger as she walks back to the study with the tray of herbs.

When the tray is placed in front of him, he smells the strong aroma, and his eyes light up.

'Sit still,' she says, and he obeys.

She leans forward, holds his thumb, and examines it. 'Just as I suspected,' she says softly, 'it's infected. That's why it's still sore.'

'It does hurt a little,' he admits.

'Don't worry,' she smiles, 'I can fix it.' She dresses his wound with the assortment of herbs. With her hair tied back, her sleeves rolled, her body leaning forward, she is the picture of devotion.

'Elder sister?'

'Don't call me that,' Jiali murmurs, her eyes still on his thumb.

'What should I be calling you?'

'My name of course.' She blushes a little.

'Jiali, Jiali.' His voice becomes tender and urgent. Then she hears something familiar: '*Discarding the fan as a frivolous feminine affectation, I dance with a glistening sword to the light of ...*'

'... *the Supreme White,*' she murmurs the rest of the line. Not the most sophisticated of her writings, this couplet about the moon and stars was one of the earliest she'd written for him. She is touched that he remembers it.

'*Leaning over the window, I hear the messages from you sent by restless birds at dawn.* Jiali, I can recite them all, each and every one of the poems you sent me.'

She leans back and lets her herb-soaked hands fall to her sides. Her sparkling eyes meet his. 'Yours, too. The feeling in this line: *The delight in finding a rare echo of my sentiments in so deep a well ...*'

Out of modesty, it seems to her, he hastily interrupts. 'I have a line,' he whispers.

'Really?' She holds her breath. Just a moment ago, she had decided to let the couplets go, watching them, in her mind's eye, taking flight, floating easily above them like the burnt paper offered at Qing Ming to ancestors long departed. But now, finally ... His previous refusal had been but teasing after all. Oh, how often she'd dreamt of such a moment, composing couplets with her beloved ...

'*I wish to be the straw mat, covering the bed you sleep on,*' he starts, mysteriously.

'Oh, but this is not ...' She is taken aback.

He continues: '*Or the soft silk quilt, on top of you, sheltering you from wind and frost.*'

It is not a new couplet, as she had hoped, yet the words are alive in the air, each of them startling, caressing, teasing. She is reminded of how much she loves this poem, having long imagined the intimate atmosphere described.

'*No man alive has ever seen a sight such as this ...*'

'*No pleasure can ever match this one of ours tonight ...*' she whispers.

'Please, Jiali. Make me the happiest man alive!'

But it is not only the words of the couplet that disrobes her.

If only he knew. Deep inside her, there has been a spark, an itch, and she has been restless with it, ever since the wedding night. She glances away, but the sight of the bedspread, with its red silk embroidery of dragon and phoenix playing neck to neck, fuels the spark; then she hears her name called again.

'I wish you would put this back on again.' He holds the wedding top in his hand.

When did he get hold of that? She remembers what Lanlan said about him sniffing it in the study before he left home. She shuts her eyes: surprised at herself that such a gesture, instead of repulsing her, should now have the effect of making her feel daring and aroused.

'Do you really want me to?' she whispers.

'Please.'

She starts to unbutton her man's gown, her movements slow and deliberate; he has no idea the same request has been made of her before, in this very room, and she is reminded of Wu Fang's voice, the same urgent, insistent tone. Her skin shivers on contact with her own fingertips, still smelling of the strong scent of the herbs she had earlier used to treat him.

She is down to her undergarments, and now reaches for the crumpled top, but instead of handing it to her, he tilts his head and his eyes plead silently for something she instantly understands.

She slips into the bed, her heart thumping like a drum. Under the quilt she strips quickly and deftly. She is naked. But instead of feeling weak and vulnerable, she feels bold and invincible. And with the boldness grows impatience. The last thing she wants to do now is to put that cold and indifferent top on her soft, soft skin, the part of her that is crying out to be paid just the right attention.

'Touch me,' she whispers urgently, and he, shocked and delighted, gingerly lifts up the quilt, and tentatively puts a hand on her warm, smooth, bare stomach, rising and falling fast with her quickened breaths. She closes her eyes; from somewhere far off, a thought drifts to her: *What would Wu Fang say?* But the hand on her stomach starts to stroke her ever so gently, and she feels the spark inside her rekindle; she cannot bear to wait any longer. To hell with couplets.

Teeth chattering, she murmurs, 'Take off your clothes and get in.'

Her right nipple stiffens instantly at the touch of his cold, trembling hand; a crumb or two of the herbs she had applied to his thumb earlier fall on her breast, reminding her of his sacrifice. The ripple of desire now spreads all over her body; she is on fire. She leans to clasp him in her arms, pulling him to her; liking the solidness of his weight pressing down on her, like a promise, she puts her mouth fervently to his, to seal it. She has always been eager to learn and quick to enjoy new sensations, and, oh, she knows this new pleasure is going to be extraordinary: her life's happiness depends upon it. Spreading her legs wide, she opens herself up to her husband, to a new, exciting world.

How deep she is, she has had no idea, and yet there are still depths to her that he cannot reach. The pain is nothing like what she feared, and she arches her knees, accommodating him, drawing him in further, to her core; does he know does he know does he know? Not quite but nearly there, oh how near and yet how far; he will never get there, even though she has no idea where 'there' is, but deeper, deeper, deeper please, she begs voicelessly, with her eyes, her arms, her hips; he's getting rougher but can go no deeper, to her utter frustration.

Then, just as she is saying to herself, *don't stop don't stop don't stop*, he stops. The trickle of liquid flowing between her legs feels warm, thick, and sticky; now his weight becomes a burden, and she pulls herself away.

He smiles tenderly at her, but she avoids his eyes; she can't help feeling that she has been used for his pleasure alone. She is but a wife after all.

6

How wide and spacious the temple, but how suffocating; the curving roof spreading territorially over the faithful beneath reminds Jiali of a giant bird of prey sheltering her young under powerful wings. Thick white curtains of incense form further protective shrouds for the worshippers — every one of them married, and female, like her. Standing by the ancient pine in the courtyard, Jiali has no idea that she causes quite a stir. There is something odd about this young woman, the other worshippers puzzle: they tell themselves it is her unbound feet, square and unsightly. Other reasons for their unease are not so easily identified, though they are more deeply felt: perhaps it is the way that, while other eyes are cast either up fervently to heaven for favours or down humbly in self-abasement, hers stare irreverently forward, curious, questioning.

She strides into the darkened inner hall, as reluctant and ill at ease as her mother-in-law is eager and at home. The sea of praying women around her, rising and falling, fills her with distaste. Is she to become one of them? She kneels and closes her eyes and remembers Yanbu's ecstatic face hovering above her last night, entreating his 'elder sister' not to get up too soon. If she stayed lying down, his seed would have more chance of staying planted.

How ardently he desires a child, a desire surely even stronger and more personal than tradition and convention dictate! She wants, if she can, to help him fulfil that desire. But what of that special pleasure the ancients sing and write poems about? Each night, getting ready for bed, she is aware of a longing, growing stronger as she waits for him, reaching breaking point as he caresses her; but then she feels her desire abating as he grows redder in the face and rougher in his embraces. It is as bizarre and desperate as if she were shivering from cold while he toasts by a fire. Then he is in another world, moving to his own rhythm with a joy that is alien to her. When they are at their most intimate, she feels the furthest from him.

Help! the voice inside her screams, and she wonders if the gods here hear it. What are the other women praying for? A much-desired son, as her own mother-in-law is so keen for, the reason for this visit to the temple? Yanbu had departed for the college yesterday, concluding his wedding leave. Could she already be carrying his child?

She turns to look for her mother-in-law, and, once again offended by the sight of the prostrating women, leaves the hall without a backward glance. Outside, she carelessly casts the bundle of burning incense sticks in her hand into the giant smoking urn in the middle of the courtyard, scandalising a woman praying fervently next to it. The sudden rise of the dry, suffocating heat stings her face, causing her to cough.

No pleasure can ever match this one of ours tonight, the line by Zhang Heng he had quoted that first time haunts her, and the next line makes her wince, *such pleasure that I shall never forget, even when I am a toothless old woman.*

How the ancients fuss! How the couplets make something out of nothing; how trivial those beautiful words; how meaningless this temple, that pine; how false her marriage!

She hears her name called: her mother-in-law, emerging from the hall leaning on the shoulders of the maid Wang Ma.

'The Buddha here is especially attentive,' says Mrs Yan. 'I was helped, and I show my gratitude: the Yan family sponsors a permanent lamp at this temple.'

'The old master always wanted a son, but had no luck, until our old mistress came to the Yans,' Wang Ma is all smiles. 'The old mistress is the most devout worshipper of Buddha.'

'Didn't the other ...' Jiali stops herself just before the word 'concubine' escapes her mouth. Mrs Yan had been one of two concubines, only promoted to the status of 'old mistress' after both the old master's wife and first concubine had died. 'Didn't the other old mistresses pray, too?' she asks innocently.

'Oh yes, they most certainly did,' smiles Mrs Yan.

'And they both died childless,' Wang Ma adds hastily, almost gleefully, 'But for the Buddha to grant your wish ...'

'... your heart needs to be pure,' says Mrs Yan, fingering her praying beads, her eyes fixed on Jiali, making her feel uneasy.

While Mrs Yan goes to meet with the presiding monk to discuss the renewal of her sponsorship, Jiali slips back into the hall and kneels down. For Yanbu's sake, she tells herself.

'Been praying hard, child?' inquires Mrs Yan, as they meet again in the courtyard.

'I tried to,' Jiali answers truthfully.

'Remember, you heart must be pure when you pray.' Mrs Yan's cold voice continues, 'The Buddha's eyes are wide open. No one can fool Buddha. You will be punished, if you are false.'

Jiali puzzles over her mother-in-law on the sedan ride back. There were hints of a threat in her words at the temple, but what of? What did she mean by 'false?' But Mrs Yan is prone to strange outburst from time to time, and soon Jiali is distracted by her almost-girlish chuckling, as she nods at amusing street scenes Wang Ma points out, the whiteness of her teeth contrasting with the black widow's gown she always wears; she is a severe and strict woman, and yet how little it takes, Jiali marvels, for Mrs Yan to be happy.

*

At first, she takes it for a cat meowing. But the cry persists, sounding ever more piteous; presently Jiali hears Wang Ma hissing, 'Stop fussing! You will wake up the old mistress from her afternoon nap, and then you shall pay for your insolence!'

It is not difficult to follow the voices, in the stillness of the afternoon, to find the girl, the youngest of Mrs Yan's adopted daughters, her hands tied, a handkerchief stuffed in her mouth, huddled by the large porcelain fishbowl. Jiali pulls the handkerchief out, and tries, but fails, to untie the tight knot of rope.

The girl gasps for air.

'Wang Ma, did you do this to her?' Jiali turns to the maid, furious. 'How could you!'

'Young Mistress should not worry herself about trivial matters.' Wang Ma avoids Jiali's eyes.

'Untie her!'

Wang Ma remains motionless.

'I said—'

'We have to do this, Young Mistress, for her own good.'

'How is this good for her?'

'It's her feet, Young Mistress. We started the binding last week. Naturally they get itchy, and she will not leave them alone; her elder sister has had no trouble keeping her hands off, but Mochou is fussier, so we ... Old Mistress' orders. Old Mistress has only the girl's best interest at heart.'

'Untie her, now!'

'I wouldn't dare. Old Mistress will not be pleased.'

'Do it now. I will be responsible.'

Slowly Wang Ma gets to work.

*

The summons does not take long to come, the message delivered by Wang Ma, who would have lingered, but is ordered out of the old master's study, where Mrs Yan reclines on her husband's ancient, threadbare armchair. Jiali has heard much about this room: its four walls fortified by scrolls and pictures, still and imposing as judges, it is a shrivelled, dried-up hole for spiders and mice, quiet as death. The room holds secrets, since not one, but two ghosts of past mistresses haunt it. The young Yanbu used to have nightmares of the stuffy room and is still reluctant to enter it. And yet, of all the spaces in the large sprawling Yan residence, this is where Mrs Yan always chooses to have her afternoon nap, sombre and still, mothlike in her habitual black widow's gown.

'Mochou is only six, Mother,' Jiali implores, 'surely too young to start all this.'

Mrs Yan stares ahead. 'She will weep, as I did when I had mine bound, but she knows the pain will be worth it in the end. Your meddling will only delay the inevitable.'

'Mochou is my little sister, and I cannot bear for her to be hurt.'

'Nonsense. As her elder sister, you should be helping me.'

'Mother, this is a cruel and outdated practice! And no, I will not be helping you to make Mochou miserable.' Overcome, Jiali finally bursts forth bitterly: 'It's just like Wu Fang says, we women are doing this to other women!'

'Not everyone is born into a Hakka family, nor to parents who will indulge their every whim,' Mrs Yan says coldly.

Jiali's back stiffens.

'My parents brought me up to be proud of our ancestry. We Hakka women do all the things that men do, thanks to our unbound feet. As for being indulged, I thank Ma and Pa for letting me be who I want to be — they never once made me feel lesser because I am a girl.'

Mrs Yan is silent.

Jiali softens her voice. 'Things are changing, Mother. Some families have stopped this practice altogether. My little sisters could grow up educated, and free of shackles.'

Mrs Yan waves a hand impatiently. 'Yes, but then who will marry them?'

'I have unbound feet, Mother, and yet I am your daughter-in-law.'

Mrs Yan draws in a sharp breath. 'If Yanbu had not begged … You have no idea what he means to me, do you?'

This catches Jiali by surprise.

'I know Yanbu is your only son, Mother, and that you care for him very much.'

'You have no idea,' whispers Mrs Yan, as if she hasn't heard Jiali.

A long silence follows. Mrs Yan closes her eyes. After a while, believing the older woman to have fallen asleep, Jiali turns to leave, only to be drawn back by a sudden, hushed voice: 'Stay.'

Curious and apprehensive, the girl stands by the door and watches her mother-in-law, still with her eyes closed.

'He used to sit, the old man, on this very chair, and give orders. One in particular, which I shall never forget, was to cook and bring a bowl of chicken soup, here.'

The chair creaks. The air is dry and tight. Mrs Yan's voice, usually high-pitched and thin, now takes on an unreal quality, a slow and dreamy cadence; Jiali has the curious urge both to run and to stay.

'So I made my best soup, and brought it all the way from the kitchen, burning my hands, because I wanted him to have it while it was still hot. I wanted … you see, I hadn't been allowed into his bedroom for quite a while.'

'Mother …' The intimate revelation makes Jiali cringe, and she suddenly wishes she had slipped out when she'd had the chance.

'Don't interrupt,' the voice snaps. 'I knocked on the door, and heard him say, "Come in", and I found him sitting right here on this chair, with the first concubine on his lap. The soup was for her. You have no idea how ridiculous they looked together, she as big as a melon, and he a small, wrinkled walnut!'

'I am not sure …' Jiali whispers, but she might just as well have not spoken.

Mrs Yan's eyes open suddenly, and she leans forward, her voice becoming fast, urgent, and passionate: 'Do you know how it feels to wait on a woman who is ugly, ignorant, and not worthy of wiping your feet on? A woman who has taken your man, your hope, and your happiness away from you? Do you know how it feels then to be told that you have not done a good job and to have to apologise to her? The soup was too hot! It burnt her lips! Oh, I apologised all right. I should have known better than to upset the expectant mother, so close to giving birth. Of course it would be a boy, the feng shui master had been consulted. He was adamant that any slights, especially from a female in the close vicinity, could cause an *unpredictable* birth.'

Though uncomfortable, Jiali is also fascinated. Never has she heard her mother-in-law speak so many words, with such animation. But there is also lunacy in the widow's gleaming eyes and gesticulating hands. Jiali eyes the door, even as her ears are glued to Mrs Yan's hypnotic voice.

'On my hands and knees, I begged for forgiveness. On my hands and knees, I remained outside her bedroom all night, praying loudly for the safe delivery of our much-desired son.'

The look of sarcasm on Mrs Yan's face is plain, and Jiali can't help asking, in a low voice: 'Did you really?'

'Do you think I had any choice?' Mrs Yan snaps. 'The old master would have beaten the daylights out of me if I had done anything less. I had to show that I was repentant, and I was good at it. I've had good practice. It was not the first time he'd ...' Mrs Yan stops suddenly, and sighs deeply, as if exhausted. 'Really, when I think back on those days, I marvel at my own patience.'

'Are you all right, Mother?' Jiali whispers. To hear her own voice echo in the study is a strange sensation.

Mrs Yan laughs unexpectedly, a loud, thudding cackle. 'Me? Never better! Oh, how good it feels to be telling you all this. You know, I prayed for something else that night, too. I told you:

your prayer will be answered by the gods if your heart is pure.' She pauses, and then, keeping her eyes on Jiali, breathes out the words slowly and thickly: 'My heart was pure all right, and I got what I wished for.'

'Oh Mother, what did you do?' Horror stricken, Jiali grips the door behind her for support.

'What did I do?' chuckles Mrs Yan. 'I told you, I prayed.' She resumes an ordinary voice: 'The day the boy was born was also the day that woman died.'

'What did you do to her?' Jiali asks again.

Mrs Yan smiles serenely. 'Nothing at all. That stupid, good-for-nothing woman died in childbirth, not at all a pleasant sight, for she screamed and scratched, refusing to go, all in vain of course. Women do die in childbirth, you know, though we tried our best to save her, Wang Ma and I.'

Mrs Yan's face, Jiali notices with a shudder, has become smooth and radiant.

'My poor husband followed her soon after, the old wife, too, not long after that, leaving me to raise our only son, the son I had always longed for, such is the will of Buddha.'

She seems to be in another world. Jiali wonders why her mother-in-law is telling her all this. Perhaps it had all been too much, the horror and oppression she had suffered at the hands of the old master; it had been chilling to hear, and gave an insight into the widow's coldness of heart. But even as she feels pity for her mother-in-law, Jiali senses menace, too. There is a warning in the tale, and Jiali is determined not to seem intimidated by it. Keeping her voice steady, she speaks calmly: 'So Yanbu isn't your child.'

'How dare you say such a thing? Of course he is mine. Do

70

you not hear him calling me "Mother"? Wasn't I the one who raised him, and made a scholar of him? I lived for the boy, and he is perfect. Isn't he the best of men? Aren't you the luckiest of women?'

'Does he know that he was born of another woman?'

'Oh yes, but he remembers nothing of her of course. He doesn't even know her name. I am his mother.'

Her tone of voice triumphant, Mrs Yan reaches out a long-nailed finger to smooth down an invisible stray hair, then, letting the hand drop abruptly, her icy eyes now set on Jiali.

'Yanbu did not take you on the wedding night. That blood-soaked bit of cloth he showed me the next morning could not fool even Wang Ma. Servants are not stupid, and neither am I.'

'You spied on us.' Jiali despises her.

'What an ugly accusation. I consider it my duty to ensure that you behave as a wife should and that my son does what he's meant to do. He is tofu-hearted when it comes to the people he really cares for. That is the one thing in him that I cannot seem to correct, however much I try.'

'That is why I like Yanbu: he is kind. Are you disappointed he didn't force himself on me?'

'I endured the old man using me as a spittoon, why should you have it easier?'

'Because you suffered, I shall have to suffer, too?'

'All men take their brides on their wedding night — who do you think you are?'

'I am Shen Jiali, and we live in different times now. Mother, I know you haven't had an easy life, I understand. But this chain of suffering, it can't go on. You mustn't do to other women what has been done to you. You are ...' she takes a step closer, but is forced back by the icy look of her mother-in-law.

'I know who I am.' Mrs Yan stiffens her back, her voice stern. 'I am your mother-in-law. What my son is too soft-hearted to ask, I demand: you must please him, and give him a son, within the year.'

'And if I don't?'

'Then I will send you home and get him a concubine. There are many women who would be only too happy to serve such an exemplary young man.'

The women's eyes meet. It occurs suddenly to Jiali that her mother-in-law has no idea about the latest development in their bedroom — perhaps her spy Wang Ma had not been as vigilant the last few days, and so the consummation of their marriage is still a secret. At this realisation, a strange sense of alliance with her husband grows in Jiali. After a short silence, the daughter-in-law says quietly: 'Yanbu would never agree to it.'

Jiali jumps aside as a stream of beads flies out of Mrs Yan's hands — in fury she has torn her string of prayer beads apart, each one a capsule of anger, spinning furiously over the floor. Some reach their target, hitting Jiali's feet, though many more disappear into the far corners of the vast room.

'Wang Ma! Wang Ma!' shrieks Mrs Yan, stamping her feet.

'I will send for her,' Jiali speaks calmly, bows, and leaves the room.

7

The bedroom is in disarray: silks strewn about, cases opened, and books pulled off shelves; the maids tiptoe around their young mistress, whom they address as 'Master', who is huddling, uncharacteristically still, in an armchair. Young Master Wu always used to be pleased to get notes from Mistress Shen, but the latest, sent two days ago, has put her in a very dark mood. Several times the maids have been instructed to pack 'for a very long journey', though moments later, she changes her mind and orders them to unpack again. One bold maid dared to inform Wu Fang's parents, and the resulting recrimination sent the whole household into a spin. The Wus have no idea why their long-absent daughter has suddenly decided to leave home again, 'to go anywhere but Fudi', when only days ago she had told them she was so very happy to be back where she belonged. 'What has changed?' they ask, but can get no answer.

At dusk, a maid enters timidly and announces a visitor.

'I don't wish to see anyone,' Wu Fang waves a hand impatiently.

'Not even me?' says a familiar voice.

'You? What are you doing here?' Wu Fang stands abruptly, dropping the note she has been drafting and redrafting to the very person standing in front of her.

73

'I've come to see you of course.'

'What have you come to see me for?' Wu Fang frowns. 'Aren't you happily married now? You should be with your beloved.'

'Yanbu left yesterday.'

'Having given you the time of your life.'

'What are you talking about?'

'I read your note.'

'Oh that,' murmurs Jiali. 'You conclude from that one line that I have been in marital bliss.'

'How else am I to interpret: "Yanbu has matched my couplet!"'

'It wasn't quite true.'

'What do you mean?'

'*Nearly*, I wrote, nearly!' Jiali cries: 'Didn't you read to the end?'

'Small point,' Wu Fang protests weakly, her face brightening.

'He didn't match my couplet, it was some old lines from our past correspondences, and he quoted Zhang Heng, and then …'

'I see.' Wu Fang nods slowly.

Jiali bursts into tears. 'I feel so cheated, and in turn I cheated you — us — I was weak.'

'Come, that we can fix,' Wu Fang rises decisively, taking Jiali's hand. 'We will be at the stone boat,' she turns to her maid, waiting discreetly just outside the bedroom, 'bring our things there, including the candles.'

'Yes, Young Master.'

*

While Wu Fang busies herself ordering the maids to place food, papers, and various other objects here and there, Jiali stands at one end of the stone boat, breathing deeply. She knows every nook and cranny of the boat, built on a small island in the middle of the artificial lake in the large Wu grounds, accessed by hidden stepping stones; occasionally it served as a stage for operas, but more often the two of them would recline there, composing their lines.

Behind Jiali rises the distinctive scent of sandalwood incense. She closes her eyes. How young they had been, swearing allegiance to eternal sisterhood in this very place.

The novel sensation of the crisp, stiff man's gown on her skin — the first time she'd worn one; her finger tingling with the sharp sensation of being recently pricked; her heart fluttering with excitement at the sight of her own crimson blood mixing with that of Wu Fang's.

They watch in silent awe as their blood mingles.

Then, in unison: 'We swear to be eternal sisters. We shall never part, whatever happens ...' They keep intoning, their voices rising and falling, echoing in the large stillness of the lake: so sincere, so naïve.

She opens her eyes with a start and meets Wu Fang's gaze. They kneel in the centre of the boat.

Incense hugs the two figures just as it had done twelve years ago, though earnest girlish voices loudly proclaiming eternal sisterhood have now been replaced by a pregnant silence.

Then Jiali rises abruptly, haunted by the image of the women kneeling and praying in the temple.

'No.' She puts a hand on her friend's shoulders, resolute. 'Get up, get up! We don't need any of this, Wu Fang. We are not little girls anymore — what we have is beyond pledges.'

*

They share Wu Fang's large bed that night.

'So it was underwhelming.' Secretly pleased with what her friend has confided in her, Wu Fang nonetheless keeps her voice flat, even sounding bored. The room, having heard so many secrets from the two before, holds its breath in conspiracy.

'I realise, on reflection, that one must not expect too much on the first night,' Jiali declares, feeling a need suddenly not to paint Yanbu with too dark a brush, out of vanity, perhaps — he is, after all, the husband she chose.

'He stayed several days, no?' Wu Fang tries to sound nonchalant.

'The first few nights, I mean,' Jiali adds hastily. 'And he is clever and kind.'

'So you tell me.' Wu Fang nods slowly.

Jiali suddenly despairs: 'What if we never get there? Oh Wu Fang, what if Yanbu and I are simply not meant for each other?' She stops, frowning. 'Or perhaps the ancients have got it wrong, waxing lyrical about this so-called pleasure ...'

'The ancients are not wrong. There is such pleasure.'

'Then why can't I have it?'

Wu Fang's anger bursts from her, despite herself. Unable ever to find faults with Jiali, she directs her wrath at Yanbu: 'I hear Yanbu is an experienced man, he should really be the one showing you. Didn't you tell me that his mother sent him a maid when he was only twelve, to instruct him on bedroom matters?'

'Indeed, Yanbu was traumatised. He told me the maid was old and ugly and used him like a toy! But that is not his only experience ... The brothels ...' Jiali rolls her eyes.

'What?' Wu Fang is scandalised. Yanbu has admitted to going to brothels? It is an outdated practice, though still common, for a young man to receive instruction from an older woman in these matters — and in this case it had not been Yanbu's choice — but to visit prostitutes and boast about it?

'He didn't say anything of the sort, of course,' Jiali clarifies, 'but Lanlan heard it from Wang Ma. It happened before we were married of course, in Shanghai.' It is humiliating to be confiding this to Wu Fang, but she is too miserable to care.

Such entitlement! And you still think marriage is a good idea?! Wu Fang watches Jiali, her eyes accusing in the dark, though she doesn't say a word. But Jiali's sad silence moves Wu Fang, and soon pity overcomes all other sentiments.

'Jiali,' she calls softly.

Silence.

'Jiali', Wu Fang calls again. 'Listen, I've got something to tell you.' Her voice becomes mysterious.

Jiali raises her head from the pillow.

Wu Fang smiles. 'The body is a wonderful thing. Let me show you.' She can give her friend this, at least.

Wu Fang turns on the lamp, gets out of the bed, finds a piece of paper, and starts drawing. 'There,' she points, 'this is your yin passage, your ...'

'Yes, I know, of course,' Jiali nods, looking vaguely at the paper, though not really knowing what it is she is looking at.

'Here,' Wu Fang moves closer to show her.

Two black-haired heads lean together; suppressed giggles and gasps of surprise soon ensue at the impromptu anatomy lesson.

*

The night deepens but neither is able to sleep. After a little while, Wu Fang whispers, 'What you said, earlier, about your mother-in-law, it must be unnerving that she knew what was going on in your bedroom.'

Jiali muses, 'She is jealous of me; I think she might even hate me, but she is also fascinated by me. It's … it's not a cold-hearted hatred.'

'Wake up Jiali, she is a crazy, cruel woman who is going to give you hell — she more or less promised it! What she said to you in the old man's study could not be plainer: she killed Yanbu's mother!'

'She is indeed cruel, and I hate what she has done to Mochou, but she hasn't had an easy life and I don't believe she is a murderer.'

'You think too kindly of everyone, Jiali. I really can see her disposing of the other woman, it is in her character. What happened to the first wife, I wonder?'

'Didn't she die of food poisoning?'

'Maybe Mrs Yan slipped something into the women's food? Into her famed mushroom soup perhaps?'

'How terrible if that were true. Just because she herself wasn't …'

'… loved.' Wu Fang nods.

'But she dotes on Yanbu. She knows how to love, fiercely.'

'That's different. She wasn't loved, not as a woman, and definitely not as herself.'

Somewhere in the dark of the night, an owl hoots, and though the two have been lying side by side, talking aloud to the ceiling, now they turn to each other.

'She is so unhappy,' Jiali says.

Wu Fang sighs. 'I do not care about her happiness, but your happiness, my dear, that I do care about, very much. Just how happily married are you, really?' She pauses, then leans closer. 'Patience is not a virtue; it is much overrated. Look at your miserable mother-in-law — you will never be like her, of course, but this sort of life grinds you down, and I can't bear the thought of you being unhappy, not even for a second.'

'I am not unhappy,' Jiali answers, after a long silence.

'You have just got married; you should be ecstatically happy.'

'I'm not unhappy,' Jiali repeats her mantra, but the lie burns her lips.

*

As Wu Fang slumbers, Jiali lies wide awake. Her friend's words ring loud and clear in her ears. In her mind's eye, she sees Mrs Yan: her thin pursed lips, her smooth and spotless hair, her cool, staring eyes. Jiali shudders.

That itch she had felt since her wedding night had never been scratched. Several times Yanbu had come close, but always, at the crucial time, he'd stopped, almost as if to spite her, and the flame was extinguished. Now the itch has grown, consuming her, demanding her full attention, and she can no longer ignore it. She thinks of what Wu Fang drew on the paper: surely Yanbu knows all this, so why doesn't he seem to want to please her?

Jiali drifts off just as day dawns and swims in dreams. The faces of Yan mistresses past and present hover menacingly, though vaguely, then fade; more vivid images emerge, and she sits up abruptly with the last still fresh in her mind: that of the ocean man, naked, holding her tight, kissing her passionately on the lips, jolting her from sleep.

Putting a hand to her fast-beating heart, she peers around guiltily. Really, how absurd! She doesn't even remember the ocean man's name, and they have hardly talked, not since the day she rescued him. Certainly a most strange dream, she puzzles, then settles on the explanation that this is really about her marriage and not the ocean man at all: she wants someone to be intimate with, it could have been anybody, Yanbu even.

Though when she closes her eyes again the scene of the ocean man kissing her returns.

8

It was bad enough to be called to sea from his newly warmed marital bed; now there's a storm.

Shivering below the darkened sky and towering waves, Yanbu barks instructions that the pupils largely ignore — he has no authority with them and is only on this particular expedition because their usual teacher has suddenly fallen ill; instead, they turn their young, scared faces to the ocean man. Charles' commands, though precise and effective, are peppered freely with curses and damnations in his ocean language, as if the sea could be scolded into submission. For the pupils, though, there is something strangely reassuring about the incomprehensible obscenities.

Shouts, screams, the smell of leaked engine oil; blasts of wet, salty air so thick one can hardly breathe. Nausea renders Yanbu powerless, even as he attempts to rally. But when Charles tries to tie a knot, Yanbu reaches out a trembling hand to help, and when two wet knuckles knock on each other a brotherhood is formed. Indicating that Charles should concentrate on giving command to the pupils, Yanbu succeeds in tying the knot himself, earning a thumbs up.

That is all the encouragement Yanbu needs, for even as he is nervous of water, he is no coward. He remembers what he learned in his student days, takes out his logbook, and, on unsteady feet, attempts to write in it. Then, miraculously, the storm becomes less threatening. As it subsides, they let the pupils take charge of the ship; the two teachers wipe their brows and steal surreptitious glances at each other. The storm has swept the little distance between them away with its giant, careless hand. Such a trial by providence is exactly what was needed for the budding friendship to blossom.

*

On the island, the two men lead different groups: there are navigations to complete, observation logs to fill in, shipping matters to settle. Towards late afternoon, their tasks completed, they reunite on the beach. Yanbu is shocked at the almost indecent practical skills Charles seems to possess: rustling up a fire, killing and skinning a rabbit, scaling and grilling a fish; he would expect this from a servant or a coolie but not a gentleman. Charles does it deftly, confidently, and without ceremony or embarrassment. Won over, Yanbu shows off too: a delicious hot vapour rises from the bubbling pot as he nonchalantly chucks in the wild mushrooms he's picked, and he pretends not to be overjoyed at Charles' exclamations of surprise and gratitude. The purpose of the practice trip being to prepare the pupils for emergencies, they have deliberately forgone the ship's supply of food and kitchen utensils. But the large cooking pot was carried off the ship, at Yanbu's insistence. Having cast doubts at the time, Charles is now glad he yielded. Not very professional of him, he knows.

'Sir, can we take off our uniforms?' a student asks.

'Permission granted.' Yanbu nods, as Charles starts to undo his own buttons, whistling happily.

That the obedient, passive students have suddenly come alive on this deserted island is no surprise to Charles, though he is delighted at their unexpectedly good culinary skills. It seems that each and every one of these Chinese boys has been trained by an expert chef to magically produce dish after dish of deliciousness. Numerous Chinese must have quoted to him that saying: 'For the ordinary people, food is their god.' *Can eating be both the journey and destination?* Charles ponders. Food is certainly much more than mere stuff to satiate or enable a conversation. Food is the path to ancestors, to God, the last rite for men awaiting execution; Charles has even seen supremely enticing plates of food left in neat reverence in the deserted, godless pagoda. Raggedly dressed beggars huddled together still manage to give the impression of a rich banquet with salvaged food. You cannot be in this country for long without succumbing to the temptation yourself. Charles is not religious, but surely there is something not quite moral in this, he thinks with half-hearted guilt as he swallows yet another mouthful of wild mushroom fried with garlic.

Yanbu's widowed, devout Buddhist mother taught him how to identify edible mushrooms, Charles learns. They are her meat substitutes. She has many different ways of cooking mushrooms, so they taste sometimes like chicken, sometimes like pork. It's no mean feat, as some mushrooms can be deadly, though Mrs Yan has never, Buddha be thanked, made a mistake.

But how strange to want to be reminded of meat when you are a vegetarian, Charles muses innocently, to which Yanbu does not respond. He thinks the question odd.

'My mother is a first-rate scholar, too.'

'Yes, so I remember you saying. You had to be tested on

classical Chinese for the college and she helped you with that.'

'I owe her so much.'

'And your wife Jiali is also so accomplished.'

'I'm afraid she is not as good a cook, but she does have other attributes.'

'Such as being the most marvellous poetess and excellent swordswoman, I hear? Not to mention her skill as a herbalist. If it hadn't been for her and her father, and Wu Fang ...'

'I am so very pleased they were there for you, Charles, though I am not so sure about Wu Fang; since her return from Japan, Jiali has done a few things, no doubt influenced by her old friend, that my mother found offensive — she is an old-fashioned woman with traditional views, and Miss Wu had been unnecessarily blunt with her; they have crossed words quite a few times. The latest development is Wu Fang interfering over my youngest sister, Mochou. You see, Wu Fang has an issue with the girl having her feet bound.'

Charles laughs. 'Miss Wu is truly exceptional.'

'I hadn't realised you were an admirer of hers.'

'How can I not be? She's refreshingly unlike any other woman, Chinese or otherwise, that I have ever met.'

'You thought her a man, and Japanese, when you first met.'

'She is full of surprises, Wu Fang, isn't she?'

There is a sudden eruption of boys laughing, as one of them, a small, well-built lad with oily, dark skin, starts and fails to do a somersault on the sand. Their tummies full, adventure awaiting, their faces relax into expressions of ease that Charles is pleased to see.

'That one,' says Yanbu of the boy, frowning, 'he is trouble.'

'Shuisheng is never still, for sure. He is a sailor's son.'

'In class he misbehaves, it's all a question of attitude. To be attentive is respectful. These boys have it all too easy, Charles. When I was their age …'

'Of course, you all had to take the imperial exam.' Charles nods in sympathy. The exam, fiercely competitive and notoriously difficult, lasting days, used to be the only route to official posts in the kingdom, and young Chinese boys spent years preparing for it. But things are changing now, he knows: 'I hear the emperor is thinking of abolishing it.'

'I never took it myself.'

'Didn't you?'

It won't do to say that he is no good at reciting classics or composing couplets, both essential components of the imperial exam — the ocean man will not understand. So Yanbu tells of how he came to be enrolled in the naval college, which does not require the same level of competence in classical Chinese as it is science based, in a way that makes Charles see quite clearly that he was far too young to resist an over-anxious mother — who agreed for him to attend the college on condition that he never be sent to sea — and yet old enough to know that such a choice would be beneficial to the country, much more so than the imperial exam, a traditional route to officialdom adopted by most others.

'A fortune teller my mother consulted warned that I am at particular risk of being drowned. So my mother begged Director Zuo to never let me go on sea trips! That is why I ended up teaching at the college, instead of joining the navy like the rest of my classmates.'

'Gosh, so this expedition … how come Director Zuo let you go on the boat?'

'There was no one else he could call upon. So I volunteered.'

'That is very decent of you.'

'My mother must not know, or she will be worried sick,' Yanbu laughs.

It occurs to Charles that more mention has been made by his friend of his mother than of his wife.

The sailor's son, having gathered up his courage, joins them. Now that he is bare-chested — all their wet, storm-drenched clothes are drying by the fire — they see the solid bronze cross dangling from his neck. Deliberately ignoring it for now, Charles asks if he likes going to the Mazu Miao, the Sea Goddess Temple.

'We pray there each time father goes out to the sea, to the goddess. We saw you there once, sir!'

'And you go to the church as well? How often?'

Before Shuisheng is able to answer, the tall boy standing next to him asks in a small voice, 'Why are ocean men so keen for us to worship their God?'

'Some ocean men,' Charles corrects him.

'Don't all ocean men worship their God and want us Chinese to do so, too?'

'Some do, some don't. I don't.' Charles grins. 'Just as some of you believe in Buddha, some of you believe in Confucius, and some,' he smiles at Shuisheng, 'pray to Mazu. If I were Chinese, I would pray to her. She is bound to do better for you than the ocean men's God.'

He waits for their reaction and is not disappointed. He said things they did not expect an ocean man to say. He knows he differs from many of his kin on this, but he doesn't care. He's not living away from his people to be told what to do and how to think by them. He is in a good mood. The pleasure of knowing other minds is as rewarding and thrilling as knowing new mountains; what can be more adventurous than being intimate with people from a totally different culture and background from oneself?

Shuisheng again: 'We go to the pagoda as well.'

'The one near our college? Lovely view from the top.'

'We saw you there, too, sir. You run very fast,' admires another boy.

'Did I?' He doesn't always run, but admits that he is always in a rush to get to the top.

'Sir, have you heard the story?' whispers yet another boy conspiratorially — now they are crowding over Charles.

'About the temple?'

'About the pagoda.'

'Yes, I know it well.' Charles shifts subtly, to include Yanbu in the circle. 'There was once a black snake with magic who changed shape into a beautiful woman and seduced an honest scholar. Then one day a Buddhist monk told him the truth …'

The boys nudge each other. Shuisheng, growing bolder, grins.

'Sir, with respect, you have it all wrong. It was not a Buddhist monk, but a Taoist priest, and it was the white snake that seduced the scholar, the black snake was her sister …'

'No, they were friends, best friends,' someone disagrees.

'I prefer the black snake anyway, she was fierce and loyal, just the sort of friend one needs. If it hadn't been for her, the baby would have died.' Shuisheng gives his opinion.

'A baby? Was there a baby?' a boy asks.

They start chatting excitedly among themselves.

'That was because she wasn't the one in love with the

scholar. Being in love makes you weak.'

'What do you know about being in love?'

'The priest was evil. No one likes Falao the priest. Served him right to be changed into a crab.'

'The scholar should have been turned into one, he is such a coward!'

Yanbu murmurs to Charles dismissively, 'Ah, there is such a story, and it is very well known. It has been made into operas. But the story is not of this pagoda, it's of the one near the famed West Lake.'

'There seem to be many versions of the story …'

Yanbu interrupts, 'There certainly are, but do you know the background to the story is that in the previous life, the white snake was indebted to the scholar — he saved her life.'

'So she repaid a debt.' Charles smiles.

'Exactly. Repaying a debt of gratitude is an important part of our culture.'

'Can a snake really love a human?' a tall, timid boy asks suddenly.

'Love is love, whatever and whoever!' declares Shuisheng.

'Can a man love a man, a woman a woman?' asks another.

'A man can definitely love another, haven't you heard of the story of Broken Sleeve, that tells of the affection of an emperor for his favourite servant?'

'But they are not really like a husband and wife, he is just the emperor's plaything.'

'There are others, I am sure,' insists Shuisheng, 'not that I love another man.' He pauses, then smiles innocently: 'Nor a woman. I love my dog.'

They all laugh.

*

Dusk. They sip tea, the sea and the sky calm and still, spreading out in front of them like a painted scroll. Stars already. Proctor and Humboldt had been right — Charles thinks pleasantly of the two astronomers whose books he had recently read — the stars in the tropics are indeed brighter, even at this early hour. This is what Humboldt must have meant by the 'peculiar calm and serene character to the celestial depths in these countries'. A row of islands — the nearest one, their next day's destination — crouches in the distance, composed and orderly, their clear outline reminding him of the stone tortoises he has seen outside ruined temples. Even nature is elegant here. He hasn't drunk anything — not while he is on duty — but he feels intoxicated.

A massive war ship sails past, all the more menacing for its silence.

'One of yours,' Yanbu says, a little piqued that the presence of a foreign war ship no longer surprises him.

'Perhaps we should get one of the pupils to identify it?' Charles, whose back is turned to the sea, glances back, then chuckles: 'But they are all fast asleep.'

'I've heard rumours.'

'Yes?'

'Your country, and my country …' Charles must know. One of his closest friends, he had told Yanbu, is the consul of his country.

'That's nothing to do with you and me.' After a long silence, Charles whispers this, as if addressing the whole darkening island.

'But it's hard not to think of what might happen sometimes.'

'What will happen will happen, but if you ask me nothing will happen.'

'It's easy to say that, if one is well paid and has the freedom to come or go.'

Charles frowns. 'I keep forgetting, sorry.'

'Can I ask, Charles, if it's not too rude. The world is big, why China? For you?'

Charles shifts uneasily. Sooner or later, such a question is asked of one by a Chinese friend. He has a stock answer, though even as he gives it, he hears the shallowness in it.

'I have loved reading about China ever since childhood. Its culture and language fascinated me, always has. It so happened that I studied astronomy and there was a vacancy here and the pay is good. I get paid much better than I would at home.'

'Still, why China? I often hear many ocean people prefer Japan.'

'It is true. For better or worse, Japan has adapted to our ways, the way China hasn't and never shall. But now that I am here, I far prefer China.'

'You mean you like us as we are: backward, superstitious, dirty, oppressed, and enslaved by an alien ruler?'

'But also wise, civilized, warm, and generous to a fault. Yanbu, no country is perfect.'

While his Chinese pride is pricked, another part of Yanbu is touched by Charles' honesty. How often Yanbu has cursed Chinese falsity! People never tell the truth about anything, always too polite, especially in front of others — 'Family ugliness must not be known outside.' Now here is Charles, saying truthful things only a genuine friend would.

'Why can't the other ocean people be like you?' he blurts out.

'I can't speak for others, but I know how lucky I am to … to have met such a kind friend as you.'

Yanbu shivers. Charles is a charmer, but how nicely he does it! Yanbu reciprocates, and confides: 'Me and Jiali … we are trying for a baby.'

'Oh,' says Charles, 'how nice.'

'The thing is, Jiali complains, that mother is putting too much pressure on her, at one point even threatening her, which I find hard to believe.' Jiali also hinted in her letter that his mother might be a little deranged, a point Yanbu strenuously disputed, but that is of course something he does not wish to share with Charles.

He is expected to commiserate, but Charles is lost for words. Yanbu's news touches a nerve. He starts thinking of his late wife, Anne — no, that's not true, he never stops thinking about Anne — but this revelation, that the young couple is trying for a baby, is too hard to take. If he is being honest, it's also a little too intimate. 'It must be difficult for you' is the only comment he can muster.

'Mother-in-law, daughter-in-law, the bane of family life. I tried to keep the balance, when I was at home, but I gather that now I am back here, things are not easy for either of them.'

'I understand.'

'Women. Can't live with them. Can't live without them.'

'Indeed.'

'But Charles, I don't know anything about your family.'

Charles sighs. Now he has to tell.

Confiding to Yanbu about his grief feels different from telling Wu Fang. Instead of relief and a sense of being understood, he feels burdened. The revelation shocks and embarrasses Yanbu, who doesn't know what to say; clearing his throat, he suggests they look through the telescope at the night sky.

The lonely figure of the ocean man carrying the telescope on his shoulders, shuffling hesitantly across the sand, casts a long, ominous shadow in the moonlight and in Yanbu's heart. Awed and moved, Yanbu rises, intending to help, but his awkward gesture is ignored. Breathing heavily, Charles sets the telescope down on the sand and silently adjusts the lens. The touch of his fingers on the cold metal, an absorbing mechanical process, is a welcome distraction. Then he steps back, and beckons to Yanbu. Yanbu hesitates before standing closer, then leans forward, his back tense, ready to stare into the darkness that they share.

For a second or two, the warmth of their breaths stirs both, and Charles is strangely soothed. Since Anne's death, he has claimed the dark of the night as his private time of grief, and avoids company in the evening whenever he can, so as to best indulge in memories. This is the first time in a long time, after that night up the pagoda with Wu Fang, that he's shared this sacred time with another human being. As Yanbu steps back, his gentle, good-looking face glistens in the moonlight, and Charles realises, with a sudden catch in his throat, that he likes the scholarly young teacher.

He likes Yanbu during the day, too, but liking someone in the quiet of the night feels so differently from liking someone in the day. It is ever so much more intimate.

9

She misses her bleeding for the second time, and over the coming weeks becomes thin, pale, and dispirited.

'What will help?' Wu Fang asks, when the nausea becomes too much.

'To get away from the house, and to be near water,' Jiali answers.

So Wu Fang arranges a trip. To get Mrs Yan to agree, they concoct a message from Father Shen, begging Mrs Yan to allow her daughter-in-law to visit his ailing aunt in Shanghai. At first furious that permission even needs to be sought for Jiali to leave, Wu Fang is nonetheless appeased by the thought that she will have her friend all to herself for a good part of a month.

Fudi is already out of view, the only reminder of it the pagoda, and even that just a speck, a lingering wave, words mouthed but not heard. Happily, Jiali ignores it. In her mind, she closes the door to the Yans' house, slots it back into the black-and-white-roofed row of homes crouching low, receding on the horizon, the irritable growl of her mother-in-law muffled and faint. Ahead of her, the vista opens wide as the river swirls here and there, seemingly at will, trailing a longer and broader hem. The prospect of adventure excites. She had dreaded motion sickness, but the sickness stops almost the moment the boat leaves land. The stillness captures her just as suddenly as the whirl of nausea had once taken hold. Leaning back, she dips her fingers in the water, and feels the river's firm, reassuring grasp. It is tremendous. Something of the water permeates her veins. It is a kind of coming home.

Wu Fang, watching Jiali, is more than a little pleased with herself: this is more like it, the friend she knows — her gasp when a fish steals up from the depth below, the shout for Wu Fang to look as she withdraws her hands sharply; her unguarded laughter, her smile. Her happiness matters more than my own, Wu Fang thinks, with a quick jolt of her heart.

They could have gone to Shanghai much faster by ferry, but the smell of the engine would have been intolerable to Jiali; plus, the boat family has ferried the Shens on this route numerous times before, never failing to deliver them to their destination. Surrendering to their skilful steering is one of the pleasures of the trip. Wonderful, the ease of the boat woman rowing, standing cormorant-like with one bare foot folded over the other, a toddler strapped to her hips. Her face, roughened by constant exposure to sun and wind, wrinkles into sudden tenderness as she lowers and smiles at her child; wonderful also is the woman's sense of total autonomy over her own destiny. The whole family is on board: husband, wife, young son, and elder daughter, all, bar the toddler, sharing the rowing, going about it with quiet dignity. Though the labourers and the mistresses are of different classes, there is a sense of kinship. On the great Yangtze the boat floats as a flat thin leaf, but in the firm and assured hands of the boat woman, all feel safe and snug.

Wu Fang sits opposite Jiali, the boat woman's toddler on her lap.

'That is a rare sight,' Jiali laughs. 'You always said you have no patience for the little ones.'

Playing with the boy's fat little fingers, Wu Fang laughs, but does not answer, to herself she says: *You gorgeous being, is this what Jiali is going to have?*

Lanlan takes the toddler from Wu Fang so the two mistresses can have their dinner.

'I see, twice the portion for her,' Wu Fang picks up the bowl.

'Eating for two, I am.'

'Hakka girls are so coarse.'

'And proud of it!'

When Lanlan is out of earshot, Wu Fang leans closer.

'Does this mean you have decided to have the baby?'

Jiali sighs. 'I am torn: the more my mother-in-law threatens me, the less keen I am to do her bidding. She demands a grandson, and talks as if I am just a vessel, a tool for the Yan family to have an heir.'

'She doesn't need to know. It is your decision and yours only. But bear in mind,' Wu Fang lowers her voice, 'if you decide not to keep the baby, there are things I can do to help.'

'I don't know yet what to do.'

'You've got some time, though not long. Just don't tell anyone.'

'It's not just my mother-in-law ... Yanbu ... I sometimes think he married me only so he could have a child, a boy of course.'

'I have done it before.'

'What? Oh that.'

'Yes. There are things you can take, but the earlier the better. You remember Yueyue, the girl whose father used to work for our family as a stable man?'

'Tall girl with long straight hair, sparkling eyes? Very pretty …' Jiali stops: 'but I thought your father fired the man because …'

Wu Fang shivers. 'That man is a beast. She came to me for help, scared that she might be pregnant by him, and I gave her a draught to take.'

'I see.' Jiali is silent for a breath, then, glancing up, she says: 'There must be something more we can do for her. I mean, her home is not safe for her, who's to say he won't do it again.'

Taking Jiali's lead — for it's obvious to Wu Fang that Jiali is uncomfortable talking about her own predicament — Wu Fang nods. 'Exactly. I was going to talk to you about this: I want to set up a girls' school in Fudi.'

'But that is a wonderful idea.' Jiali's eyes brighten.

'Our school can be a sanctuary for girls like Yueyue. We will make sure they are safe.' Watching Jiali's animated face, Wu Fang grows excited herself. 'Lanlan can join, and the two Yan sisters.'

Jiali looks at Wu Fang: how well her friend knows her. 'Can't wait.' She beams, 'Why don't we start now, this trip? Can we do useful things to prepare for the school while we are in Shanghai?'

*

At night, disturbed by the toddler's coughing, Jiali tiptoes out of the small cabin she shares with Wu Fang. Cloaked in moonlight, the intimate picture in front of her unfolds and compels like a prophecy: the muscly arms of the mother that firmly gripped the oar in the day now rest tenderly on the boy; the father curls foetus-like to one side, his back to the rest of his family; the elder daughter lies spread-eagled in the middle, the casual, shameless exposure of her body a contrasting, though integral, part of the family as a whole. Jiali steps back, stirred: though they are humble, they are also fearless, because they trust; perhaps so should she. Somehow reassured, she goes to sleep, too tired to ask what or who it is that she should trust. No decision is made about her pregnancy, for how could she?

Morning brings grave distractions: the toddler is not at all well. His cough has worsened. Learning that Wu Fang is a doctor, the mother turns her beseeching face, her arms loose, her shoulders hunched. The elder daughter cries; the father turns hastily to light incense to placate the angry river god who has brought about this misfortune, and clumsily knocks down one of the two wooden oars, creating further upset. Wu Fang's treatment, though effective, does not restore calm. Calamities can strike out of nowhere and no one is spared. The family rallies to row on, stoically facing the river ahead, though forever glancing backwards at the boy. The oar is retrieved, but fear reigns the rest of their journey to Shanghai.

*

'It's all my fault', Jiali says unhappily from the carriage once they have disembarked, peering back at the boat pinned helplessly between two large ships. 'When I held the boy, I let his scarf loose. His mother protested, but I laughed at her.'

'Nonsense! You wanted the sun to shine on him. Absolutely the right thing to do. There was hardly any wind. Stop blaming yourself,' orders Wu Fang. 'I will send Xiao Mei to check on them. But he will be fine.'

'He does look a sturdy little fellow.'

'Trust a doctor. The poor are tough, they have to be. The child grew up on that boat and is practically fed by wind and rain.'

*

Wu Fang transforms in the city. Even in the carriage, her eyes narrow, squint, and sharpen. Something heavy and hard sets all about her; she grows rough edges. Her voice, too, becomes harsh and shrill as she spits the high-pitched Shanghai dialect Jiali, at first, finds difficult to follow. Shanghai is bad-tempered, a faceless giant quick to take offence. It snarls indiscriminately, and demands one to be loud, abrupt, and larger than life; Jiali is in awe as her friend negotiates with coolies, servants, and red-turbaned Sikh policemen to get them to their hotel, though Wu Fang's boldness contrasts with her own nervousness, and makes her feel a little inadequate.

This is not Jiali's first time in Shanghai. As the carriage trundles through the streets, memories are jolted. She was but a girl then and had noticed different things: the way the women dressed and held themselves, the dust, the smells. She'd had a carefree mind. But her mind is pre-occupied now, for the trip to Shanghai has a new purpose — to prepare for the Fudi girl's school. They discuss many practical errands — getting stocks of textbooks, chalks, boards; securing speakers — but Wu Fang also insists on interposing these with visits to parks and gardens to amuse her friend.

'Isn't it just like the old days?' Wu Fang enthuses, beaming from the top steps of an ocean-style hotel, by the gate of a grand bank, at the end of a fierce haggling session over the price of chairs. Jiali nods in assent; since her marriage she is quite the mistress of deception. Wu Fang is loud and jolly, but she has secrets, Jiali concludes, as she tries to hide her own.

*

The days pass pleasantly enough. Then, the evening of discovery starts with Wu Fang's maid Xiao Mei knocking on the door of Jiali and Lanlan's room, adjacent to theirs, with a message from her mistress. She receives no answer. Wu Fang asks the hotel staff if they have seen anybody leaving the room. Two young gentlemen left an hour or so ago, says the porter; he heard them giving the waiting carriage an address in the harbour. The address is in the part of town famed for cheap prostitutes, which the sailors frequent. The porter nods in a knowing way. Always the same address, he claims, the last three evenings. So this is where Jiali and Lanlan have gone each time Jiali claimed tiredness and wanted to retire early.

Wu Fang knocks on the battered door. They had walked past endless rows of low, darkly lit huts spilling with music and merry laughter, and are now in the quiet, residential part of the district, no less poor, though more decent looking.

Lanlan herself opens the door, dressed in men's clothes. Before surprise can register on the girl's face, Wu Fang pushes her aside and strides into the narrow passage. It is not the first time she's been here, and she is relieved to note the place, though small and modest, remains clean. A strong odour prevails — a herbal concoction. The toddler, cradled in the arms of the boat woman, is turning his face away from Jiali, a bowl in her hand, the elder girl and the father coaxing the boy to turn back. Wu Fang walks over to the toddler and strokes his cheeks as she speaks to the mother in a calm, reassuring manner. The arrival of the two newcomers distracts the toddler, and Jiali takes full advantage of this and tips the rest of the concoction into his open mouth.

Back at the hotel Wu Fang dismisses the maids. They did not talk in the carriage.

'I would have told you,' Jiali starts.

'I gave them medicine and told them how and when to administer it!' Wu Fang sighs.

'So you have, and they are ever so grateful, not just for the medicine, but also for the roof over their head and the money for food. You have done so much for them, but I couldn't convince them to take your medicine.'

'I knew it. The capsules are too foreign looking, aren't they? They took the herbs willingly on the boat.'

'That's just it. They are suspicious. I thought of treating them myself, but then I grew doubtful … The herbalist I consulted was a trustworthy one, I have made inquiries. The concoction is working, isn't it? I saw you checking the boy out just now. Tell me he's getting better.'

'He seems to be,' Wu Fang concedes.

Jiali whispers, 'Then please, please forgive my interference. I simply wanted peace of mind. I couldn't enjoy Shanghai, and our hard-earned time together, without being assured that the boy was going to be all right.'

'Okay, but let me take over from now on. The harbour is no place for you.'

*

Days later, at the sight of the lone, tight-muscled man waiting for them by an unfamiliar boat Jiali knows all is not well but is too scared to ask. When they dock for the night, Wu Fang finally tells her: 'The boy had an underlying illness, long before we even boarded the boat. It couldn't have been helped ...'

'So he died, after all.'

'Yes, two days ago.'

'He might still be alive if ...' Jiali's voice breaks. 'I fear we brought them bad luck.'

'Nonsense. We are not gods.'

'How matter of factly you talk, Wu Fang.'

'They abandoned the house I rented for them and went to stay in the derelict Earth God Temple at the end of the street. Someone had told them to pacify the god with prayer, and that's what they did, night after night. When I got there, I knew straight away the boy was not well and arranged for a carriage to take him to the ocean hospital; I have a friend who'd agreed to treat him. But you should have seen the look on their faces.' She bites her lip. 'Terror. It was as if I wanted to send the boy to hell. The very place the boy would have the best chance to be cured was, in their mind, the worst place he could be.'

'This is terrible, terrible.'

'It makes one mad to think of it! The boy could have lived.'

'Wu Fang! Oh Wu Fang, what have we done!'

'This is exactly why ... This is the sort of thing that ...' Wu Fang swallows, overcome. 'When I first got to Japan, my aim was simple, as you know — become a surgeon, cure people; but the longer I stayed, the more I saw how things were done there, the angrier I grew with what's happening here, in China. Their people are fed, educated, and respected, and ours poor, ignorant, and despised. So what if our bodies are healthy, but our minds are diseased? How can a surgeon help with that? There are so many things wrong here, our people are sleepwalking to their graves. How do we make them see light and sense, instead of ghosts and incense? I realised, you see, that being a doctor is not enough.'

'I know.'

'What do you mean?'

Jiali glances at the far end of the boat. Certain that she will not be overheard, she whispers: 'I know about your revolutionary work.'

'How?'

'Those boxes at the docks you went to inspect; the men arriving at night, all wearing the same yinyang symbols on their left shoulders, the same as the men surrounding our house when Charles was attacked. Is it a particular fashion among Chinese students in Japan?' Jiali lists breathlessly. 'I have eyes. Why didn't you tell me?'

'I was never going to lie to you,' Wu Fang sighs, 'but I had hoped to leave it as late as I could.'

'Don't you trust me?'

'I thought you would try to stop me.'

'Then you don't know me.'

'Jiali!'

'I admire you for it. The unjustness of it all, the suffering. Yueyue, Lanlan, that poor boat family, even my mother-in-law: this rotten so-called tradition that twisted her mind and poisoned her heart. All of this must end, and not a day too soon!'

'It's like surgery, some brutality is absolutely necessary.'

'I understand. I want one thing though, one thing only.'

'Yes?'

'Promise me you will be safe.'

'I will be careful.'

'Promise.'

'I won't take unnecessary risks. As to being safe, who can be safe nowadays? Besides, safe is boring, safe is not doing anything and that's not me. You cannot ask me to be less than who I am.'

'But you are all I have! You are the one person I can tell all my secrets to. Not Yanbu, definitely not him, not even my parents. I can't bear to lose you, Wu Fang!'

'You won't.'

At some sound from the other side of the boat, they glance up. Then, lowering her voice, Jiali says, 'Why not include me? Let me be part of it. That way, I can be helpful. Though I worry I might not be good enough.'

'You, not good enough?' Wu Fang shakes her head, 'I don't want you to take the risk,' she puts a hand firmly on Jiali's arm, 'and you can help in other ways.'

*

It pours. The boat rocks in the wetness. Wu Fang goes inside the cabin; Jiali stands a while and watches the boat man sullenly tighten the rope and settle the boat for the night. Though well-built and obedient, he has an air of indifference that makes Jiali keep her distance; there is hardly any communication beyond the absolutely necessary. As Jiali turns from the man, the image of the boat family sleeping together on their journey to Shanghai comes to her, and she sheds a tear. The death of the little boy, whom she was very fond of, casts a shadow on an otherwise good trip. The world, never a just one, is an even harsher place now; Wu Fang's confession has given her a sense of danger and uncertainty, though the sharing of the secret brings her even closer to her old friend.

*

Wu Fang works long into the night in the small cabin they share, by the light of the candle perched on a small stool, papers spilling onto their shared, makeshift bed. The errands in Shanghai to garner support for the girls' school were a big success, but they also generated more work for Wu Fang.

'Lanlan has learned accounting. She can add it all up tomorrow,' Jiali says as she enters.

'It can't wait, the workmen building the school need to be paid on time.'

Later, drifting back to consciousness, Jiali hears the creaking of the bed and smells a strong scent of burnt candle wax. A few breaths later, all is dark as Wu Fang snuggles down next to her.

'How did you join?' Jiali whispers.

'The Society for a New China? A fellow student recruited me, when we were playing chess at the Chinese Students' Club in Tokyo.' Wu Fang chuckles, recollecting. 'A lot of the overseas Chinese students have joined, our members are from all over China. We all have work to do upon returning.'

'Is that why you often disappear into the countryside and the nearby towns?'

'Yes.'

'I guessed as much.' She pauses, then says, 'Aren't you scared, sometimes?'

'Not for myself, no. It feels good to be doing something, but I do worry for those I care for. You, my parents ...'

'What about your brother? He holds such an important position in court.'

'He is not in the movement, not officially, though my sister-in-law is. It is better that way. He can get the latest news from the court, and she will pass it on. I am in contact with them often. Nobody is to know any of this of course. Especially my parents.'

'Of course.'

'A family of traitors, we are,' Wu Fang jokes.

'And yet you don't want me to join,' says Jiali, jealous.

'My parents would be worried to death, I don't want to add yours to the list!'

Jiali's hands seek Wu Fang's in the darkness, and having found what they are looking for, hold them tight. She whispers, 'I have decided.'

'About the baby?' Wu Fang's voice is alert and cautious.

Jiali sits up.

'It wasn't conceived in love. I can't carry a life inside me without feeling I have actively wanted it; I am not just a vessel.'

'Indeed you are not.'

'I won't be bound. I want to be free.'

'Good. Are you sure?'

'Very. It's not right to keep it, because I don't feel a connection to it, none at all.'

'Then I shall help you get rid of it.'

'Sorry it took me so long to make up my mind.'

In Shanghai, things would have been easier, they both know.

'It's a big decision. I understand.' Wu Fang says softly.

A long silence. Just as Wu Fang believes her friend has fallen asleep, she hears supressed snuffling.

'Oh Jiali.'

'I am sad, too.'

'Of course you are, of course. Ssssh.'

The river rises to rock them, swaying a long, firm arm of deliberation, pushing and tilting the two bodies together, one half asleep, one half awake. Aided by the motion, Wu Fang wraps her arms around Jiali and rocks the same rhythm as the river; she is not letting go.

10

What are her ears for but to listen to every single word uttered between laboured breaths by the ocean surgeon; what are her hands for but to swiftly and accurately act on his instructions. Beyond these, Wu Fang does not exist. Her world narrows as she focuses inward, to the small, square space in front of her, the patient draped with a white sheet lying on the steel bed, the rugged wound on his leg exposed, red and raw, pulsating, steaming, smelling the way flesh does. Fellow students in Japan, grown men, had fainted upon first sight of a wound, but Wu Fang's hands are steady and her heart rejoices: no one Chinese, however well trained, has ever been allowed to assist in an operation by an ocean surgeon before, but there is a shortage of medical staff at the hospital in Fudi due to Europeans going off to the hills to cool down for the summer, 'and so it seems, Miss Wu, that you might need to step in and lend me a hand with this procedure'.

The operation is over, seemingly in seconds. It feels like a dream. When she had finally plucked up the courage to meet the surgeon's eyes, Wu Fang wasn't quite sure whether it was a smile or a frown she was getting from underneath the white face mask and bushy eyebrows. Now he is gone, and she stands dazed; finding her eyes and face itchy, she realises she is soaked through with sweat. But a weight lifts, and she goes about with a song in her heart. A Chinese nurse enters, and Wu Fang gives instructions, surprising herself with her eloquence and detailed knowledge. The patient is wheeled out and she begins to fill in the paperwork; only then does she discover his identity: the doctor had said something about the naval college, she now recalls. Too nervous at the time, it had hardly registered.

Shaken by the discovery, and tired beyond words after the operation, she sinks into the bench on the corridor outside the operating room, thinking she will take a moment's rest. She loses track of time. When she stirs from her awkward position, stiff and sore, it is already dark. Feeling as though she has been in a battle, and survived, she becomes vaguely aware of a familiar figure standing beside her.

'How did it go?' the man asks.

'All right, I think,' she answers modestly, taking him for a fellow doctor.

'Wu Fang, don't you recognise me?'

She rubs her eyes: 'Charles! What happened to your beard?'

'I reckon I can get away with a shave, with all my countrymen leaving Fudi, including my consul, and it being so, so hot! Will you stop staring at me?'

'You look much younger without all those hairs on your chin.' Wu Fang sits up.

Charles grins, then his face grows serious again.

'So how is Yanbu?'

'Ruptured artery ...' she explains. 'He will be awake in an hour or so. A close call though. What happened?'

'A most unfortunate accident. Yanbu was hit by a cannon fired by one of the students during a shooting practice.'

'Poor man!' Wu Fang is genuinely concerned. Never a huge

108

fan of Yanbu, she nonetheless does not wish such a misfortune to fall on him.

'A huge shame,' he shakes his head. 'Everything before then had gone so well. Yanbu was not even meant to be on the mission — he isn't experienced in military procedures — but when he was called, he stepped up, a most decent thing to do.'

'You got him here just in time. Any delay, with that much loss of blood …'

'Thank you for saving him, Wu Fang.'

'I didn't do the operation itself, but it was my first to assist.' She beams. 'I think I did all right.'

'You did more than all right.'

'How would you know?'

'Dr Johnson, the surgeon, said so.'

'He never told …'

'It would never do to praise someone Chinese in their earshot, a woman, too, in case he or she gets above themselves, but one can be honest with a fellow ocean man.'

'Me being a woman was never an issue for them, Buddha be thanked. It is one of the advantages of working in a Christian hospital.'

'You know that I disapprove of a great many things my people do here in the name of religion, but I whole-heartedly applaud the hospital.' Charles smiles. 'Anyway, the surgeon told me in my language, which you wouldn't have understood, and you were asleep.'

'Well. I am glad, to assist him made me feel very special.'

'That indeed you are.'

The admiring gaze Charles gives her, so open and unguarded, makes her change subject.

'Does Jiali know? Has Mrs Yan been informed?'

'Yes, yes, they have all been told; Mrs Yan, especially, had to be amply reassured that Yanbu will be sewed back into one piece again. She is nearly hysterical.'

Wu Fang nods sympathetically. 'Did she give you a hard time? I can imagine. Is Jiali coming here? Soon I hope.'

'I believe so. At least ... that's what she told me when I saw them earlier. She was a great calming influence on her mother-in-law. I tried to explain the procedure to Mrs Yan, but it was only with Jiali's help that I was able to convince her. She was terrified by the thought that Yanbu had to be cut—'

'So Jiali is on her way?'

'She will come as soon as she is allowed to visit. Shall I go now and tell her?'

'Do!' Wu Fang rises to leave too, but is held back by the look in his eyes. 'Is there something else?'

'No.' Charles seems suddenly flustered. 'I will just go and see if Yanbu is awake first.'

*

The smell of disinfectant and the stillness of the recovery ward reminds Wu Fang once again of her student days in Japan. She'd enclosed all memories of China in one huge bubble with Jiali at the centre, and held it close to her chest, drawing comfort from it from time to time; she hadn't found any aspects of overseas college life, so often complained about by other Chinese students, too hard to bear. Of course, compared to the majority, who were on the Qing government scholarships, she lived a comfortable life, thanks to her father's wealth, but she couldn't understand the fuss the others made of the endless exams and the austere life of an apprentice doctor. She had welcomed tasks others thought beneath them and relished the schedule others found punishing. She had simply wanted to qualify as a surgeon, and to go home to be with her best friend.

She is impatient to see Jiali, partly to discuss the termination of Jiali's pregnancy, which is becoming more urgent by the day. Wu Fang had favoured meeting in her own house, away from the prying eyes of Mrs Yan, but now, waiting for Jiali, she wonders if the hospital itself might be the place. Having completed Yanbu's operation, the surgeon has set off for the hills and Wu Fang is the most senior staff member left. She so wants Jiali to witness this, her moment of pride — to have assisted in her first real operation. She had not thought it possible, but the two have grown even closer after the trip to Shanghai. How good it had been to have Jiali all to herself again, to sleep next to her, breathing in as she breathed out ... A sudden image comes to Wu Fang, causing her to stop in the middle of the corridor — an image of herself kissing Jiali on the forehead, as they lay together that last evening on the boat. Did she really do that? If not, why is the image so clear? She must have done, and yet she has folded the kiss into the layers of darkness, so that awake, she herself is at a loss to find it. She is sure Jiali was not aware of it, and now, the thought of seeing her again — they haven't met since returning from the trip, over a week ago — triggers in Wu Fang a strange set of reactions: clammy hands, a sweaty brow, and a fast-beating heart. What is the matter? Wu Fang wonders if she is quite well ...

There is Charles by Yanbu's bed, a devoted friend if there ever was one, but as his eyes raise at her footsteps, she recognises the look that he gave her earlier, that had made her turn her eyes away, knowing suddenly what it is. She leans down and checks Yanbu's pulse, nods, then beckons to Charles. The two tiptoe outside the room.

'Go fetch Jiali. He will wake very soon,' she says in the reassuring tone of a doctor.

'You look tired yourself, get some rest while I am gone.' He urges in a tender, concerned voice.

She shakes her head. 'I don't need rest,' she pauses, thinking carefully about what to say next, 'I need some advice.'

'What kind of advice?'

'I've had a letter from someone I knew when I was in Japan, a fellow Chinese student.'

'What does he want?'

'To marry me.' She is surprised at her own calm. To lie so outrageously seems too easy, but then, she tells herself, it is for Charles' own good. Besides, she did receive a few proposals in Japan, all of which she refused.

'I see.' He drops his eyes.

'It is not the first time he has proposed.'

'He must love you very much.' Charles' voice is low and coarse.

'He is certainly very stubborn and will once again be disappointed.'

'I see.' His voice, though low, becomes curious and hopeful — the reason for her to speak fast and straight.

'He never seemed to believe me when I told him I could love no man. It's not him, he is a handsome and clever young man, someone I think many women will easily fall in love with.'

'I ...'

'If you say, "I see" once again I shall have to knock you down!' she threatens gently.

'I was only going to ask: no man at all?'

'I can't help it. I was brought up differently: I see men as my kind, I feel a kindship to them, I feel as if I am a man myself, you see ... You must believe me. I haven't told many people this, not that I am ashamed of it, but they won't understand; I am telling the truth. Charles.'

The grace and sincerity of her tone of voice moves him so that, though sobered and disappointed, Charles is not disheartened, and is saved from despair. He manages a quick smile, and to say: 'I am very honoured.'

Then he remembers this is exactly what she herself said to him on the pagoda when he confided in her about the death of his wife. Lost for words, he gazes at her in silence.

'Have you any advice? What shall I say, to convince him once and for all that marriage is not for me?'

Their eyes meet, and hers stay on his with a frankness that makes it impossible for him to ignore.

'Are you sure?'

'Don't you know me at all?' she whispers. 'He is a dear friend; I do not want him hurt.'

Charles pauses, then says, 'Tell him you are in love with someone else.'

'Why not the truth, surely that will hurt him less?'

'The truth is you are not in love with him. Love is love, as you told me on the ship. It matters not whether it is with a man or a woman, or even with a snake. Tell him you are in love with someone else.'

'You are very eloquent!' she laughs.

'Aren't you?'

'Eloquent?'

'No, not that,' he shakes his head vehemently, a little impatient. 'In love with someone else. You can tell me, truly.'

So he doesn't believe her, after all.

'No,' she says firmly, exasperated, 'that would be a lie. I am not in love. I don't know what love is.'

'Don't you?'

'No.' Wu Fang's voice becomes slow and serious: 'But you do. You must, you must know what true love is. What you had with Anne, surely nothing else can compare?'

Charles opens his mouth, and then sighs.

By evoking Anne's name, she had meant to make him see how fleetingly his fondness of herself is, but little does she realise how much the look on his face affects her.

'It is brave of you, Charles,' Wu Fang whispers, 'to have loved. I salute you.'

'It is not bravery, Wu Fang,' Charles cries, 'I couldn't help it. And neither will you, when it comes to it.'

Wu Fang falls silent. Then, in a softer voice: 'I just hope it's not too late to tell him, that I don't — can't — love him.'

Charles shakes his head. 'Not too late.' He licks his dry lips. 'Didn't you say he's clever? He will soon see sense. Anybody who knows you would want to keep your friendship, at whatever cost.'

'You think too well of me, Charles.' She smiles, shaking off the thoughts that are spinning round her head. 'You should go to Jiali now.'

Wu Fang watches Charles leave, feeling relieved: the ocean man is grieving still, and his attachment to her can't have been formed too long; a short hurt is preferable to a long pain. Some love easily and move on quickly, and the young ocean man had better be one such person.

*

Wu Fang does her round of check-ups later in the evening. The nurse on duty reports on the excellent progress of patient number four: not only is Mr Yan recovering well from the operation, he is also an exemplary gentleman. He has swallowed whatever is given him, no crying out for attention, no complaining of pain. Wu Fang nods.

Yanbu's eyes have been following her from the moment she entered the ward; now she is by his side, he makes an effort to rise, and is firmly told to lay back by the nurse.

'Welcome back,' smiles Wu Fang.

'I am so grateful, Wu Fang. They told me you were the one who operated on me.'

'I was only assisting. The person you ought to thank is Charles, who got you here just in time. You have lost a lot of blood and would have been in a much worse situation if there had been delays.'

'Charles is a true friend.'

'You were lucky ...'

'Very lucky!' A breathless new voice joins in; it is Jiali. 'I came as soon as Charles told me it was okay,' she says, 'That was a close one, Yanbu, but thank the Buddha you are all right now.'

'Where is Charles?' Wu Fang asks.

'Oh, he had some stuff to deal with at the college, but he will visit later, he said.'

'Have you been worried?' Yanbu asks Jiali tenderly.

'Naturally.'

Wu Fang steps back and watches the two leaning together and talking in eagerness, to onlookers a perfect picture of marital harmony: the doting wife with her ailing husband. She keeps away deliberately and stops the nurse on duty from disturbing the couple.

'Give them time,' she says, feeling momentarily apprehensive for what she is about to help Jiali do. It is, of course, Jiali's own decision, but isn't it rather a convenient solution to her own dilemma, too — wanting Jiali all to herself? A child would bring the couple closer; indeed, the birth of a child can save a failing marriage. Jiali claims not to love Yanbu now, but what would happen if a child were born?

Wu Fang glances up and catches a flash of Jiali's smile; she remembers again their time together on the boat. Her heart hardens.

*

When Jiali leaves an exhausted but pleased Yanbu, Wu Fang walks abreast of her. Finally, she can have Jiali all to herself: to be congratulated by her, and to plan ahead with her. The two will have so much to talk about. But Jiali does not slow down, even as she turns and thanks Wu Fang for her part in the operation.

'So you've heard.' Wu Fang beams.

'Charles told me that it was the first you have assisted in.'

'Did he?'

'Congratulations! I know how much this matters to you. Charles was so impressed.'

And you? But she doesn't say it loud.

'He looks so different.'

'Who? What are you talking about?'

'Charles. His face, without the beard. I nearly didn't recognise him at first. My mother-in-law thought it impossible that he should be able to speak Chinese, so I had to translate everything he said, even though, well, you know how good his Chinese is. It was actually quite funny ...'

Wu Fang slows down, *Charles this, Charles that*, really, sometimes Jiali can be so easily distracted. Brushing away the disappointment that she hasn't yet been properly congratulated by Jiali, she calls after her friend.

'Jiali.'

'What is it?'

Wu Fang lowers her voice. 'About that matter that we talked about on the boat?'

'Oh.' Jiali bites her lip. 'I thought we were going to discuss it at your house ...'

'I know, but ...' she quickly scans the empty corridor, 'I've got all the stuff ready, here.'

'Wu Fang, I ...' There is no mistaking the sudden look of alarm on Jiali's face.

'You have changed your mind.' Wu Fang's heart sinks.

'Can't I decide later?'

'Later will be too late. In fact, later means never.' It is the truth, but the sharpness in her voice makes Jiali wince; Wu Fang continues mercilessly: 'So it's now or never.'

'On the boat, my mind was clear, and everything seemed so straightforward,' Jiali says slowly.

'But now it isn't?' Wu Fang purses her lips.

'You saw him lying there, Wu Fang, so helpless, so happy to see me, to be alive.' Jiali pleads passionately: 'He wants a child desperately and I have the means to make it happen. How can I not give it to him? There, I am weak, I cannot help it. I am so sorry I failed you.'

Wu Fang steps back, a flash of impatience makes her speak fast. 'You don't have to justify your decision to anybody. But, forgive me for saying this, feeling sorry for Yanbu is not a reason to have the baby.'

Avoiding Wu Fang's eyes, Jiali's voice becomes urgent and miserable. 'I don't know anything! I just know I don't want to hurt him.'

11

All his life, Mrs Yan had obsessed about a calamity befalling Yanbu and finally it has happened. Thank the Buddha he is alive, released all in one piece from the ocean hospital, accompanied by his ocean colleague. In a glowing voice, Yanbu reveals how Charles saved his life: 'Did he tell you how he pushed me out of the way where the cannon was to land? He himself could have been hit. I don't know how he knew, but if it hadn't been for him, it might not have just been my left thigh that was injured. The cannon made a hole big enough to sink a man where I had been standing.'

Mrs Yan declares eternal devotion to Charles. For a mere drop of water, the Yan family will pay back a flowing fountain. Does the ocean gentleman know there is no limit to what they will do in gratitude?

Blushing, Charles murmurs, 'Mrs Yan. Yanbu exaggerates! I did nothing worth mentioning.'

'He is so modest, and kind beyond words,' says Yanbu.

Out of danger now, the invalid sits grandly on his bed, is daily fed nourishing chicken and mushroom soups, and receives a constant stream of visitors. Important-looking carriages and sedans weave busily in and out of the modest, narrow lane like dragons in a small pool. Wu Fang, the other person the Yans are indebted to, though this is not as enthusiastically acknowledged, drops in regularly to change his dressings; Director Zuo sends warm messages and home-made cures for a speedy recovery. The Yans might have an injured son, but it looks to envious neighbours as if the family has gained good fortune. Such an erect back and look of importance on Mrs Yan's face. A *Renao* — the warm, bustling atmosphere, peculiar to a prosperous family filled with important comings and goings — is something she'd long given up hope for, and yet here it is. She most certainly approves of the speed with which Jiali learns wound dressing from Wu Fang and takes over the task; Mrs Yan looks on favourably also at the fuss Jiali makes of Yanbu, all positive signs of her daughter-in-law's increasing devotion to her husband. What Jiali does still falls far short of Mrs Yan's standards, of course, but her expectations of Jiali have never been high.

Only Wu Fang discerns the sad truth — that there is more love in the wife for the husband in the dressing of his wound than in all their previous intimacies added together. Healing gives unadulterated pleasure, she well knows. She senses also that Jiali's conflicted mind and vacant heart welcome the responsibilities of caring for Yanbu and the management of the household. On Ancestor Worship day, the Yans' is quite a place for sore eyes: large, firm grapefruits, hollowed and filled with incense, hang off beams and down walls on colourful threads, their fruity scents warm and welcoming; small and large pagodas made of little trinkets have been placed in various corners and on the stone tables in the garden, to bring in and retain good luck. Yanbu's two younger sisters, dressed in festive gowns, run with happy smiles, holding more trinkets in their hands; giggling and animated, they are no longer shy. Servants walk purposefully with dustpans, vases, and various other objects. All seem to know what they are doing; all seem to obey invisible commands. Yanbu does not recall his home being so richly decorated and the festival so ably managed, so lavishly celebrated; and when he announces his praise aloud to his wife, in front of all, no one can doubt, surely, that he is the most content man in Fudi.

*

Yanbu is nearly fully recovered, when a new visitor is announced: Li Jian, one of Yanbu's old school friends, just returned from Shanghai. Stout, flamboyantly dressed, and carrying himself with a quiet swagger, Li Jian dominates the conversation as the two reminiscence about the time when both were pupils at the naval college.

'All the Fudi boys ganged up against me, except you, Yanbu, for that I am eternally grateful,' Li Jian laughs heartily.

'You were the tallest in the class then, and you talked fast with your Manchu accent, you really stood out among us Fudi boys,' remembers Yanbu.

Wu Fang watches coolly. Despite the familiarity, she senses an awkwardness between the two old friends; she is also not at all sure of the repeated glances Li Jian throws at Jiali, even though his words are addressed to Yanbu.

'So what brought you to Fudi, Mr Li,' Mrs Yan asks politely.

'I came to Fudi because of my father, Mrs Yan,' he speaks in a confiding tone.

'What is it your father does?'

'How could you forget, Mother?' Yanbu turns to Mrs Yan, impatient. 'Li Jian's father is the Mayor of Shanbei.'

'Oh, silly me,' says Mrs Yan, 'of course. Shanbei is a bit too far to travel easily to from Fudi, which was why you stayed with us during the holidays sometimes, I remember ...'

Li Jian smiles. 'Actually, my father's no longer the mayor there. He's got a new position elsewhere.'

'So where is he working now?' asks Mrs Yan solicitously.

'Here in Fudi.'

'Fudi? But I don't understand. We don't have a mayor ... Oh ... you don't mean ...' Mrs Yan gasps.

'Yes, he has been promoted. He is the new governor of Fudi.'

Mrs Yan is beyond herself. This precious *guanxi* — connection — with the son of the governor, is another piece of good luck coming the Yans' way, well worth cultivating. After a few flustered words, she settles to ask: 'Did your father come here alone, or with the Old Mistress?'

'Father has brought his third concubine ...'

'Ah, plenty of officials do that.'

'... without telling my mother!' Li Jian barks.

'A man of his age would need looking after, and it is wise of your father to choose someone young and energetic. The Old Mistress would not have taken the journey well, even though it is not that far, but your third mother ...' Mrs Yan soothes understandingly.

'Well, if only the woman would look after him!' Li Jian lowers his voice. 'This is strictly between us, mind: I never could stand her.'

Yanbu glances away. A change of topic is called for. Fortunately, Li Jian himself loses interest. He winks at Yanbu. 'Enough said about her, anyway. Not everyone is as lucky as you, my dear brother.' He looks pointedly at Jiali. 'I am a huge fan of your beautiful poems,' he bows deeply to her.

Wu Fang frowns and Mrs Yan purses her lips; Yanbu, face reddening, says, 'He means the ones that are widely circulated among the candidates for the imperial exam of course.'

'Naturally.' Li Jian nods.

Wu Fang does not like the look she sees the men exchange.

A proposal to climb the pagoda the day after is suggested by Li Jian, who seems keen to rekindle his old friendship. Mrs Yan expresses concern for her son's fitness to climb so soon after his operation, but Yanbu declares himself able, and suggests that his colleague Charles, who is not present, but who loves the pagoda, be invited too, so it will be a party.

*

The day dawns bright and promising. Impatient as ever, Jiali is the first to reach the top.

How familiar the view, and yet how different. The fields rise and arrange themselves in brown and green checks, as shapely and clearly defined as a large chess board; the hills in the distance beyond the fields stand erect and serene as ancient wise men holding scrolls in the folds of their elbows, partially obscured by the late morning mist. The world is immense and mysterious, and yet Jiali, watching, does not feel diminished. At a stretch of her hands, she would be able to move the chess pieces; at the stir of her lips, converse with the elders. The vast sky is but a soft piece of blue silk she can wrap around her, and the warm air a friend whispering intimately. Everything seems possible and within reach, all claim a connection, eager to communicate with her, because she is with child.

And feels fitter than ever. She tires easily, of course, but the sickness, which she had feared returning after her Shanghai trip, does not return; and as a result, her appetite increases enormously, even though, typical for this stage of pregnancy, she does not show. Her energy, a little waned in those earlier days of pregnancy, is restored, to her delight. She resumes sword practice daily, which she had stopped doing for a while in those days of sickness.

She is herself again, and more.

Now she is breathless with joy, she cannot think how the idea of terminating the pregnancy ever occurred to her. What a ridiculous and cruel plan. How she'd nearly ruined her chance of happiness. Oh, to be a mother, to carry a life inside one, this life: what an honour!

But even as she is engulfed in the tremendous surge of this newfound confidence and happiness, she is also easily affected, and prone to mood swings as only an expectant mother can be; the same role equips her with sharper eyes and ears, and she becomes more observant. Yanbu's recuperation at home has brought all of them together in such close proximity and, watching Charles, Jiali believes she knows what the ocean man is going through: a gesture, a sigh, a glance, and a whisper, nothing escapes her, everything is noted and keenly reflected on. Wu Fang has no idea, Jiali has concluded, and she has resolved to do her best as a friend to bring the two together. She has quite dismissed the dreams she herself once had of him — silly fantasies, unimaginable to her now, though she does like his face without the beard; it is more open somehow.

'Did you say you'd like to learn more about Chinese poems, Charles? You could do worse than starting with the Ballad of

Mulan. It is one of Wu Fang's favourites,' she had suggested, knowing her friend unable to resist the role of a teacher; then, for days afterwards, she'd sat back and listened to the two:

'*I don't hear the sound of weaving, I hear only the girl sighing. I ask what is she thinking? I ask why is she sighing ...*'

'No, not *sighing*,' Wu Fang's voice, correcting him. '*I ask what is she remembering.* Mulan does not just sit there sighing all the time!' A laugh, a pause, then praise for his ability to memorise the lines so fast.

'Any poor devil learning your language has to do it the hard way. My Chinese teacher used to make me recite chunks of the *Three Character Classic*, which I still just remember ... *When first born, a man is kindly disposed ...*'

'Stop, Charles, stop. I've had enough of Confucius. I'm afraid he's not very popular with us.' Wu Fang's laugher, then: 'Now quick, the next line.'

'*Last night came the war summon, the Khan having inspected his ... troops?*'

How endearing the hesitancy in Charles' voice, the unusual emphasis, not yet knowing the full meaning of the words he pronounced, she'd declared to Wu Fang. Wu Fang had nodded and Jiali'd felt smug: she'd surely created a most romantic atmosphere for the two. But as she turned from them, smiling, there suddenly followed a sense of loss, of loneliness, which she couldn't account for. Perhaps it was to do with being pregnant, the strange mood swings, as Wu Fang warned her of, she'd told herself, and carried on matchmaking.

*

A fluster of feathers disturbs Jiali's thoughts: a startled pheasant taking flight, shocked by the sudden ascent of the group. Jiali leans over the top of the pagoda: there are her two little sisters, Mochou and Moli, just getting out of their carriages. They don't often have the opportunity to come outside. Jiali waves: the grins, the clapping of hands. How wonderful the touch of freshness the sun gives to their young, upturned faces.

Now Wu Fang's quick and passionate voice swirls up the steps of the pagoda: '... what do you say? Science, English, Chinese, any subject! How can we call ours a civilised country when we only educate our boys? It is surely a crime that only the rich can afford for their women to learn to read and write ... Ah, there you are Jiali, ahead of us again.' Wu Fang's face emerges.

'I started off earlier than you lot since you told me to slow down ...' she stops herself, remembering that Yanbu hasn't yet been told of the pregnancy.

'Because you are always in a rush!' Wu Fang quickly covers for her, and the two exchange a look. Really, now that she has decided to go ahead with the pregnancy, there is no need to keep it a secret from Yanbu, and yet Jiali guards the news jealously. Why? Jiali asks herself.

'Where will the school be?' Yanbu, unsuspecting, asks.

'Down by the harbour, not at all far from the market, on the site of the old Christian girls' school,' answers Wu Fang.

'Oh yes, the old building was burnt down by angry townspeople, after the rumours of them abducting virgin girls for sacrifice spread. I hear my father mention that case often,' Li Jian adds authoritatively, 'as an example of the necessity for balanced governance. The ocean people built roads, and the peasants condemned them for destroying good feng shui; they built lighthouses, and our sailors decided they were to guide the foreign ships to invade us; they connected us with the world using telegraphs, and the town accused them of sending evil messages ...' Turning solicitously to Charles, he laughs: 'You poor devils! It seems you can never do right!'

'We were not meant to be here in the first place,' Charles says with balance, 'so the responsibility lies with us to keep trying, until we get it right.'

'The ocean people are not always at fault,' Wu Fang declares. 'Take our hospital. As outrageous as it sounds, some ignorant townspeople still believe we gouge out children's eyes as offerings to the ocean people's God because the hospital was set up by the Christians. How many townspeople do you know who dare to send patients to us? I can vouch for all the doctors there. They are just like me, wanting to help, but because they are ocean people ...'

'There, there,' soothes Yanbu. 'Education, education. Our people need enlightenment, and we must all do our bit.'

All through the conversation, Jiali is aware of the eyes of the son of the governor on her. Uncomfortable with the close attention, she makes a point of showing the Yan sisters the view now that they have caught up, moving to the other side of the pagoda.

'There, our house; there, the Earth Temple; and there, the harbour,' Jiali points at the place in the distance where the many sails of the ships gather, compact as packets of needles.

'Where is the college our brother works in?' asks Mochou.

Jiali is at a loss, 'I know it must be near the harbour, but ...'

Then she becomes aware of a voice she has come to know well lately: the slow, steady tone of the ocean man, always reminding her of a free-flowing, enigmatic river.

'Can you see the flags waving in the wind, that's the main college building. The staff rooms are on the very top floor, yes, that one right by the flags with a window open, that's where me and Yanbu work, side by side. We share a desk actually.'

'Is our brother a good teacher?' Mochou smiles shyly.

'The pupils call him the "Merciless Master", for he has high expectations.'

'That sounds scary!' Moli laughs.

'What about you?' Jiali asks, unable to resist the twinkle in his eyes. 'What do they call you?'

He grins, and waves a hand, 'Oh, I am the "Taoist", for I let them be, which is a sign of my incompetence as a teacher ...'

'Don't you believe a word of what he says!' shouts Yanbu, catching Charles' words. 'If the numerous banners and couplets of praises from the pupils do not reassure you, I do not know what will. Really, I am quite envious.'

Now the rest of the group gather around them. Wu Fang asks for a show of hands for teaching at the girls' school.

Yanbu shakes his head, citing his busy schedule at the college. But would he consent to his wife teaching there, Wu Fang asks?

'Assuredly,' he glances affectionately at Jiali. 'Whatever she wants. She is her own mistress.'

'I would also like to help out,' declares Li Jian.

'Don't you have to go back to Shanghai for business? I thought you said you had to return quite soon,' asks Yanbu, looking strangely crestfallen.

'I haven't had time to tell you, things have changed at home, I need to stay a while in Fudi.'

The women turn their faces to the ocean man.

'Count me in,' Charles says.

'Wonderful!' Jiali beams; Wu Fang will be so pleased, she tells herself.

12

The feeling of exuberance, inspired no doubt by the open vista of the pagoda, stays with Jiali, and the next day Wu Fang learns of her decision to definitely keep the baby.

'So you've made up your mind.'

'Yes.'

'As long as you are sure — I mean, for the right reason.'

'I was wrong before — to keep the baby for pity, and for him. But now I know I want the baby for myself. I love carrying a life inside me, I look forward to being a mother.'

'Then I will support you, all the way.'

*

The trip to Shanghai has inspired several ventures. The petition to unbind women's feet that she and Jiali start runs out of pages on the third day of its public display at the marketplace. Men and women, old and young, sign it. The *Fudi Women's Journal* — Jiali being the editor and main writer — is oversubscribed as soon as it is published. Who doesn't want to read about new ideas from an accomplished poetess? But the school for girls is where their hearts truly lie. It is Jiali's idea to hold a series of fundraising events, attracting large groups of distinguished guests, thanks to the Shens' literary fame and the Wus' generosity and wealth.

Very often Jiali takes centre stage, and Wu Fang steps willingly back to let her friend shine — she is used to it.

'Miss Shen has been standing far too long,' Wu Fang says to a maid at one of these events, 'make her sit.' Then, a moment later, grabbing another maid, she tells her: 'Take another tea to Miss Shen, and don't leave until you see her drinking it!'

The other guests laugh indulgently at the attention their hostess pays to her friend, but think nothing of it; the closeness of the two is well known in Fudi, no eyebrows are raised. The Wus' grounds are large, but wherever she is, Wu Fang is always pulled to her friend's familiar voice, and administers to Jiali's comfort. The pregnancy is still a secret shared only by the two of them — another reason for Wu Fang's buoyancy. The longer it is kept from the Yans, the happier Wu Fang is.

*

The opera, staged on the stone boat, starts. Wu Fang strides past the moon gate to be near Jiali's group: women, all friends of similar ages and backgrounds, oblivious to the old-fashioned songs. Their topics are more contemporary: the latest reforms and girls' education, spiced occasionally with quotes of couplets and girly giggles. At Wu Fang's advice, Jiali wears female garments all the time nowadays, the better to hide her new shape. But to Wu Fang's knowing eyes, a small bump is already visible, and Wu Fang smiles to herself each time her friend's right hand reaches out to smooth her lower belly. All voices dim for Wu Fang as soon as Jiali speaks, and she finds Jiali's recitations particularly pleasing today. Catching her friend's eye, Jiali excuses herself and the two walk side by side towards a small crowd in front of the round pavilion on a raised platform. An ocean woman stands in the centre, dressed in a long, flowing skirt, speaking through a Chinese translator.

'That is the ocean lady we met in Shanghai, in Zizhulin park,' says Wu Fang, 'Do you remember?'

'Yes, yes, the one who door-stepped the Minister of Culture himself to persuade him to support the cause of anti-foot binding,' Jiali nods eagerly.

'I wrote to her, on the off chance that she would come and support us.'

'And she came all the way from Shanghai!'

'See that fan she holds in her hand? It is signed by him. Officials used to ignore her, but now, doors are opened everywhere!'

'That's admirable, and she's not even Chinese.'

'They are indeed freer than us,' sighs Wu Fang.

'That's the way we should all live …' Jiali trails off, then says, cautiously, 'There is something I want to talk to you about.'

'Is it to do with the pregnancy?' Wu Fang's voice is ordinary enough, though she knows what's coming.

'Yes.' Jiali watches her friend's face closely, looking for signs of upset, but all she sees is tenderness. 'Wu Fang …' she starts hesitantly.

'Tell Yanbu. It's time.'

'You … you don't mind?'

'Why should I?' Wu Fang replies with mixed feelings. 'It's joyful news, and you have made up your mind.'

'Oh, thank you Wu Fang, thank you! I am so relieved.' Overcome, she hugs Wu Fang. 'I wouldn't know what to do if you had said no.'

'What an idea! Why should my opinion matter so much?'

Wu Fang protests, even though she is pleased.

'Because it does.' Jiali declares simply. Now her voice is light and fast. 'His sick leave is over, and he is going back to college tomorrow, I … I want him to hear the news before he goes. He'll be so pleased!'

'I should think your mother-in-law will be pleased, too. Perhaps she will be kinder to you.'

'She will indeed be pleased, and I will be glad about that. But Wu Fang,' she claps her friend's hands, 'their happiness is nothing compared to how I feel! Here,' she brings Wu Fang's hands to her chest, then to her lower belly. 'Seriously I have never known joys like this. I could fly, I really could. And I want to shout the news to the whole world!'

'Do, you will make the most wonderful mother.' Wu Fang sighs, once again struck by the realisation that Jiali's happiness brings about her own: what pleasure it gives her to see the beaming smile on her friend's face.

'Go tell him, now.' she urges.

*

'How well Jiali looks!' Wu Fang's mother comments.

'It's the marriage,' says her father, 'She is a woman fulfilled.'

'Is she now?' Wu Fang laughs.

'Quite true,' says her mother pointedly, 'and it will be your turn soon.'

Wu Fang claims she is needed somewhere else urgently, and makes for a group of Chinese men in Western attire and women in high-fashion clothes that combine traditional Chinese and Western styles. Speaking to a friend on the edge of the group,

Wu Fang admires one of the women at its centre.

'Don't you know who that is? They are your guests.'

Wu Fang shakes her head.

'That is the famous courtesan, Rouge. Apparently she is living with the new governor's son.'

'Not Li Jian!' Wu Fang exclaims.

'Yes, him, the flamboyant playboy. He is her patron.'

'Ah yes, I did invite him, but I didn't realise he has a concubine.'

Wu Fang gives Rouge closer scrutiny: 'She has bound feet inside her high-heeled leather shoes, I can tell. I have many women patients who come to me wearing those kinds of shoes. They keep big wads of soft cotton inside to fill up the space.'

'Why on earth did you invite them?'

'He asked to be involved in my girl's school and I agreed because he is the governor's son, a powerful patron. But the courtesan business is new. Where is he? I shall have a word with him about it.'

*

The playboy himself is standing underneath a Banyan tree, explaining his set-up to his old friend Yanbu: 'All men are entitled to a concubine. As the famous Mr Fan claimed, "A teapot has to be matched with 6 teacups, not vice versa." It is a fact of life. Nothing to do with progress or anything else. It's nature. Actually,' Li Jian laughs, 'you met her, last time you were with me in Shanghai.' He points at the most fabulously dressed woman in high-heeled shoes among the cluster of fashionable-looking people. 'There she is.'

'Rouge?' Yanbu narrows his eyes, then exclaims, 'Well I never!'

Yanbu has been admiring the group from afar, never gathering enough courage to go over. With an air of possession, Li Jian smiles: 'She dresses differently nowadays, keeping up with the latest fashion, you know.'

'Yes, yes, I do see that. Women must. It's just that ... last time we met, she ... she was the epitome of traditional elegance.'

'So she made an impression on you. I'm glad.'

Yanbu is silent. Rouge had more than made an impression. At the flower wine party held in Shanghai before Yanbu's marriage, which Li Jian had hosted, gentlemen were accompanied by their favourite courtesans. Yanbu had been placed next to Rouge. A flash of pink silk sleeves, a face hidden behind a fan, a soft, lingering gaze were all it took for the nervous provincial boy to be captured. Such a skill these courtesans had, of making one feel special.

'I had no idea that you ... that she ...' Yanbu apologises. Thinking of her, his heart beats fast.

'No need to worry. I wasn't her patron then,' Li Jian waves his hand generously.

'Rouge is the most perfect woman any man could wish for!' This is a heartfelt statement. What a memorable night Yanbu had spent with her. Thanks to his mother, most anxious for her son to acquire bedroom skills in order to produce a much-desired son, Yanbu had slept with quite a few women of pleasure, but Rouge put them all to shame. How much she knew about his own body, and how to both give and receive pleasure. The girl had practically squealed for joy, and thanked him profusely for giving her the time of her life. Why couldn't his wife feel the same?

'She is indeed lovely, but with Jiali you have struck gold. Just how ... well she looks!'

Their eyes now drift to Jiali, standing in the middle of a cluster of women, a bit further apart from the group Rouge is a part of; Jiali leans slightly forward, listening attentively to another woman. She is modestly dressed in a traditional gown, the pink floral patterns creating the image of a perfect blossom in full, gorgeous bloom. A mischievous smile emerges on Li Jian's face — he's downed three cups of strong, spicy yellow plum wine in quick succession. The appearance of the smile puts Yanbu, who knew the look well from old, immediately on guard.

'So, you succeeded in capturing the famous Jiali? Shame I couldn't come to the wedding. That trip to Guangzhou cost me a whole month in bed, ill with flu.' Li Jian is slurring his words.

'You had to go. Business is important.' Yanbu purses his lips and is brief; he is not in the mood to reminiscence, especially with Li Jian.

Li Jian winks. 'To hell with business. I would rather have had the pleasure of conversing daily with such a literary talent. My dear brother, such enviable luck.'

'If only I were with her daily. I have so few home leaves.' Yanbu blushes.

'Still, when you are together, I wonder if you appreciate the good fortune of having a beauty to cut candle wicks with?'

'Li Jian, I shall never forget all the help you've given me in the past. But ...' Yanbu's voice becomes sterner, with a vague sense of threat.

'But what?' Li Jian raises his eyebrows provocatively.

'I fear you are a little drunk.' Yanbu chooses his words

136

carefully. 'You might regret saying certain things when you are sober.'

The two eye each other.

Li Jian suddenly bursts into a giggle. 'Oh, old friend. You know me. I like to joke, but I don't mean any harm. Surely you know the saying: when one's drunk, one has no virtue.' He puts both hands up. 'I will stop teasing you, right now. Come,' he calls to a nearby servant, 'bring tea!'

There is a truce. The two sit silently while the tea is served.

*

Yanbu thinks of the courtesan with warmth. Jiali is stunning, of course, and has so many attributes: chastity, cleverness and, since the operation, devotion. And yet …

How come Jiali never seemed that keen to be with him?

He stares at the wine glass in front of him. His last night's leave. Earlier, chancing upon his wife in a crowd of her admirers — all women clambering to show her their couplets — she'd taken him aside and told him the news of her pregnancy. Watching her excited, beaming face, he'd been touched. When he'd sat down with Li Jian, he'd wanted to share the good news, but now … It's a momentous event — he is to be a father — but Li Jian is the last man in Fudi he wants to get drunk with.

He wishes Charles were here.

'What are you thinking?' Li Jian asks.

'Oh, some joke I heard earlier,' Yanbu lies.

Li Jian drops his eyes and gulps down a whole cup of the strong wulong tea. Glancing up, he catches sight of Wu Fang in the distance talking to a well-built man in military uniform, and muses: 'Our good headmistress is so well connected, don't you think?'

Yanbu looks up. 'Isn't that er ... Commander Shu of the Eighth Battalion? I recognise him since he came to inspect one of our ships with Director Zuo.'

'It's General Shu,' corrects Li Jian.

'So he is, now I remember, he has been promoted since that battle with Charles' country at the border. A most heroic and patriotic man.'

'Heroic no doubt, as to his patriotism, well, I hear he has said unflattering things about us Manchus.'

'Oh,' Yanbu keeps a watchful tone.

'A troublemaker. Wu Fang really shouldn't be too friendly with him.' Li Jian's voice becomes severe, sounding even a little menacing to Yanbu. 'Wu Fang is a most extraordinary woman, but she can be just a little foolish sometimes.'

*

Yanbu is relieved when Li Jian does not return with the rest to the Yans' that evening. He has finally been called back to Shanghai. With Li Jian gone, the atmosphere lightens. The news of Jiali's pregnancy is announced, prompting Mrs Yan to call for a banquet to celebrate. Not content with the tender, red braised pork, steamed fish, fragrant beef, and various assortment of chicken and duck dishes the servants have cooked, Mrs Yan personally makes her famous 'Monks' vegetables' using wild mushrooms she has picked herself, to universal acclaim.

After the evening banquet, while Wu Fang and Charles are engaged in a heated discussion about education, Yanbu finds

Jiali alone in their bedroom and tells her Li Jian's warnings about Wu Fang.

'She should watch out. Li Jian might speak of reforms, but deep down, he is a reactionary; he is vain too, and takes offence easily.'

'I will tell her, Yanbu,' she nods, 'Thanks for looking out for her. Wu Fang might have a sharp mouth, but she really is kind-hearted. She said your mother would be pleased with the news of my pregnancy.'

'You saw mother tonight at the banquet, I've never seen her happier. It is kind of Wu Fang to think of her.'

'She's had a hard life; I am glad to be making her happy.'

'Yes, mother is pleased, as am I ...' Drunk and emboldened, he strokes her face, but the image of Rouge appears. Guiltily, he closes his eyes, only to feel his hand gently moved away.

'We mustn't.'

'Why not?'

'Wu Fang said that no lovemaking should happen at this stage of the pregnancy.'

'Wu Fang again!' he curses. 'Mother is right, Wu Fang is such a busybody!'

'I wish you wouldn't say such things about her.' Taken aback, Jiali bites her lip. 'Wu Fang's my best friend, and she is a doctor ...'

'Would-be doctor,' he mocks.

'She's like a sister to me. She only ever wants the best for me,' she asserts.

'I don't doubt it,' Yanbu sighs, 'but however good a friend, Jiali, there must be a limit.'

'What do you mean?'

'I meant what I said. She is interfering! What right does she have to tell us what to do, what not? We are husband and wife, no one should come between us. Oh Jiali, sometimes, just sometimes, I wish Wu Fang hadn't come back from Japan. It feels almost as if she is the third person in our marriage.'

He stops to gaze at her.

His hurt look touches her, and there is truth in what he said. But in her heart's heart, she knows that Wu Fang's recommendation is just an excuse, the real reason for her refusal to sleep with him is simply that she no longer desires it. Pregnancy gives her the right to autonomy over her own body, and she instinctively seizes the opportunity.

'Wu Fang aside, for the sake of the baby, it's best that we are careful,' she says gently, mindful of his feelings.

But the night is not such a chaste one, for she dreams again of Charles, doing the most intimate acts with her. Horror, oh horror! To have had such dreams before had been bad enough, but to dream of him again, when he is so obviously claimed — by none other than her best friend — and with her husband sleeping next to her ...

Feeling guilty, she banishes Charles from her thoughts and is extra kind to Yanbu the next day, though being careful not to get his hopes up. But pride ensures that he does not broach the subject again for the rest of his sick leave, and when he feels desire rising, it is the passionate, alluring Rouge who appears in his mind, telling him what a wonderful lover he is, not his wife. The more he thinks about it, the more certain he is that the ecstatic cries of the courtesan could not have been faked: it was not as if he was a rich patron she needed to please. And if he could give such a sought-after courtesan in Shanghai a good time, he is surely good enough for any woman.

Just not his wife. How sad it makes him.

13

The following night, after dinner, Charles sets off reluctantly for the International Club; reluctant because it means he has to wear his stiff, formal Western clothes, also because he would rather spend the pleasant late-summer evening alone. But the consul of his country has requested the meeting, a request that Charles does not feel he can refuse. Like other ocean residents in Fudi, he has long stopped being amazed by the sight of the many European-style buildings dotted among the quintessential Chinese houses this side of the hill, though he finds time to pause to admire the many-coloured blossoms sprouting from two square tubs in front of the Western-style stone columns. Those you wouldn't get back home.

Pierre, the smartly dressed, well-connected tea merchant, is the first foreigner he meets inside.

'You used to talk about leaving, Charles, what now? Have the women proved to be irresistible after all?'

'Don't jest Pierre, you know I travel light.'

'Chinese women are not at all demanding. They ask so little of you.'

'All the same, I like being on my own.'

'Quite right. Can't live with one now.'

Pierre winks and turns back to the billiards table. A long-term Fudi resident, Pierre is not constant with women — his concubines come and go. He boasts a large collection of 'spring court pictures' in his well-stocked study. The meticulously drawn scenes depicting explicit lovemaking are not to everyone's taste, though Pierre is unapologetic. Charles was invited to view them once and found them unremarkable. Desire, not always for his late wife, he certainly has, wave after suffocating wave riding on the tide of grief, but the supposedly exotic pictures did not arouse him.

The club is unusually full, crowded with people returning from their summer hill retreats. Charles searches for Paul, the consul. In the next moment he hears Pierre exclaiming, 'Paul, old man, how are you getting on with your translation?'

'Painful as a toothache.'

'But it's just your thing: political intrigues, strategies, kingdoms fall and emperors die. You look surprised. Yes, I do know some Chinese. Once upon a time I nurtured such literary ambitions myself, but business got in the way.'

Charles guesses the book. He happens to be reading it in the original, having been lent it by Yanbu. He hasn't yet been able to get beyond the first few pages, with its enigmatic Taoist quotes. Persevere, Yanbu beseeched him, pointing out to him the number of Chinese operas based on excerpts from the book. He will better understand the Chinese psyche that way. Charles is trying, though would have preferred to read something he enjoys. It is an exercise in willpower, he supposes.

Around him, the conversation is about the new Fudi governor, a Manchu with exquisite taste in Peking opera and concubines, and whose favour, it seems, is easily bought with invitations to polo matches, a novelty for the Chinese. Charles sits brooding, unwilling to attempt conversation. The animated, chattering crowds around him speak his own language, and yet how brash their gestures, how blindingly narrow-minded their speech. He misses the undulating Mandarin tones mixed with the odd Fudi dialects he's become used to hearing over the last few months. Oh, the joy of learning the Mulan poem! It has been a most refreshing experience being instructed by the two women: one strict and efficient, the other quietly commanding. He is sure he has benefited from both in different ways.

Finally, Paul catches his eye and the two sit down in a quiet corner. Paul turns to Charles. 'Did you really spend all summer here marking pupils' workbooks, or perhaps you found other engagements? They must have been enticing since you turned down the use of my chalet in the hills ...'

'You know how grateful I am for the offer, but you seem to have forgotten that the college doesn't take summer breaks. As an employee, I had no choice.'

'They must have kept you busy,' Paul smiles, his easy manner suggesting he's got all day. How are things going at the college, he wants to know. Does Charles get the sense that the director is still supportive of the bid for their country to continue the partnership in its running for the next five years? What do Charles' Chinese colleagues think of the latest imperial decree, reforming the imperial exam? Had it been a long-anticipated decision? How would it impact on such a beacon of New Learning as the naval college?

Charles is only half listening. For, despite Paul's outward friendliness, he senses the increasing distance between the two. They used to get on; Paul had been the man who had first greeted Charles at the club upon his arrival. For the first couple of months of his Fudi life, introductions to people who mattered, both Chinese and ocean, were made through this quietly spoken, learned fellow, who, as well as being a most competent consul, is also an avid amateur translator. And yet the longer Charles lives in Fudi, the further the two drift apart. Who is to blame?

'Pardon?' Paul has said something he has missed.

'We are really pleased the small difficulty of the field trip has been cleared up, Charles. We won't forget what you did, very decent of you.'

Their government has a big stake in the naval college and Paul, as its representative, wants things to run smoothly, just as the Chinese do. Charles understands that. Already, fingers are being pointed at the ocean firm supplying the cannons. Had the Chinese deliberately been sent inferior products? Whose fault was it that the cannons were slow to fire, causing the pupils to lean over and check, resulting in casualties? In a climate such as this, the less tension there is, the easier everyone's life is.

'We need more of your sort.'

'I happened to react quicker than the rest, and managed to push my Chinese colleague out of the way just in time. Really it was nothing. At any rate, I have been given enough medals and scrolls from the Chinese to last me to eternity.' He rises. 'Look, Paul, it's getting late. I've got lessons to prepare for tomorrow, so if you will excuse me …'

'Charles … not so quick … Tell me about your involvement with the girls' school.'

So this is what the meeting is really about.

'The headmistress, Miss Wu, is a dynamic reformer, whose energy and determination I greatly admire.' Her astonishingly loud, open, disarming laugh also, but he is not going to tell Paul that. He won't understand. 'My teaching at the college does not take up all of my time, as you know. I wish I had your patience and superior scholarship to translate books.'

'A mere hobby, interesting only to myself.' Paul lowers his head modestly. Then, 'There's quite a group that meets at your Chinese colleague's house.'

'I go to deliver Yanbu, my injured colleague, the books he wants to read while convalescing.' And sit by his bed, reading to him, watched by his pregnant wife.

'And?'

'Sometimes Miss Wu is there,' arguing with Jiali, with him, with everyone, arguing and laughing, the two women's laugher infectious and delightful, 'and sometimes Mr Li ... but you wouldn't be interested ...'

'It's our business to know, especially where our compatriots are involved. Mixing with the wrong lot might get you into all sorts of bother.'

'Meaning?' Charles sighs deeply, trying to suppress the rising anger in him.

'Reform in this part of the world can be a double-edged sword. These new schools sprouting up around the country are places where unsavoury characters can hide. Agitators, you know, wanting to be rid of the Manchus.'

'You need not worry. These admirable young reformers want only to help poor girls. As to the Manchus, well, to my taste the sooner they are rid of them the better.'

'Change will be sure to come. But what then? Chaos, chaos, the last thing China's people need,' Paul says. 'Charles. Listen. You and I care about China. Unlike many others here we speak the language and pride ourselves on knowing a little of its culture — as well as any poor devils are able to. I appreciate your feelings with regard to the Chinese. You are their employee, you mix with them daily, affections naturally grow, and you are admirably understanding of their sensitivity. I really do see all this. But, dear Charles, speaking as a friend as well as your consul, I beg you to be more sensible. By all means be civil, but do, do keep your distance.'

*

Charles steps out onto the balcony on the second floor and stands in a quiet dark corner by himself. Paul's words are heartfelt, he knows, and it is precisely for this reason he is upset, for their conversation has reminded him of the deep chasm between him and his fellow countrymen, even supposedly sensitive and sympathetic ones like Paul. The consul sees the Chinese as being fundamentally, irrevocably different to them, and, therefore, beyond intimacy, and in appealing to Charles, assumes that he agrees.

The only other person in the vast empty space is a Chinese servant watering the giant porcelain pot of canna lily. Charles has to check himself not to start a conversation with the middle-aged man with a kind round face and immense dignity. How different a world this is from the college, Yanbu's home, and the girls' school, where Charles cannot go two steps without being greeted solicitously by his pupils and fellow teachers. Here, surrounded by people of his own race, he has to remind himself to keep his distance, to behave as the customs of his culture dictates. How lonely he feels: jealous of the intimacy into which all the Chinese around him seem to be able to fall so easily, held back because he is an ocean man.

This time yesterday, he had been dining at the Yans' again. It was Yanbu's last day of leave. Everybody seemed extra kind, even that miserable Mrs Yan, whose wild mushroom dish was simply to die for; everybody drunk and exuberant. Not even in Charles' country, supposed to be more liberal, had he ever seen such a set-up. Wu Fang, tipsy, had suddenly turned on Charles, and asked him to 'compose a poem' or 'sing a song', neither of which he was capable of doing on the spot. The punishment was more plum wine drinking. All the foreign etiquette he'd been warned of, all his own previous perceptions of Chinese women, has been turned upside down since he came to Fudi; he is the one who is shy and ridiculed for it, while the women laugh at his expense. Oh, these extraordinary Fudi women! He is sure he is totally over his infatuation with Wu Fang now, in its place is huge admiration. One senses such intimacy and trust between the two women, enviable, really. A glance, a sway of arms, and the two understand each other perfectly. Wu Fang is gregarious, outgoing, and Jiali supremely self-possessed. And Jiali! A most enigmatic woman. He realises, now, that though she had often seemed partially obscured while he was with them, he has indeed been seeing her, always out of the corner of his eyes, just as he always saw Anne.

He had said his late wife's name last night, a couple of times, too many times probably.

'Stay the night, Charles. You are too drunk,' Yanbu had insisted, knowing what the word Anne meant to him. He was indeed incoherent — intoxicated not only with the sickly sweet plum wine but also with everyone's praise of his recitation of the Mulan poem. A maid helped him to undress, and he'd thanked her, but she didn't leave after that. Old Mistress said for me to warm your bed for you, or Old Mistress said for me to be your companion, or some such. And then she had moved the light to herself, so that Charles could see her face. Not Jiali's maid, Lanlan, who is beautiful but sharp-featured and hardly smiles; this girl had a soft round face, was all smiles. Hers was an intelligent face, with an expression so intimate that Charles felt ashamed and had to glance away. She might have been one of Mrs Yan's maids. Was that the Yan's way of consoling him?

Anne, how could you have left me alone to temptations like this!

The wide elevated space of the balcony suddenly expands all around him. He closes his eyes. He is back at sea, on the top deck of the ocean liner they had sailed on. The brightness of the moon and the night sky framed her face, a face fresh and new and full of stories she would tell him. Even on the night she died, Anne had still more of her life to reveal to him. How quickly it had all happened. How could fever have taken one so young? They were on their honeymoon, for God's sake!

He only realises he is crying when the tears become cold and hang heavy and uncomfortable around the corners of his eyes. He shakes his head and wipes the tears away; looking up, he stares straight into the pagoda standing opposite the club, how small and weak it looks, he thinks; then, how homely and comforting, for he feels he knows it well now.

'That old boy is to go,' whispers a voice next to him, another ocean man with a cigar, pointing at the pagoda.

'What?' Charles is taken aback.

'Ah, all you old China hands are so nostalgic.'

'Why?' Not at all an 'old China hand', Charles nonetheless feels instinctively protective of the pagoda.

'They are replacing it with a lighthouse, now that is

something useful, isn't it? It will save lives.'

Charles is rendered speechless. Some aspects of old China — its long, complex history, its sense of moderation and balance — appeal strongly to the scholar in him. They make him feel at home, not *home* home, but a spiritual, worldly home that he can carry with him wherever he goes.

'I know of a legend,' he starts, but stops himself. The pagoda is squat, mute, pitiable, but it holds the memories of his times there with Wu Fang, Yanbu, and Jiali, which are his own.

*

Nowadays, Charles dreams in Chinese, waking up to the shapes of characters, some he doesn't yet know the meaning of. Oh, how sudden and overwhelming these foreign assaults on his senses are: the ceaseless chorus of the frogs at night, the indescribable scent upon waking, the enviable ease of an old man's steady, agile gait, the porcelain perfect skin of the women. Already he recalls blossoms at home with a sense of distance, not being able to remember their fragrance, even those that he'd once loved. Replacing them are jasmines, gardenias, orange blossoms, lilies, numerous others he knows not the names of … Scents bold and thick, not at all refined and gentle. Voices also, his own having taken on the high low sing-song of the local dialect; donning Chinese gowns on his non-teaching days, he feels the strange new rhythm in the long and slow sway of his limbs. Late afternoons, he steps into the long gallery upstairs watching the rolling clouds: shape-shifting dragons from the mythical legends he is reading.

I have arrived, he tells himself.

Then, *Arrived where?*

In the middle of the night, he wakes. He has left the window open, and the breeze brings in a sort of flapping sound. He follows the sound to his study: a scroll, hanging just above his desk; it was a present from Jiali. He has no recollection of asking for it to be hung in so prominent a place, Lao Lin, his servant, having once again overstepped the mark in his devotion to his master. Charles sighs, exasperated. He has been given so many scrolls lately, for saving Yanbu's life, but more often before that, from grateful students and their parents; all ceremoniously presented, extravagantly praised, then discreetly folded up and put away. He can't possibly display them all. He will make sure Lao Lin takes the scroll down in the morning — for it unsettles him.

He returns to the bed. But with each flap of the scroll, he is distracted. More details of its composition and presentation come to him. She made it as a thank you for saving her husband's life, over a couple of evenings alone at her desk. As the rest of the group chatted, he had glimpsed her occasionally looking up at him, but quickly dropping her eyes when she caught his. He had not realised she was doing something for him until he was presented with it. Even now, he could not recall her words, just a memory of her shy smile and the strange firm pressure of the scroll as it was pressed into his hands. Her elegant, almost reticent presence is always a contrast from the dreamlike, fast-moving creature that is Wu Fang. Oh, these women, they excite and puzzle him deeply. There are things Charles feels that he cannot articulate, but as he pulls his mind reluctantly but forcibly away from Jiali and her scroll, he has an impression of her having a secure and firm place in his consciousness, necessary but invisible, like peace.

14

Smelling of disinfectant from the hospital, Wu Fang pauses a few steps from the door of the classroom. There is Jiali, standing at the front, wearing the shawl knitted by her student Yueyue, the blue of the wool the colour of the sea, circling, enlivening the paler, plainer hue of her gown. The bump is growing, but more noticeable is Jiali's smooth glistening skin and bright sparkling eyes. Wu Fang leans back; that familiar feeling she has had lately — a sense of pride, almost of ownership — returns: *this radiant being, mine, my very own, for she confides in me. I am the keeper of her utmost secrets.*

Kingdom, Broken, Mountain, River, Remains. Long, slender bamboo-shoot hands draw the characters on the board with quick elegance and confidence, then the clear, bell-like voice rings the words, the cadence rhythmic and seductive: '*Though the kingdom is broken, rivers and mountains stand; spring deepens in the conquered city, grass and trees darken. Lamenting the sad times, the sight of blossom brings tears to my eyes; Reluctantly separating from loved ones, the singing of the birds breaks my heart; Beacons burn continuously for three months, warning of war, and a letter from home is worth ten thousand gold* ... The last line, what does it make you think of?'

'A man losing his hair, getting old and bald!' giggles a pupil.

'I think he is worried, very worried,' nods an older woman slowly.

'I don't get how easy it is to read such a famous poem. To me, it means the poem is not good enough. It is too simple,' says another voice.

'Yueyue, what do you think? Yueyue? Speak up,' instructs Jiali.

'I think it really affecting,' says the tall girl at the front in a low, shy voice.

'How so?'

'Take the first line. Though it tells you all about what remains, it really makes you think of what's not there. It is like the place is haunted. It makes you feel sad.'

Good girl, Wu Fang tells herself, Yueyue is really coming along very well.

A hand raises tentatively at the back, then she hears Charles' hesitant voice.

'I have a question, Miss Shen ...'

Wu Fang steps away, a trace of a smile on her lips. What's Charles doing in Jiali's class, and what do the girls make of this giant crouching clumsily on a chair too small for him, learning a poem written 800 years ago with them? Since Mulan, there seems to be no stopping Charles in his pursuit of Chinese literature. Wu Fang likes him the more for it. Not everyone takes rejection — however subtly she had tried to mask it — as well as he has done; she had expected things between them to be awkward, but was pleasantly surprised. Charles has carried on as if nothing happened.

*

Later, from the window of the staff room, Wu Fang watches Jiali lead the morning stretch. Bending down must take some effort now; still, the figure in front of the girls is quick and agile, the shawl flapping like wings as Jiali stretches her arms. The exercise combines Chinese tai chi moves with modern gymnastics, intended to strengthen the muscle and clear one's brain. That is the idea, Wu Fang muses, though when she learned it in Japan, she simply copied without thinking about what she was doing. Jiali has given the form so much grace.

'Miss Shen is quite the picture of a free, strong, modern woman. I have in mind a painting I can do of her, which we can hang at the school, as inspiration for the girls,' enthuses the new art teacher, who Wu Fang has engaged to come in once a week.

'Why don't you?' Wu Fang turns to him eagerly. 'I have long imagined a group of portraits hanging along the corridor, this could be a start.'

'Who knitted the blue shawl that so becomes Miss Shen?' asks Charles, also admiring.

'A girl with chilblained hands,' Wu Fang answers.

'Yueyue, the tall girl, always sitting at the front of the class? Poor child. I heard her mother died when she was young. She has an invalid father and a younger brother to look after, and she's only, what, twelve?' He pauses, then says, 'She writes about her home life in her essays.'

'There are things she would not write,' Wu Fang sighs, 'that will make your blood boil. I will tell you one day, if you have the stomach to listen.'

'Such a lovely gesture, the shawl. In my country it would have been an apple. I've done it myself.'

'It seems the girl has a soft spot for Jiali, but fortunately I am not at all jealous!' Wu Fang smiles.

*

'I saw Charles in your class,' Wu Fang says to Jiali, when the two are alone in the staffroom that afternoon.

'He asked out of the blue, I didn't have the heart to say no. Should I have let him?'

'Of course! I don't have a problem with it, and I believe the girls like him.'

Jiali becomes coy: 'And you?'

'We both like him, don't we? He's so different from the other ocean devils.'

'I've seen the way he looks at you.'

Wu Fang laughs, then shakes her head.

'You have been blind,' Jiali insists.

'Not in the least,' Wu Fang protests. 'I am not in love with him, nor him me.'

'How can you say that, when he watches you all the time, his eyes full of admiration.'

Wu Fang laughs. 'Does he? How would you know?'

'Well,' Jiali blushes. She can't very well say she watches Charles all the time.

Fortunately for her, Wu Fang does not seem to notice. She waves a hand. 'I told him that I cannot, and will not, love a man.'

'Really? You talked about it?'

'Yes.'

'Did he, did you …'

'Of course I didn't ask if he was in love with me, I am not that vain; but I saw the way he looked at me and I warned him off in a way that could leave no room for misunderstanding.'

'And he took it well?'

155

'Most certainly.' Wu Fang smiles. 'I feel for him as a sister does a brother. I should hate to lose such a good friend; fortunately, I think we are all right. No, we are more than all right. I feel most at ease with him, and him me, I am sure of it.'

'Wu Fang, that's such a relief,' Jiali beams.

'We don't meet ocean men like him every day. Charles is very special.'

'Indeed he is,' nods Jiali emphatically, feeling suddenly light-hearted. Then, as if to make certain, she asks, blushing again, 'But what's wrong with him?'

'Nothing. It's not him. It's me. I shall never marry. You know that.' Wu Fang seeks Jiali's eyes.

'You just haven't met the right person,' Jiali whispers, meeting Wu Fang's eyes with her usual open gaze. 'Perhaps Charles isn't the one for you.' She sounds sadder than she feels, and hopes her friend does not notice.

*

As she travels the country, mobilising and attending meetings, the image of Jiali in the blue shawl stays with Wu Fang, distracting her from whatever she is doing. The urge to change the world is very much still there, but the joy of saving lives in the hospital and giving the girls a better future increasingly trumps plotting to overthrow the Manchus. Though a woman, Wu Fang is well respected among the tough men of the revolutionary movement, but more and more she finds that her heart is not in it. What seemed noble and grand in Japan, in the field is much more complex. The men talk constantly of destruction and revenge, while Wu Fang's heart grows soft and gentle at the thought of the girls, her patients, and above all, her friend.

Back home, Jiali watches Charles with fresh eyes. She has watched him before, so many times, but how different he looks to her now he is no longer Wu Fang's beloved. Perhaps it isn't him, she concedes, it is her: she is bolder, less guilty, and her eyes follow him ardently. Not when he is in her classroom, mind; there, she never glances his way, for fear that her face will betray her. But how distracting having him so close by! Sometimes she thinks the whole class can hear the heavy thumping of her heart.

*

Now she watches him, hidden from view, by the door, teaching his own class. A familiar sight: the ocean man sinking down on his knees, being a clown, reducing his height so he does not appear intimidating to the girls; can this be the same giant who sat upright and serious on a small, low stool in her lesson just now? Such a transformation seems to come naturally to him. *Merrily, Stream, Life, Dream*: the words are written in Charles' language neatly enough on the board, though the class is in disarray, girls falling all over laughing, pointing at their ocean teacher on the floor, propping himself up with his elbow, his knees up, head thrown backwards, every inch of his muscles enjoying the farce as much as the girls. Jiali finds herself laughing, too. How infectious his playfulness.

Now she hears, with a tinge of jealousy — for the girl, though loving and respectful, rarely laughs in her presence — the high note of Yueyue giggling, and the calm baritone hum of Charles. His voice, how well she knows it now. Hearing it always gives her the sense of being near to adventure, and she is reminded suddenly of the Chinese word for soul mate: *zhi yin —* *someone who knows truly the other's voice.*

What is she doing? She chides herself: *Pull yourself together.* *You are a married woman, with a baby on the way.* Besides, Wu Fang was his heart's desire, and even though she has rejected him, can Jiali be sure that Charles does not still harbour hopes?

15

Though he is not a big man, Li Jian's presence somehow fills Charles' study.

'Jiali and Wu Fang,' says Li Jian to Charles, 'are no ordinary women.'

'Indeed,' smiles Charles, adjusting the calligraphy brush in his hand, copying Li Jian. 'Is it the feng shui here in Fudi, perhaps? They are both so supremely self-possessed,' he admires, 'mistresses of their own destinies.'

'You can say that again,' Li Jian nods. 'I have no time for women who manipulate men with their come-hither looks, nor taste for those slave types who pine for their masters with sick submission. I love a woman who knows her own mind.'

'You have your Rouge, and she strikes me as a remarkable girl.'

'It's good to know that someone else, apart from me, appreciates her; I do admit that compared to many of her sort, she is different.'

'Far more than that, surely. There is a quiet dignity about her, I have nothing but the utmost respect for her.'

'She is respectful now, living with me; I provide for her, I've done right by her. Still, put her next to these two … there is something wanting.'

'In status? She can't help that.'

'I don't hold it against her. It irks me, though, that Wu Fang stopped me from teaching at the school because of it.'

'Well, I suppose, as the head of a girls' school, Wu Fang has to …'

'Oh, Miss Wu finds many faults with me, even though I admire her, both her and Miss Shen, greatly!'

Lao Lin brings in tea, and Li Jian stands to admire the ornaments in Charles' study; for some obscure reason, Charles finds himself hoping Li Jian will not notice the scroll that hangs right above them, the scroll from Jiali. Why on earth does he keep forgetting to ask Lao Lin to put it somewhere else? He is relieved when Li Jian asks casually, 'So what's new at the school?'

'Nothing much. Miss Shen is blooming, the picture of good health, and despite her pregnancy, still comes in to teach from time to time; Mr Lu, the art teacher, that pleasant old Confucius gentleman, is doing all of our portraits; he's already completed one of me; oh, and Wu Fang is troubled because she is due to go to Beijing to run some errands for her hospital, but she is finding it difficult to leave Fudi — there is the school, Jiali is pregnant, and I can't be there all the time.'

'Miss Wu is a busy woman, isn't she? Needed everywhere and by everyone! I do wonder, sometimes, if all this is too much for her?'

'I thought you were an admirer?'

'I admire her energy, hugely, but I thank God not all women are like her. No man would dare marry them! I say, Charles,' he smiles, 'have you ever felt tempted to take her on?'

Charles laughs. 'Why, are you matchmaking now, too?'

'Who else has tried?'

'Jiali,' he pauses, then, 'For a while, anyway. She thought

she was being subtle, but I guessed it straight away. Anyway, she has stopped trying, thank heavens.'

'Has she indeed?' Li Jian laughs. 'I must say, I find the idea of Jiali matchmaking for Wu Fang quite a curious concept.'

'Curious indeed.'

Li Jian raises an eyebrow, and nods slowly, 'Well, aren't you a little bit besotted?'

'By Wu Fang? To be perfectly honest with you, yes, I was. I was very much attracted to her, when we first met. It's not every day that you meet a woman like her: original, brave, big-hearted, but she is not for me.'

'Why not?'

'To start off, she has made it very clear that she isn't in love with me. It's no fun pursuing a girl who is not keen on you.'

'No fun? That seems all the more fun to me!'

'Don't joke, Li Jian. I also know now that I was not in love with her, not really, I've simply been dazzled by her personality, and I thank her for making me see that, and not letting me make a fool of myself.'

'Did she now?'

'Yes. It was most handsomely done. She put me down most emphatically but gently, and told me that she could never love a man.'

'Interesting.'

'It's a lie of course, she just didn't want to hurt me. She's so remarkable, she just hasn't met the right man to match her brilliancy, I am sure of it. In the meantime, you and I, ordinary mortals, will just have to admire her from a distance.'

'Wise counsel, my friend, for brilliant as she is, she spells trouble to me.'

'Why do you say that?' Charles's voice is alert.

'Just a hunch, nothing more.' Li Jian laughs mysteriously.

*

When Li Jian leaves the study, Charles puts the brush down, and breathes the curiously intoxicating scent of the ink in deeply. This is Li Jian's third weekly visit as Charles' calligraphy teacher. At first, Charles found the young son of the governor shallow, but no one can stay uncharmed for long by Li Jian's quick and ready friendliness.

It is getting dark outside. Through the open window, the chorus of the cicadas pours right in, accompanying Charles as he works. The sound soothes, just as once it grated. On the wall opposite him are star maps and diagrams illustrating celestial phenomena; familiar images with new-to-him Chinese names. The room is austere, but he has long ceased fantasising a capable feminine hand arranging his things. When he returns from work, he likes his environment unobtrusive. Too elegant and beautiful surroundings will cause him to be sentimental, which he has no need for at the moment.

He pauses to read through what he's copied. Earlier, Li Jian hinted at some daring words, but it seems to Charles that, although most of the couplets are about courtship, they seem pretty mild. He can't see how they would offend even the most modest of women.

Your face flickers in the candlelight.

moon

blossoms

The usual stuff. His mind wanders as his hands are busy copying.

A pure jade buried among common pebbles.

Jade. Curious the Chinese attach such importance to this particular precious stone. Jiali wears one, so does Wu Fang, and Yanbu's two little sisters, who, unusually, now come to both the morning and afternoon lessons at the girls' school. But what improvements already to their personalities. It heartens one to see their open smiles. Both now have unbound feet. Another fierce battle won by the admirable Wu Fang and Jiali against that miserable Mrs Yan.

He glances down and studies his own writing against the original. Proudly he picks two pages out. He will show them to Li Jian tomorrow, to see if he can tell them apart.

In one hand you hold a sword, in the other, a book on the latest in science. Discarding your rouge, you outshine the men; humbled in front of your brilliance, I am willing to grind your ink for you.

He puts the brush down and stares: *sword, science book, ink.* Ordinary enough references, and yet he can't help conjuring up the quiet, enigmatic figure standing in a man's gown, her hand habitually on her small bump, her feet firmly on the ground, laughing heartily at something Wu Fang has said. How strange that it is Jiali's image that is conjured up by the couplets, even though he and Li Jian had been talking about Wu Fang all this time. He has lent Jiali astronomy books at her request, but ... mere coincidence, surely.

I really must stop thinking that everything is about her, he chides himself.

He leans back as a gentle breeze blows through the window, causing the scroll above him to flap again. Closing his eyes, Charles listens with a sense of familiarity and possession. The last thing he would do now, he realises, is to ask Lao Wang to remove the scroll. He'd grown used to the sound and sight of it. It's become part of his home.

16

Your face flickers in the candlelight ...

Hands on her mouth, Jiali gasps. The thin rice paper, on which the words are written, smells faintly of something familiar. Bringing it close to her face, she thinks she ascertains, with a delicious thrill, the indescribable scent that wafts towards her each time she walks past Charles in her classroom. How clumsily and yet endearingly he folds his long limbs: arms crossed, legs bent. She brings the paper closer to her face, feeling the rough grainy surface rubbing against her cheek, and inhales.

In a little while, she opens her eyes, and greedy for more, reads on:

In one hand you hold a sword, in the other, a book on the latest in science. Discarding your rouge, you outshine the men ...

Is that how she appears to him? The words are a little over the top, she supposes, but for an ocean man, to write as well as this ...

... humbled in front of your brilliance, I am willing to grind your ink for you.

Heavens! Pages and pages of words flattering her in refined, elegant writing that she laps up, as a camel thirsts for water in the desert. Twice Lanlan tiptoes in, and twice she waves the maid impatiently away. Finally, reluctantly, cheeks burning, Jiali slams the paper down. To read on is to be led down a very dangerous path, an indulgence she cannot afford; but how tempting to let herself believe for even a second more that this really is from him, to her.

But it is from him, to her. There is no doubt about it. The meticulously written couplets were neatly slotted inside the blue-covered book on astronomy he had lent her. The book came a couple of days ago and had been sitting on her desk untouched, until just now.

For a breath or two she stands in the middle of the room torn; it can't have been, Charles' Chinese wouldn't have improved so much in such a short space of time, and yet love does the strangest things to people. Love creates miracles.

Love. Could he have been in love with her, all this time?

She needs to know, now.

*

She hardly registers that she is standing before him in his study, and then, only then, does she become alarmed, but there is no retreating now.

'I've come to ...' Looking up to the wall opposite them, she exclaims, 'There's my scroll.'

And he, in shock at her sudden appearance, glancing from the scroll to her, and then back to the scroll, is struck by the thought: *Peace, I am with peace.* His spine tingles. Speechless, he stands and stares at her, so fresh and early on this summer morning. Something is glistening on her and he is not sure what — perhaps the dew, he thinks wildly.

She takes a long breath and puts the book in front of him.

'You can't have finished reading it already?' he asks conversationally, collecting himself.

'I am returning the book,' she points at the book with a trembling hand, 'because of what was in it.'

'I knew the language would be difficult,' he says, smiling, 'but I had hoped that the pictures of stars would engage you.'

'It's not the book,' she pushes the book to him, 'it's what's inside it.'

Puzzled, he picks it up, and the papers float out as feathers. Catching one, his eyes lighten.

'Where on earth did you find these sheets of mine?'

'So you don't deny it, they are yours.'

'Assuredly. The papers are mine.' He studies the paper in his hand.

'And the words?'

He laughs that she thinks so highly of his Chinese. 'Not mine. I copied them.'

'And you didn't put the papers in the book,' she murmurs, her cheeks burning.

Suddenly he realises the implication, what she clearly suspects, and his own face turns crimson, too.

'Goodness me, no!' he cries, horror stricken, then, quickly, 'but I suspect Lao Lin might have something to do with it.'

Lao Lin is called for, and the mystery is solved: after the papers on which the couplets were written had dried, the servant, thinking it a shame to throw them away as instructed, had taken the initiative of putting them inside the sleeves of selected books and not informed his master. Charles curses gently to himself — he'd quite forgotten about the reverence, especially from the illiterates of this country, held for the written word. He himself has often dropped coins into the open palm of the beggar outside the college, a bamboo basket on his back, a long stick with a sharp tip in his hand, which he uses to pick up straying bits of papers strewn on the path to be burnt in a respectful way so as not to offend the literary god.

Lao Lin indicates that there are more, and before long, the two are shown book after guilty book, their sleeves and pages slotted with strips of couplet papers; in no time at all, Charles' study resembles a prayer room adorned with words of praise for the exalted guest standing in the middle of the room, bewildered at what she has read. Though the handwriting is Charles', the words are ...

'You can go now,' Charles dismisses Lao Lin.

They stand awkwardly apart, each cringing at the thought of how the other must have viewed the whole episode. Jiali breaks the silence with a hushed voice.

'Where are the words from?'

'I have no idea. You'd have to ask my calligraphy teacher.'

'You took up calligraphy?'

'Why, yes, since learning the Mulan poem, I thought to improve my Chinese further, and so when Li Jian offered to teach me calligraphy ...'

'Li Jian?'

'Yes.'

'I see.'

But she doesn't see, she doesn't understand how couplets between her and Yanbu could have ended up in Li Jian's hands.

'I only understand some of them, and gather the words are personal, but are they ... that bad?' The pallor of her face concerns him.

'Not bad so much as ... they are private correspondences between me and Yanbu, from before we were married.'

'Courtship poems — love letters!' he exclaims.

'You could call them that.' She smiles weakly.

'How did Li Jian get hold of them?' His voice is serious and scandalised. To have intruded on something so personal, so intimate.

'I'm just wondering,' she hazards, 'there are a few that are about ... now.'

'The lines about reading science books?'

'Yes,' she says, not looking at him. 'That's what made me think it was you ...'

'I, too, thought of you when I copied those ...'

He also glances away.

Acute embarrassment is genuinely felt by both. For a long time, neither can bear to glance up. He feels naked, exposed, which curiously emboldens him finally to blurt out, 'I'm not ready for this, not now, not today!'

She steps back, her eyes enlarging at his outburst, and at the sight of tears streaming down his face.

'If I have offended you by suggesting ...'

'No, no, no,' he shakes head vehemently. 'It's not that, not at all that! It's ... It's ...' He breathes deeply, strides over to a drawer, pulls out a framed photo and places it in front of her. 'Meet Anne, my late wife. Today would have been her twenty-second birthday. She died on the ship we travelled on; we were barely married. I was ... remembering her, just before you came ...' He turns his face away.

She picks up the frame reverently, holding her breath. What little she heard from Wu Fang about Charles' tragic short marriage often made her wonder about his wife, and now she stares straight into the face of a golden-locked young girl, sitting sideways on a low stool. As is the custom, she looks reserved and composed, but Jiali can see, from her curved lips and dimpled cheek, a smile about to burst through.

'Charles,' she whispers, her eyes on the photo, 'she is beautiful, and I feel I know her well, already.'

He remains silent, stunned by the words and her voice. A few others, when shown pictures of Anne, had said similar things, but they always sounded hollow, and seemed to him polite words to comfort; but somehow, when Jiali says this, his heart melts. Jiali speaks the truth: Anne was beautiful, and the two would have got on swimmingly. The thought compounds his feeling of loss, even as he finds genuine solace in it.

Fearing she has caused offence, Jiali quickly puts the frame down. 'I'm sorry.'

'Whatever for?'

'I don't want to remind you of …'

The sight of her tearful face gives him the urge to embrace her, knowing the gesture will comfort himself, too; but he holds back; to put her at ease, he turns away from her and puts the photo back in the drawer. Jiali watches him in reverent silence. Never having been in love before, she, like Wu Fang, is in awe of Charles.

He stands by the drawer for a moment, liking the comfort her silence creates. Presently, feeling able to speak more calmly, he says, 'I have not mentioned my brief marriage and Anne's death to many people here, hardly. My consul knows, two of my countrymen, my servant Lao Lin, Yanbu, you, and Wu Fang.'

'Yanbu?' she asks, suppressing a sudden, surprising burst of jealousy.

'Yes, but I don't think he knows how to handle it,' he muses. 'I think it embarrasses him, my grief.'

She lets that go. 'I hope you don't mind, but Wu Fang had told me a little …'

'Wu Fang was the first person I told. Even before my consul.' At the mention of her name, Charles becomes animated. 'I trusted her; one does, with Wu Fang. Even when we first met, on the ship, even before I knew her well.'

'When you thought her Japanese, and a man?'

The atmosphere lightens as he laughs, shaking his head at his own folly. 'Please don't embarrass me further, but then, I am not so easily embarrassed now. I've learned a few lessons in humility. At one stage, I don't mind telling you now, I thought I was in love with Wu Fang!'

'Really?' she keeps her voice cool and ordinary.

'Come Jiali, you must have noticed it, too.' He speaks quickly now, feeling more at ease. 'I think it started after I told her about Anne. Wu Fang showed me such genuine kindness, just the right kind, and I was touched.'

'And you mistook that for love?'

He nods. 'But I am not in love with her. I am dazzled by her. Who isn't? Wu Fang is so special, we must all thank heaven for the gift of Wu Fang to the world.'

Sighing with genuine relief and grace, she breathes out: 'Thank heaven indeed.'

She becomes silent, and he is struck again with the thought that he is in the presence of peace, peace disturbed, but peace nonetheless. Her presence is all presence, and his whole being is consumed by it. Something invisible links his fate with hers, inevitably, and he wants to surrender to it. Realising the danger just in time, he pulls himself up. 'Will you have tea? I will call Lao Lin.'

'No need. Charles. I must go.' She hesitates, then: 'Will you … not say anything to Yanbu?'

'Of course not.'

She turns to the door.

'Wait!' he calls. He collects the sheets of couplets, as silently and quickly as he can. Though the papers are light, the words in them, as he recalls them, feel weighty in his hands. Soon a thick pile is gathered, and he hesitates before placing it on the desk in front of her. 'Take them with you. They are yours.'

*

'Something most strange has happened,' she later tells Lanlan, who has come into the room to help her get ready for bed.

'What is it, Mistress?'

She shows her the roll of couplet papers.

'Ah, your poems. I remember these lines,' Lanlan studies the papers. 'But who copied them?'

'Master Cha.'

'Such good writing, Mistress, don't you think?' Lanlan admires.

'I agree, they are not bad.'

'But,' Lanlan frowns, 'how did he get hold of them to copy? I know he and the master are good friends, but surely the master wouldn't have given these to anybody else to see, not even Master Cha!'

'The master didn't give them to him. Charles never knew these were my poems, he copied them from Master Li Jian.'

'I wonder how Master Li got hold of them. It wouldn't have been from the master. He knows what the couplets meant to you. It must have been Wang Ma — she takes things from your quarters sometimes.'

'But how ever would the lines get from Wang Ma to Li Jian?'

'I don't know, Mistress.' Lanlan glances at the papers again and smiles. 'Master Cha is so different from the other ocean people. He even walks like us.'

'How do you mean?'

'When he wears the Chinese gown, from the back, you can almost believe he is one of us, you know, the way he leans slightly back, and sways — it is something comical to watch.'

Lanlan does an impersonation, and makes her mistress giggle, 'Stop, Lanlan, stop!'

'Something else, too.'

'What is it?'

Lanlan becomes coy. 'But you will forgive me for saying this?'

'It depends on what you are going to say.'

'Master Cha can't take his eyes off you!'

'What nonsense,' Jiali scolds, though she can't help the smile in her eyes.

'It's not only me, Yueyue has noticed it, too. Mistress.'

'Liar, liar! Get out this instant, I don't want to hear another word!' Jiali's protest is so forceful that the maid hangs her head low, ashamed.

'Beg your pardon, Mistress.'

'Don't you dare say a word about any of this to Mistress Wu!'

'Of course, Mistress.'

Jiali sleeps fitfully that night, the words of the couplets swimming in and out of her dreams, mixed up with images of

Charles and Anne hand in hand. She wakes with a sense of deep longing. Seeing Anne's photo has made her feelings for Charles more concrete. He has loved, and grieving, loves still, and that she finds irresistible.

17

The truce between mother- and daughter-in-law is short lived, and it is most unfortunate for Mrs Yan that that ever-present, hateful friend of her daughter-in-law's, Wu Fang, is always there to witness their altercations. Walking into the inner court, Wu Fang hears immediately Mrs Yan's high-pitched voice: '... and what business is it yours, to interfere?'

'None, except that I can't bear seeing a girl being used in that way.'

'I am her mistress — I do whatever I want with her.'

'What about her feelings?'

'Her what?'

'Her pride then.'

'Nonsense. We owe the ocean gentleman a favour for saving your husband's life.'

'Yanbu would be horrified!'

'Would he? Don't be too sure.'

Grinding her teeth, Wu Fang steps into the middle of the courtyard and speaks in a voice loud enough for all to hear.

'Do I hear right? How dare anyone talk to an expectant mother in this shocking manner? If you want her to have a miscarriage, you could not have done more!'

Her words induce an instant silence.

'Thank goodness you have arrived, Mistress Wu!' exclaims

Lanlan, when they are back in Jiali's quarters.

Still fuming, Jiali nods to Wu Fang. 'Sending a maid to "warm Charles' bed" was apparently her way of thanking Charles for saving Yanbu's life! She did ask for Lanlan, but I refused, and had thought that was it, but then she sent Lulu, who is only fifteen!'

'When did this happen?'

'The night Charles stayed here. I've only just heard.'

'Surely Charles didn't ...'

'Of course not! But she's still furious at me for criticising her.'

Wu Fang sighs. 'It is despicable, what she has done, but next time, try to get someone else to intervene. This is such a crucial time during your pregnancy. You can't afford to be upset.'

'I will try, but it's hard sometimes.' Jiali concedes.

'Do it for my sake, if not yours. You must be careful. My trip to Beijing. If anything like this happens again, I won't be here to help.'

'Don't be silly.'

'Let me check you once more.'

'Whatever for? I am as fit as a cow, as you often tell me. Anyway, didn't you check me only last week?' Jiali protests, though, at Wu Fang's insistence, submits by lying back in bed.

'Still,' Wu Fang sighs, after she has examined Jiali to her satisfaction, 'how can I leave you?'

'You must go. You always go in the autumn. Your brother expects it. Your mother depends on it. I would go with you if it wasn't for the school and this,' Jiali points at her belly.

'That's exactly it though — how can I leave when you most need me?'

'Really, it will be no time at all. I'm not due for another three months and you will be back in two. I can look after myself, and the school, for that matter.'

'The last thing you need, right now, is more responsibility.'

'But I feel more energetic than ever. And there are other teachers.'

'Yes, about that,' Wu Fang's voice becomes hesitant, 'I've reinstated Li Jian. Perhaps he can deputise during my absence, if I do go.'

'However did he redeem himself?' Jiali raises an eyebrow.

'He is not living with Rouge anymore.'

'Really?'

'He said he realised that it was wrong to keep Rouge without marrying her so he gave her a large sum of money and sent her home to the Jinxing countryside to live an honest life. It's all true, I have checked.'

'What an extraordinary transformation.'

'And he is asking his father to divert funds to support our school. Li Jian being there will also be a great safety measure, for who would dare to cross the governor's son? What is it Lanlan?'

Lanlan looks worried. 'Forgive me, Mistress Wu, for saying so, but there is something about Master Li that I am not sure of.'

Wu Fang hangs her head and sighs. 'You are right. It all sounds too good to be true, somehow. Who am I kidding? I don't trust him either. But we cannot say no after what he has done for us.'

'Look at you two,' laughs Jiali. 'What harm can he possibly bring?'

*

Wu Fang returns to Jiali's room that evening, her face dark and furious.

'No, I am not leaving,' she declares.

'Why?' Jiali cries.

Wu Fang turns to Lanlan. 'I came straight from the hospital and am starving, any chance of something to eat?'

'I will get to it right now,' says Lanlan, pleased to be doing something for Wu Fang.

As soon as Lanlan is out of sight, Wu Fang says to Jiali, 'I found out about the couplets. From Charles.'

'Oh.'

'Why didn't you tell me yourself?'

'I'm still trying to think things through,' Jiali whispers. 'So what did Charles say?'

'He was most ashamed.'

'But it was not his fault.'

'Exactly. He copied from Li Jian, so I went to see the man himself.'

'Wu Fang!'

'To give him credit, Li Jian came clean the moment I said the word couplets. It almost seemed as if he had been waiting to confess, then I realised he was so vain he saw this not as cheating but something to show off with!'

'Yanbu showed my couplets to Li Jian, I guessed as much.' Jiali says, indignant, ' But what has Li Jian got to show off with?'

'Oh Jiali, you have not guessed the worst! Yanbu never wrote the couplets he sent you in response. Li Jian did! That's what he wanted to boast about!'

'What?' Jiali exclaims in shock and disgust. 'How dare …' She swallows hard.

'How dare they indeed.' Wu Fang sighs, indignant. 'I so wanted to slap both of them. I nearly slapped Li Jian.'

*

'Then there never was a courtship, was there? Not with Yanbu, anyway,' Jiali murmurs, breaking the long silence, her face burning at the thought. True, she was never really in love with Yanbu; still, he'd wronged and humiliated her, with Li Jian as witness. All those knowing looks Li Jian gave her, now she knows why. It makes her feel sick to think of it.

'I've always known there was something odd going on between them,' Wu Fang declares, trying not to sound too triumphant. She would have said *I've always known that Yanbu was not good enough for you*, but mindful of Jiali's feelings, she holds her tongue — Jiali has been punished quite enough.

It seems, though, that Jiali has read her mind. 'You are so right, Wu Fang. You have always warned me, and I didn't listen. It's my fault, I should never have attached so much importance to words. I am so shallow, I am like the most ignorant child ...'

'How could it ever be your fault when it is Yanbu who has deceived you? He has so much to answer for! Li Jian, too, though he protested his innocence most strenuously, heaping all the blame on Yanbu. But they are as bad as each other. I have told Li Jian that under no circumstances should he stay at the school or even in Fudi. And I will not be going to Beijing.'

'What? You are cancelling the trip?'

'I can't leave now, with all this going on! Li Jian has designs on you, I am sure of that, this ... business with the couplets must

179

have given him ample opportunity to indulge in his sick fantasy — I could see it in his eyes.'

'But you've already ordered him to go away, Wu Fang, so he won't have the opportunity. Besides,' Jiali shakes her head, 'Li Jian is no threat, I am only weak with people I love. I don't care for Li Jian, and so he can't harm me. What could he do? Let him stay. We could do with the help.'

'He is not staying. After our talk, he agreed to leave for Shanghai.'

'However did you get him to agree to that?'

'By being firm and straight.' Wu Fang smiles. 'He knows that I always mean what I say. That playboy does seem to have a curious regard for me, which he declared often, believing I am different from other women. Let's just say that I took full advantage of that.'

'I do have the sense that Li Jian rather admires you. Yanbu told me that the whole of the Li family were in awe of you after you cured his father's third concubine of her indigestion. But it was not just your medical skill ...'

'Let's not delude ourselves — whatever regard he holds for others, Li Jian is a most conceited and arrogant man used to getting his own way. I think the main reason he finally agreed to leave Fudi is that he has business to attend to in Shanghai anyway.'

'Then what are you waiting for?'

'What do you mean?'

'Go to Beijing!' Jiali cries.

'Well.'

'Are you still worried about the school? There are others: Charles, Mr Lu, me. We can run it.'

*

When she comes back to the room, Lanlan loudly curses herself. 'Mistress Wu gone? My fault totally! I should have realised how busy she is. I was only thinking of making one more dish for her.'

'She was in a rush. She asked me to say sorry.'

'Well then, you'd better finish all these dishes. Here's the chicken soup with bamboo shoots, here's the rice noodles, and this, look, tofu and coriander, your favourite. Smell them! I didn't overcook them this time, I promise.'

As Jiali lowers her face, a tear drops into the bowl of soup.

'Mistress, whatever has happened?' Alarmed, the girl holds Jiali's hands. 'Is it something Mistress Wu said? I knew there must have been something that she didn't want me to hear.'

'Oh Lanlan, I am a fool!' sobs Jiali. Her tears surprise herself. Talking to Wu Fang earlier, she had focused on persuading her friend to leave for Beijing without worrying unduly about her and the school, but now, her own humiliation hits home once again.

'Is it to do with the young master?'

'Yes. The young master never matched my couplets, Li Jian did!'

Lanlan is horrified, 'But ... those lines ... how much you pored over each word.' Her voice trembles.

'They mean nothing to me now.' Indeed, they are tainted by Yanbu's deceit, even the thought of it makes her feel sick.

'How can you say such a thing?' the girl practically shouts. 'I shall never forget, when I first came to you, it was your couplets that brought some meaning back to my life. Mistress, you taught me to read, remember, using your poems.'

'I remember.' Oh, how proud she was of the lines, how much time she'd poured into them, what joy they give her! They are witness to her girlhood dream of a perfect love.

'If it hadn't been for you and the old master, I'd be at the bottom of the river!'

'Lanlan, we only did what any decent human being would have done.'

'You took me in, a penniless child, and gave me shelter and made me feel safe. You've been like a sister to me. Those poems — you used to read them aloud to me, remember? They ...' she swallows, overcome '... they are not just words! They take you to another world, a nicer world ... beautiful ... like a dream.'

'They were dreams only. Love like that does not exist.'

'But it should, it does!' Lanlan holds Jiali's hand. 'Mistress, forgive me, but I have to say it.'

'Say what?'

'You and the young master, it was never right, from the very beginning. You felt it, I felt it. Now we know why. All these lies. That's not what a marriage should be like. You deserve better!'

*

Long after Lanlan leaves the room, her words stay in Jiali's mind: *You deserve better.* Wu Fang would have said the same. But what is to be done about it? Jiali goes to the window, and glances outside at the courtyard. As if to answer her question, a voice echoes, the sound of the ocean man saying the words from Mulan: *I ask what is she thinking? I ask why is she sighing ...*

Something jostles inside her. Yanbu betrayed her, right

from the start. And if she now falls for someone else, he has only himself to blame.

She is free to love Charles.

*

Later, as she tucks Jiali in, Lanlan asks, 'So Mistress Wu is not going to Beijing?'

'No. She was worried about Li Jian making trouble, even though he'd already left for Shanghai.'

'Mistress Wu is always so protective of you.'

'I don't need protection. It's ridiculous that she should stay. Her family will be so disappointed, and it makes me feel sad and a little angry that she thinks I am so weak and helpless.' Jiali is genuinely indignant, though not honest enough to admit to herself the real reason she doesn't want Wu Fang to stay.

'I know who will help persuade her.'

'Who?'

'Master Cha,' Lanlan beams. 'Mistress Wu will be reassured if Master Cha promises that he will look after you in her absence.'

'I told you, I don't need looking after, by anybody!' but the protest is weak, and Lanlan chooses to ignore it.

'It is well known that Mistress Wu has a soft spot for Master Cha.'

'Oh yes, I know that ...'

Lanlan laughs and interrupts her: 'And so do you!'

18

Deep in the heart of the hills above Fudi, the Bell Temple clings precariously to the rock, as it has done for 800 years, its black and white eaves curving delicately like butterfly wings. It is famed for its Song dynasty bronze bell, which is reputed to have taken its unique, lingering echo from the nearby waterfall; this echo is meant to impart supreme wisdom. Characters carved deep into the rock testify to the temple and bell's enduring popularity. Charles himself, woken often from his afternoon naps by its deep mellow notes, is an admirer. Back in the summer, he visited the temple almost daily, staying till late. The clear night sky offered a rewarding view of the stars, and the abbot of the temple talked of their link to and impact on human fate. In time, their exchanges became more casual, and the abbot told frivolous tales, among them another version of the snake legend that had fascinated Charles since he had heard it on the ship from Wu Fang. Charles in turn impressed the abbot by quoting extensively from Wang Wei and Du Fu to Su Dongpo, Jiali's voice echoing in his head as he recited.

But naturally the temple and its inhabitants cannot exist on beauty and prayers alone, and the abbot cannot ignore the powerful patrons that visit after the quiet summer to cleanse their spirits and donate much-needed funds. Today, no fewer than three groups of distinguished guests have been invited to lunch in the temple's small courtyard. The occasion is the Chong Yang festival: hiking, kiting, appreciating the rich adornment of autumn colours. The men around Charles, teaching colleagues from the college, wear small twigs of dogwood — green branches with red berries — in various manners. Charles is given one himself, which he hooks around his waist. Chrysanthemum wine is drunk and toasts made. He finds the taste refreshing though surprisingly bitter.

The abbot, mischief in his eyes, makes an appearance, and renews his acquaintance with Charles, taking him aside.

'I have something to show you.' He giggles, this tipsy, wrinkled old man, and takes Charles by the hand. In a side room behind the main hall, a small wooden statue stands on the purple velvet tablecloth beside a bronze incense burner. Would Charles like to have this humble gift? Really. He knows how much his ocean friend likes ancient things. What deity is it? One of the Eight Immortals, *Lanchaihe* or *Tieguai li*, due to its ragged appearance? Observe that he holds a staff and has only one shoe on ...

At the sound of footsteps, the abbot shoves the statue at him conspiratorially and turns on his heels. Charles has not much difficulty hiding it: the Chinese gown he is wearing could practically store a whole study up its sleeves, if one were so determined. He returns to the banquet feeling enriched, though a little like a naughty schoolboy.

*

'There is a poem about this festival,' Yanbu leans over, smelling of bitter wine, and launches into the line: '*In my mind's eye, I see my dear brother climbing up high; along with others he decorates the hill with branches of ...'*

A man more drunk, a fellow teacher, interrupts and finishes the line for him: '... *branches of Zhuyu, and then he realises there is someone missing.'* He laughs and points at the green twigs on Charles' waist. 'Zhuyu, this is called Zhuyu in Chinese. According to our custom, during the Chongyang Festival, you wear this to ward off evil spirits. You won't be sick for the whole year. This is a poem about deep, deep, friendship. We are your "dear brother", you know, like in the poem?'

Charles nods. He does not want to be ungrateful. After all, this is the first time an ocean man has been included in the gathering, though the many toasts praising Charles' 'heroism' on the expedition ring hollow. At the smallest excuse, he leaves the table a second time.

Walking on impulse, he finds himself outside the temple, in a small clearing among the ancient pines, holding in its bosom a flowing spring, between two low hills gazing at each other. A stillness descends. How these ancient hills stand with dignity and let him be. He used to see hills back home as a challenge and is amazed at his own lack of urge to conquer these. Something has changed in him.

'Charles! Charles! Where is Charles?' he hears faintly his name being called in drunken familiarity, and a feeling of enormous privilege and luxury possesses him — he is not merely welcomed, he is wanted. Suddenly, all the words of praise that he had found shallow just moments ago begin to work on him; the declarations of affection from Yanbu and other male Chinese colleagues, which he previously found insincere and somewhat embarrassing, are now pleasing to his ears. Perhaps it is to do with the couplets he has been diligently copying out each night; many of them are romantic in nature, but many also toast love in different forms. Chinese culture, like those of the ancient Greeks, he has learned, celebrates male friendship unashamedly; he should embrace this.

Charles is actually quite right with the world.

'Dear brother ... deep, deep friendship,' he murmurs to himself as he paces the wet mossy ground in the clearing rhythmically, liking the words more and more. *Perhaps I am drunk, too?*

The summer gone was the summer of all summers, when heat seemed to drip off the mango leaves, and dampness licked his bare arms like so many wet tongues. Butterflies beat their helpless wings weakly, fearing they might turn into ashes if they stopped. The many fruits and blossoms were weightier at night, and yet pale and unreal in the daylight, the contrast unbalancing him, making him feel unanchored. But even that now seems like a pleasure.

Since then, he has lived in confusion, with a vague sense of happiness, a feeling he thought he had long forgotten.

Is it happiness though? Something has happened between him and Jiali — a closeness, a silent understanding of a sort, though never acknowledged by either — since that day she charged into his study, accusing him of writing those damned couplets. After she left, the image of her holding Anne's photo in her hand had remained rooted in his mind and refused to go away, haunting him in his sleep and more when awake. Grief, hitherto a constant state of being, though always in the dark, had been not only brought to the open, but brought to the eyes of the most lively and vivacious woman he knew. The contrast has dazzled him, and cleared the air, so to speak; yes, he is definitely happier.

But autumn reigns now. Everything is present, instantly gratifying, like the touch of this moist, cool rock. The air is so intoxicatingly fresh that it feels as if it's never been breathed before. The crispness focuses his mind. He sees, in sharp vividness, Jiali's expressions — the way her face wrinkles in happiness — and hears the voice that makes his heart beat fast: 'It's my scroll.'

And he says to himself: 'Peace, I'm with peace.'

*

A quickening of the air, and he finds Yanbu standing in front of him. In the clear light, how smooth the young teacher's skin, how still and calm the eyes, and yet they are the eyes of the drunk, with a strange gleam of wisdom and honesty. Charles hears distant laughter, arguments, and rhythmic recitation — that peculiar Chinese game of guessing the riddles with one's fists, which he is never good at, however hard he tries, his blunders often more entertaining than the game itself. He does not feel like entertaining today. He guesses Yanbu has been sent to find him.

'They want you back — what's a banquet without the most honoured guest?' Looking around him, Yanbu beams. 'But it's so peaceful here.' His posture indicates there is no hurry.

Charles nods, his spine tingling. She appears again before him in his mind. Peace, Jiali is peace. How strange to hear this word from Yanbu.

'We Chinese can be very noisy.'

'You don't have to apologise.'

'They think they are saving the country, but all they are doing is making a racket in a quiet place.'

'It does not have to be a bad thing, having a great time.'

'You are just saying that to make me feel better.'

'Yanbu, have I ever said China was perfect?'

The women in Fudi are so much more astute than the men, Charles thinks with mixed feelings, *so much more understanding of the importance and necessity of truth, however unsavoury, in any relationship — their confiding in each other cements intimacy.* He thinks of the couplets. He'd promised Jiali not to mention them to Yanbu, but it feels wrong. He wishes he had no such burden to carry.

'Have you been home lately?' he asks.

The other laughs. 'I only left home a month ago, remember?'

'Long enough though.'

'It was generous of Director Zuo to grant me that extended sick leave in the summer; he won't offer more now I've fully recovered. It will be close to Jiali's due date when I next return. Then, hopefully, I will be a proud father!'

Hearing her name has a sobering effect on Charles, who grows silent. It strikes him as odd that Yanbu never seems to show real impatience about not being able to see his wife often, though the Yans' house is right on the other side of the town — if Yanbu were determined, he could easily be there and back in a day. In Yanbu's shoes, Charles knows he would break the rules of the naval college to see Jiali as often as possible. Perhaps, he reasons, Yanbu is simply more conscientious.

'How goes the school, Charles? Can't be easy to teach a group of illiterate girls. An uphill struggle, I suppose.'

'Quite the contrary, a delightful experience.' He tells the truth. The boys at the naval college, elites of the kingdom, are studious and stiff; the girls at the school, poor and disadvantaged though they no doubt are, surprise him with their intelligence and, once they know him, mischief. Teaching at the college is his duty, teaching at the school pure pleasure.

'You are more involved, I suppose, now that Wu Fang has left for Beijing? My mother wrote to let me know. You and Jiali are the pillars holding things up?'

'There are actually three of us,' Charles hastens to clarify, 'the new art teacher, me, and Jiali.' The art teacher is not often there, but the fact remains that there are three members of staff, he justifies to himself.

'Is my wife well?'

'Perfectly well. Now that Wu Fang has left, she is practically the head.'

She, wearing a pale green dress, smiling, always coming up with fresh ideas: 'Let's take the girls out, let's do the lessons in the yard, let's teach them dance.' Whatever she suggested on a whim, they gleefully accomplished. He'd known her to be kind; he'd seen her passionate; he'd never expected her to be such fun.

'No Li Jian?'

'He's gone back to Shanghai.'

'Oh.' Yanbu seems relieved.

'Wu Fang requested …' Charles pauses. Is it wise to confide in Yanbu what Wu Fang has asked him to do with regards to the governor's son?

Yanbu suddenly bursts out with: 'Li Jian is not to be trusted.'

Charles raises an eyebrow. 'But isn't he one of your oldest friends?'

'Exactly. I know him well. He has a lot of good points. He is generous and likeable, but he is prone to exaggeration. When we were both pupils at the college, he cheated at exams. It was well known. He copied me, my work, all the time! He is charming, as you know, and he made it easy for people to help him get what he wanted. And he also helped me, in his own way ...' He swallows. Charles' gaze unsettles him. 'What I am telling you is all in confidence.'

'I understand.' Charles waits. He feels he is on the brink of the truth. Surely Yanbu will now confide in him about the couplets. Charles had been outraged on Jiali's behalf at first, but now he is with Yanbu, he is in a more forgiving mood. What Yanbu had done was a foolish, desperate mistake, rather than an unkind act of deception. If Yanbu comes clean to him now, Charles might be prepared to plead to the women on Yanbu's behalf. Which eager lover wouldn't want to write the best lines to his beloved? He certainly would.

'My ... er ...' Suddenly Yanbu seems to despair, and Charles sees that familiar evasive look. 'I meant to ask, Charles,' Yanbu clears his throat, 'my mother wrote to me about the maid.'

'What?'

'The maid, the night you stayed over at ours?'

'I see.' Charles sighs with impatience. Fond though he is of Yanbu, sometimes he doesn't seem to know the man at all. 'Yes indeed. I am glad you mentioned it first. Forgive me for being ungrateful but I turned her away.'

'You hurt my mother's pride.'

'It wasn't my intention to upset anyone, but ...' Charles swallows, exasperated that Yanbu should have thought to mention something he had believed both of them would rather forget. Once again, he is reminded of the women: Wu Fang and Jiali would have understood him perfectly, instantly — how can Yanbu not get it?

'My mother didn't mean any harm. I know it is an old-fashioned practice, but ... Director Zuo and the governor, respectful gentlemen and reformers, both have concubines, as you well know.'

'They are of a different generation! Also, the girl was about ... what, fifteen? Really, Yanbu!'

Yanbu's face reddens, and Charles suddenly understands: feeling guilty, and yet too nervous to confess about the couplets, Yanbu is instead trying to make Charles feel guilty about something.

Such a low blow, and it has backfired, for Charles can see that Yanbu is himself embarrassed. Oh, silly man! Charles turns away, and as he does, the statue falls from his sleeve. He picks it up and thinks it wise to explain his possession of it.

'The abbot gave it to me; we have struck up rather a friendship this summer.' He smiles. 'It is one of the immortals ...'

'The abbot of this temple?' Yanbu interrupts with darkened face.

'A very learned man.'

Yanbu's lip curls. 'Why did you accept it? You hate such things. You were really angry with the governor for accepting old relics from temples.'

'The governor does a lot of things both you and I disapprove of. Or so I thought.' Charles cannot help but retort.

'What about other ocean men then? You said they were committing sacrilege by accepting such gifts. In their, no, your own, country, they would never dream of doing such a thing. It shows disrespect for our religion, you said. And I agreed with you.'

Yanbu is so indignant, so self-righteous, that Charles is tempted to expose him, here and now, about the couplets. He resists.

'It is different. I was given it by the abbot himself.'

Dropping his eyes to the statue in Charles' hand, Yanbu whispers, 'I insist that you return it. It is bad luck to take home something like this. I see ocean people taking presents from the Chinese all the time, never asking where they came from. Don't you know all objects take on something of their environment? Where do you propose to put your statue? Your house is a human dwelling, and this statue has the divine energy of centuries of worship. No human can withstand such power. You will be destroyed.'

This is heartfelt, and Charles is not unmoved by it.

'Thank you for your concern. I will keep it awhile and think about it,' he asserts convincingly, though already the statue feels heavier and sharper in his hand. There is truth in what Yanbu says, but also a hypocrisy, which he cannot stand.

'Oh, you are stubborn!' Suddenly Yanbu grabs the statue from him. 'It's theft, pure and simple.' He runs. In blind haste, instead of heading back to the temple, he disappears into the depths of the woods, holding the statue high in his hand.

Charles gives chase instinctively. Ridiculous, he tells himself, two adult men, fighting over an obscure statue he is not even particularly fond of! Cool air mops his sweaty brow, the sound of their feet on the path becomes part of the throbbing heartbeat of the hill. Ahead of him, Yanbu jumps and twirls, following the spring. Charles does the same. His feet are soaked through. This is about more than just Yanbu's guilt about the couplets, Charles now realises. He notes how Yanbu's demeanour had changed when he mentioned the abbott: Yanbu is jealous. It's nothing to do with the statue, he wants to be special to Charles. Such insecurity, and yet it pleases Charles, and makes him jump higher. Now the chase becomes light-hearted for him. 'Dear brother … deep, deep friendship,' he hums to himself as he runs. Nearing its roaring destination, the spring surges impatiently, shoving the two men, unsteady in their steps, forward. They meet at the waterfall. A homecoming. Yanbu's mood, too, changes; he turns and grins at Charles, and places the statue by a rock, as if depositing a trophy.

A truce, perhaps even a victory — whose though? The two drunken men stand still, panting.

Holding a little way back, catching his breath, Charles watches, curiously, as Yanbu stretches a hand to touch the misty white curtain in front of him, quickly withdraws, then, gingerly but determinedly, steps into the fall. Droplets of water part as they hit him; his arms are stretched wide, head up, shaking as if showering. A shiver runs through Charles' own body: in all the time he's known Yanbu, he's never seen the man so abandoned to sensation. Even on the island, when all the boys and Charles had been in various stages of disarray, Yanbu had remained formally clothed throughout. What of his fear of water? How can he breathe with all those droplets on his face, Charles thinks with concern, then with envy. The more vigorously Yanbu shakes his head, the more Charles himself is tempted. The urge to soak through is strong, as is the urge to be near Yanbu, so free now.

The bells from the temple ring suddenly: *ding dong, ding dong.*

Yanbu, wet and shivering, eyes glistening, is in front of him.

'Charles … I owe you my life. Never forget that.' He wipes his face, revealing features that suddenly strike Charles as being attractive for the first time since he has known the young teacher. It has always been a handsome face, but now, tenderness after exertion adds to it a depth and vividness that Charles finds compelling. Scared both of his own feeling and of what Yanbu might say next, he interrupts, with a light-hearted tone of voice.

'If you mention it one more time!' Charles threatens, half-jokingly, with a raised fist.

'Charles, Charles!' Yanbu puts a trembling hand on Charles' shoulder. 'Listen to me. It is fate. Three hundred years ago, we must have sailed in the same boat. It is no coincidence!' He gulps, overcome: 'You might be a foreigner, but I have never felt this way for anyone. I … you … you saved me!'

And, therefore, we are bound eternally? The ridiculous declaration hangs in the air. Charles feels oddly dissatisfied. Is this another version of *'dear brother'* or something more personal? If the latter, he should like to hear words bolder and more explicit, not that he is at all ready for such sentiments, but his heart craves clarity, even as it fears it. On the brink of more profound intimacy than he thinks he wants with Yanbu, Charles treads carefully.

'It's nothing,' he murmurs.

'It's everything.' The other grows bolder, and his hand, never leaving Charles' shoulder, now holds it with force. 'I … you …'

How direct and open is Yanbu's gaze, the sort of ocean-person gaze he used to complain to Charles about. Charles pulls away, also with force. His heart senses a momentous confession and warns of the danger of hearing it.

The moment passes, Yanbu loses courage and slips into forgiveness and understanding, feelings he is accustomed to expressing. He leans and picks up the statue by his feet: 'You can keep it, but the abbot is a real old reactionary.' He pushes the statue at Charles.

'The abbot is nothing to me,' Charles says angrily, deliberately ignoring the statue. The lie is also a truth, so he asserts it boldly. How absurd and absolutely confusing everything is!

As his eyes meet Yanbu's, a sudden image of Jiali appears in Charles' mind. Now he is filled with an enormous guilt. Theft, he has certainly attempted, not of the statue, but of something much more precious. What to do? The waterfall is to be his refuge. He turns to it. The screen of droplets blocks his way, like the porch of a church or a temple courtyard; it is imperative that one is ready to repent before one enters. But I have no sins to confess, he insists, and steps boldly into the stream. Even as she stands there, holding his whole being in thrall, they have done nothing. Even as she completely occupies his mind, he's done nothing. Nothing. He is clear as the water, he is not in love with anyone, he is ...

Ding dong, ding dong ...

Droplets slip through his outstretched fingers, like time. Eye of the hill, soul of the universe, this waterfall. Is he enlightened or more confused than ever?

Dinglingdinglin dong, dinglingdinglin dong ...

The waterfall knows that lies and truth both are in the minds of the two friends. Wisdom is said to be imparted not just in the ring of the bell, but in the echo of silence between each peal. The men pause to listen. Are they any wiser?

Charles rather doubts it.

19

Piles of letters from Jiali are already waiting for Wu Fang when she arrives at her brother's mansion in Ganbian Lane, and though impatient, she controls the urge to open them here and now. She will save herself the pleasure for when everyone has gone to bed.

The journey to Beijing had nearly not taken place, but then she'd discovered that Li Jian is not just away from Fudi, he is also away from Shanghai, on a lengthy business trip to Hong Kong, and she'd had a most reassuring meeting with Charles, who promised to be at the school every day, to watch over Jiali. She hasn't told anyone — not even Jiali, especially not Jiali — that the real purpose of her trip is to attend an emergency meeting of the Society for a United China, though getting supplies for the hospital and seeing family are perfect covers.

*

They say autumn is the best season to be in Beijing. Pomegranate trees hang low with dark-red fruits in courtyard gardens above giant golden fish bowls; gentlemen serenade their favourite caged birds with Peking operas; Manchu ladies with painted faces balance their theatrical hairdos, teetering on high platform shoes — these general impressions are well known to visitors, though Wu Fang, having stayed with her brother many times before, is blind to all. The siblings wait until their mother, who has also come on the trip, is settled and the servants sent away before sitting down to confide in each other.

'When is my sister-in-law back?' Wu Fang asks, tapping the table.

'Yingying can't wait to see you,' says her mild-mannered brother. How quickly he has lost that soft Fudi accent, Wu Fang notes, though she nods and smiles as her brother continues, 'but she will be late home. She said for you to wait up.'

'I will certainly wait up.'

'There are bound to be many messages, everyone is keen to see you again.' He is speaking carefully, even in his own house. Things must be worse than she thought.

'I will attend tomorrow evening's meeting, after I have completed the business for the hospital.' She watches her brother's face closely, then chances a question: 'So how bad is it?'

'As of yesterday, I have been barred from attending court. I am very, very lucky indeed compared to others, though — several of my colleagues have been sent into exile.'

'And Yingying is safe?'

'Yes. So far, they are only after me, because of what I said in court about further reforms, though she will be going out less now I think.'

Wu Fang understands this to mean going to fewer meetings.

'Good,' she nods. 'Are you hiding the news of your dismissal from Ma and Pa?'

'I will tell Ma in a day or two. Pa is bound to find out from the court circular anyway. Then I will write to him.' He is silent for a breath or two, then: 'But what you and Yingying do, they must never know.'

'Of course.'

'Another round of executions has been announced, now that it's autumn,' her brother says in a near whisper. 'Zhifeng, our friend, is on the list. He has a young son, only five; his family is distraught, as are we. Wu Fang, we must all be very careful.'

Wu Fang lowers her eyes.

*

Later, the courtyard house is quiet, and Wu Fang sits down with a pot of tea. Two weeks' worth of letters from Jiali await her. Keeping half an ear out for Yingying's carriage, she dives in.

… Are you in Beijing yet? I want you to be there now so your home returning will be sooner …

… what a girl Yueyue is, though I worry about her — her beast of a father was drunk again and threatening to sell her to the brothel, and Yueyue told me today she would rather kill herself. What a mad world we live in! I told the girl to come straight to me next time, but now worry that I should have done more …

… Couldn't sleep last night, so dug out all your old letters from Japan. What if I do indeed give birth before your return? I trust no one else, certainly not the doctor my mother-in-law has found. You should not have worried that she would turn nasty again for she has been kind, though manifested in strange ways, such as forcing me to eat eggs as if I am a crocodile! Lanlan says it is her future grandson (for of course I must be carrying a boy) she is taking care of, but I do feel she has mellowed somehow. Watching her, I feel great pity, for she is a lonely woman, and then I think how lucky I am to have you …

She flips through a few pages of couplets in her friend's elegant handwriting.

'*Knows, earth, tears, crossroads …*' she murmurs aloud. Good to see that Jiali is writing again.

But what is this? Wu Fang sits up.

… Yanbu wrote to me again. Rather strangely, he recalled our courtship days. I don't know what to make of it. Does he suspect that I know the truth about the couplets …

… Yanbu sent books home, but said I should not read too deep into the night …

… He's specifically requested my mother-in-law should never make me upset, not on any terms …

… Shall I ever forgive Yanbu? Charles thinks I should. He said it was understandable that Yanbu should want to appear clever to me. What he did was out of eagerness to woo me. Charles can be very persuasive. Do you know, Wu Fang, I think he is very fond of Yanbu …

Damn Charles! Wu Fang curses softly to herself. *Your job is to keep Jiali safe from unwanted attention, not to push her back into Yanbu's arms.*

*

In the crisp autumn morning, she sits upright in her brother's carriage. How deep, still, and blue the sky, how wide the road, how great the number and variety of people, how deafening the volume of traffic. The carriage sails as if on the sea, and her encounters are with both the grand and the humble: a series of elegant *pailo* gates, each bridging the road with its broad stone lintels and inscriptions in lofty, stylised characters, punctuate her journey, ceremonially ushering her towards the centre; flea-ridden beggars sun themselves daringly in the central strip of the road normally reserved only for the emperor. Fudi also possesses *pailos*, as well as beggars galore, but Wu Fang does not recall them being arranged with such shameless disregard of the contrast between grandeur and poverty. At heart a southerner, Wu Fang is used to humid air and intimate, impulsive exchanges; Beijing is the opposite: the air supremely cool, and everything about distance and formality. Long, thin lanes can be glimpsed running off the road, lined by grey-roofed courtyarded complexes, each a family home with a quietly aristocratic air. Wu Fang leans back. Her throat hurts a little; she is developing a raspy cough that reminds her that the harsh, dry wind has blown in from the Gobi Desert. The warm, humid scent of Fudi beckons, and she swallows, homesick. She hears Jiali's voice, reciting Du Mu: *To the one who truly knows me, what matters if we live as far apart as the edges of the earth? Don't let us be like those youngsters, dropping tears onto the same handkerchief on the crossroads upon the moment of parting!*

'Shall I drive the Mistress to the Tianqiao Opera House, to watch the latest opera *At the Cross Road*?' asks the driver solicitously. 'They have finished their tour of the country and have returned triumphant to the capital.'

'I have urgent business at the Zongli Yamen.'

'Won't the Mistress be buying a Ming vase or some old scripts at the stalls?' the driver points at yet another *pailo*, the gated entrance to Liulichang. To browse its many antiques stalls used to be one of the pleasures of a Beijing trip.

'Not today.'

'A shame, Mistress, you used to always go there to get little trinkets for your friend back in Fudi, I remember.'

Wu Fang changes her mind. 'Perhaps a quick look.'

*

Zongli Yamen, the government office newly set up to deal
with ocean people and their hugely varying affairs, impresses
and depresses her in turn. In vain, she explains to yet another
indifferent official the need for the Fudi hospital to have its
papers stamped so they can order much-needed medical
equipment from abroad; then, in walks another official, smiling,
who takes her aside and surreptitiously suggests how she can
get round the bureaucracy. Even when the second young official
realises that she is a woman, his face does not change colour,
and he carries on speaking to her ordinarily, with a tangible note
of admiration added to his already nice-sounding Mandarin. It
seems to be a reflection of the way the whole country is run, she
thinks, this see-saw of past and future, of outdated convention
and impatient reform.

In the early evening, she attends a banquet held in a room
in the foreigners' part of the city, not far from the Japanese
consulate. Everyone speaks in Japanese, which feels safer,
considering the topics; this also imparts a sense of freedom, as
if they are once again outside the country. Japan's reform and
westernisation has long fascinated the youth of China, their
love–hate relationship with the island country a reflection of
their own contradictions: how impressively powerful Japan
has become, and how humiliating that China has now to learn
from it. All are well aware that the Manchus are watching those
who have returned from Japan closely, for the large number of

'agitators' among them. This meeting, indeed, is dominated by the topic of reform, and Wu Fang listens in silence as her sister-in-law tells of her brother's dismissal from the court. Worse is sure to come, they agree.

Later in the evening, having said a fond and cautious goodbye to Yingying, she goes alone to another Society meeting in a private house nearby.

How much the intimate atmosphere of the room reminds her of the numerous meetings she attended in Japan: the hushed voices speaking many regional accents, the heavy smell of tobacco, eager young faces hovering over cold plates of food.

'Your brother has come off lightly,' says a masculine young man, whose profile is faintly familiar to Wu Fang. He had been at dinner earlier and has been giving Wu Fang looks all evening. 'The situation is dire. The Manchus will never listen to reason — any talk of reform is futile. It is now time for extreme measures, which is why we called this emergency meeting.'

'I have been mobilising around Fudi,' Wu Fang says, 'but I wouldn't say we are ready for an armed uprising yet.'

'Lin Zhi has good news about what's happening in Nanling, I believe,' the young man turns his face to someone in the corner of the room.

'We have been working on the troops there for quite a while now, both high ranking officers and ordinary soldiers — many now have sympathy with our cause,' says Lin Zhi slowly, 'Nanling is a foothold for the Manchus — taking it over would be a huge boost to the movement — but I agree with Wu Fang that we are not yet ready for an armed uprising. It would be too risky.'

'When will we ever be ready?' cries the masculine young

man, standing up in the light, after which Wu Fang exclaims, 'Du Wei, it's you!'

Du Wei turns and mock bows. 'I wondered if you would remember me, Wu Fang. My general is under siege still, you want to come and finish the game one day?'

After a few second's hesitation, Wu Fang laughs. 'I was under the impression you had already lost.'

'How can you say I lost when I still have my general? You never know what manoeuvre I might make next. Let's resume the battle and I might save him yet.'

'Never, never play chess with Du Wei!' complains Lin Zhi, shaking his head. 'He'll plague you forever, until he wins.' Then, turning to Du Wei, he says, 'The truth is people finally let you win, because they cannot stand it any longer.'

'That is one strategy, isn't it?' The young man grins shamelessly.

*

Du Wei was the student who had recruited her in Japan, and renewing her acquaintance with him is, at first, not at all unpleasant. Wu Fang remembers fondly many fun nights spent playing chess with this dogged young man. But though brave and dedicated, Du Wei is now a loner. Frustrated with the slow progress of the movement, he tells Wu Fang his daring plan to assassinate certain high-ranking Manchu officials himself, and appeals to her for help. To make homemade bombs, certain chemicals are needed, but how can she give away much-needed medicines that will save lives for him to use for killing, she protests vehemently.

'How many more lives will be lost if these loathed Manchus carry on ruling our country?'

'The Manchus have to go, but I can't bear the thought of such extreme methods.'

'I don't understand you, Wu Fang, why join the Society if you are so sentimental? Do you think the Manchu dogs will just step down of their own accord?'

'Of course not. I told you, I'm mobilising! We need the people to be on our side.'

'That takes far too long.'

'And those officials on your assassination list, some of them are reformers, men like my brother!'

'He's not a Manchu, is he? So he is safe. I only want to take down the Manchus.'

'All Manchus?'

'Forget it,' he says impatiently.

*

She should leave Beijing. The Society meeting is done, her work on behalf of the hospital accomplished, and she misses Fudi and Jiali desperately. And yet, how can she leave knowing Du Wei might do foolish things that will not only endanger himself, but also the cause?

'For heaven's sake,' exclaims her brother, 'you look like you have all the world's troubles on your shoulders. Why punish yourself so? Do slow down. It is not healthy, nor fair, that you work this hard.'

'*Those who are able must labour much*, said Confucius. It is one of the few sayings of his that I approve of. I want to do even more.'

'If you want to do more, isn't it time you showed Ma around a bit? She is complaining that she has been bored.'

The next day, Wu Fang takes her long-neglected mother with her to meet Du Wei, who is polite and charming, but Mrs Wu remains solemn and silent, and upon returning home that evening, when they are alone, chills her daughter with the words: 'Do warn that young man, won't you?'

'Of what, Ma?'

'A dark cloud hovers above him. Don't you feel it, too?'

'Ma! Since when are you able to tell fortunes?' Wu Fang laughs nervously.

'All mothers have certain powers when it comes to their children,' her mother carries on with a strained voice, 'Warn him. Whatever he plans, he mustn't do it. And he mustn't involve you.'

Wu Fang opens her mouth to protest, but is cut off:

'The Manchus know no mercy, and won't hesitate to punish.' Mrs Wu is more explicit now, and Wu Fang realises, with a jolt in her heart, that her mother has seen right through her, just like Jiali had.

Wu Fang goes to Du Wei late that night.

'Why did you come?' he rises.

'You must stop. It is suicide.'

'You care for me, a little, then?' he asks hopefully.

'Du Wei, we talked about this in Japan, you know I don't love you.'

'Why? Is there someone else?'

She pauses, remembering her conversation with Charles. Though she had shaped it to fit her own purposes, his advice had been genuine: yes, she ought to be truthful.

Breathing deeply, she says firmly, 'Yes.' It is not love as Du Wei understands it, but it is love nonetheless.

'Who?'

'Someone you don't know.'

'Someone in Fudi, then.'

'Indeed,' she whispers.

'The lucky bastard. Is he in the movement?'

'No.'

'No?' He raises an eyebrow. 'Does he know about your work?'

'Yes.'

'And he doesn't mind, doesn't worry, doesn't beg you to stop?'

'He ... doesn't know yet how dangerous it is.'

He studies her closely, then laughs suddenly. 'Wu Fang, you are lying.'

'What do you mean?'

'You can't love this man, or him you — not enough anyway.' He grins. 'Look around you: all of us are either single, or in it together as a couple. We do this with our heads hung by our waists. You can't be in two minds about it. If we get caught, we risk not just our lives, but those close to us. You know this, and yet this man, whom you claim you love, does not try to stop you.'

'I told you: he doesn't know how dangerous it is.'

'Come off it, Wu Fang! He can't really love you, and you can't love him, not that much,' he pauses and leans close, 'so I still have hope.'

'How dare you!' Wu Fang rises abruptly, strides to the door, and disappears into the night.

*

It is cold, and even inside the carriage, well-cushioned as it is, she feels it. The horses' hooves trot indifferently along the canal road, but what echoes within is Du Wei's sneering voice: 'You can't love this man, or him you — not enough anyway …'

Does she not love enough? Nonsense. She loves, hopelessly, for that love can never be declared.

Can it?

20

Their carriage halts to give way to a herd of twin-peaked Bactrian camels sauntering through the busy thoroughfare of the Xizhimen Gate, little bronze bells tied with red strings around their necks, ringing their busy presence. The camels have travelled down from Mongolia, the sight of them a perfect evocation of the wild north; Wu Fang's heart stirs, once again wishing Jiali was here — who else could she fantasise with about such a trip?

'You are not sorry we are leaving Beijing, then?' asks her mother, sitting in the carriage next to her.

'No. I'm ready for home,' says Wu Fang, though her eyes follow the camels.

'Thank the Buddha that friend of yours from Japan will also leave Beijing. I didn't feel easy about him staying here.'

'Don't you worry, Ma. His own mother is seriously ill, and so he had to return to Guangdong, to be with her.'

'How relieved you look, my child!'

'Oh Ma,' she settles uncharacteristically into her mother's arms, 'winter is coming, don't you feel the chill? Beautiful though it might be here, it is too severe. Let's go home.'

The camels disappear out of sight as their carriage continues south.

*

In Tianjin — the port city she had first set off from for Japan three years ago — Wu Fang watches the ships sailing away from the harbour, seeing her old self standing tall and upright on the deck, waving back energetically to her parents, who had sailed with her from Fudi to Tianjin, to say goodbye. Now, hearing talk of Japanese aggression just a few miles out to sea, she feels surprisingly unmoved. The old Wu Fang would have been outraged, would have ordered the carriage to head straight back to Beijing, so that she could join in the mobilisation to defend her country and fight off the invaders — for though she is against the Manchus, China is still her motherland. But her heart is no longer strong; it's soft as cotton. In Zizhulin, the ocean people's part of the city, where well-heeled Chinese mingle with foreign merchants, there are also rumours of a possible attack in the South China Sea by Charles' country. It's a restless and dangerous time, people sigh: China seems to be under attack from all directions. But Wu Fang orders a new, faster carriage, and they hurry home south. She curses the Japanese, not out of national pride, but for the fact that it means their journey back must be overland, and now takes much longer; the trek crosses the large Central China Plains, the Yellow Earth Plateau, then the Yangtze River valleys. It will surely take a lifetime.

The home-returning heart shoots eagerly like the arrow, or whatever the poets say! Wu Fang cracks the whips over the horses herself, causing her mother to titter. Will they never get home?

*

The soft southern sun warms their weary bones once they enter the Pearl River Delta, the Pearl River being the third, and last, great river before home. The familiar southern accents here only add to Wu Fang's impatience. Green is the colour all around them, which, after the brown bleakness of the north, soothes the eyes. Nearer Fudi, the sight of Hakka women washing their clothes in the river or working in the field, their happy, bare, unbound feet pattering, is common. At one such scene, Mother Wu murmurs, half to herself: 'They rather remind me of your friend, Jiali,' and turning to her daughter is shocked to see tears in Wu Fang's eyes.

'We are nearly home, my child. Why are you unhappy?'

Wu Fang blinks hard. 'Why, mother, these are not sad tears. I am ... relieved.'

'Whatever for?' Mrs Wu's voice is alert.

'Beijing, and all the things going on there. I am glad to be leaving those behind.'

'Oh,' Mrs Wu says softly. 'So you are not going back.'

'Not for a long time. I've got too much to lose.' Wu Fang's own voice is soft, too. The look of relief on her mother's face is almost too much to bear.

Mrs Wu is silent for a while, and as the carriage trundles, she pats her daughter's hand. 'Your father will be pleased to hear of it.'

And so ends Wu Fang's involvement in the movement — she simply cannot take it any more: her brother's dismissal, her own fierce disagreement with Du Wei, her mother's discovery, a horrific beheading she'd nearly witnessed ... but above all, the misery it would cause her beloved Jiali, should anything happen to her.

Perhaps she is weak, after all. Wu Fang tells herself. But she cannot bear to cause Jiali any pain, so be it.

212

*

They overnight in a village inn just outside Fudi. The next morning, opening her eyes, Wu Fang gazes into those of her mother's looking down at her, concerned.

'You cried out in your sleep,' says Mrs Wu. 'Was it a nightmare?'

'Quite the opposite,' Wu Fang laughs, stretching.

'What's that?' Her mother points at the white top she is clutching. 'You always go to bed with it, sleeping with it underneath your pillow. Isn't it better to wear it instead? Oh, I see, it is not a night shirt. Look how crumbled it has got. Did I give it to you?'

Wu Fang clutches the shirt tightly to her chest: 'No, it's ... something I bought from Japan.'

Mother Wu squints her eyes: 'It's the wrong size, it's too small for you.'

'Yes ... it has shrunk, somehow ...'

'And the women wear that to sleep in?'

'Eh ... no, but I do.'

'It's very pretty,' Mrs Wu observes, 'looks almost like a wedding top to me.'

Wu Fang blushes again. How sharp her mother's eyes. Wu Fang wonders if she guesses anything.

She realises she doesn't care. For Wu Fang has had such a very good dream. In the dream she had kissed Jiali, but not as she had kissed her before — and Jiali had kissed her back.

In the dream.

21

Returning to the relaxed, sleepy atmosphere of Fudi unsteadies Wu Fang at first. No one raises an eyebrow when she mentions a possible attack by the ocean country whose warships swamp the harbour below the town, even as her mother confirms the rumours. Smiling sagely, her father orders the servants to prepare a welcome home banquet for his wife and daughter, and dismisses the women's worry as 'something the idlers in Beijing make up to scare you'. Though he is upset about his son's banishment from the court, he is nonetheless relieved that he is out of the political whirlwind — the merciless struggles at the very top are never without casualties, and his son seems to have got off lightly, all things considered.

'Well then. I need to go to the school,' Wu Fang says, as soon as the banquet is over.

*

A mild, mid-winter afternoon. All is quiet. The girls must be in their last lesson of the day. Her eager eyes are first drawn to the fresh white paint on the walls and doors, glistening on all the surfaces — an initiative of Charles', she had learned from Jiali's letters. She makes an attempt to lift one of the dumbbells stacked in the yard and grimaces — again, Charles's idea. He had also

214

paid for the new equipment. Wu Fang squints at the new bright-white chalk lines on the ground: markings for running and for the morning stretch, also used for teaching the girls sword-dance. The school has transformed since she left, it suddenly occurs to her; and the generous-hearted headmistress sighs with anticipation.

Entering the darker corridor, she pauses in front of the portraits that now line the walls outside the staff room, bemused to note her own name on the top row, with space saved presumably for her to be painted upon her return. In the row below are Charles, Jiali, and the art teacher himself. Charles' portrait was completed before she left for Beijing and the rest must have been done while she was away — she wonders why Jiali hadn't written to tell her about it. Her long-absent eyes jump eagerly to Jiali's portrait: the artist has painted her friend in a standing posture, in profile, no doubt an attempt to capture the striking image of Jiali leading the morning stretch. It is a true likeness, except that the art teacher has discreetly reduced the size of Jiali's belly — her bump must be quite prominent by now. Wu Fang steps closer to the portrait, and gazes at the face she has so missed these last two months: the gently curving lips, the straight, slightly upturned nose, the eyes … how good to gaze into them at will without fearing that she will reveal too much of herself. Then an uneasiness occurs: what is that glint of excitement in Jiali's eyes? There is something new in them. Who or what has put it there? Her heart suddenly starts beating fast.

Jiali is alone in the staffroom, with her back to the door, reading something. At the sound of Wu Fang's footsteps, she turns sharply, sees her friend, and grins. The bump is indeed huge, and as Jiali strides towards her, it looks to Wu Fang almost as if she is a small boat sailing. Wu Fang feels nauseous. There is something oppressive about the situation, even as Jiali beams.

'I'm back,' Wu Fang says through dry lips, and tries to sound calm. 'Where are the girls?'

'Out in the back yard, drawing with Mr Lu. Didn't you see them? Oh, I am so glad you have returned. So much has happened. Yueyue ...'

Wu Fang watches Jiali's lips moving, though hearing and seeing nothing.

'... but is it really you, Wu Fang?' Jiali's voice seems to come from far off.

'You have something to tell me, don't you?' Wu Fang asks weakly, urgently.

'But I just told you, about Yueyue's father.'

Wu Fang shakes her head. 'Not that.'

'What do you mean then?'

'You. I mean about you.'

Jiali, taken aback, whispers, 'But how do you know?' She exclaims, 'I've saved it as a surprise!'

Wu Fang's knees give way, and she sinks down on her old chair opposite Jiali. She is too late. She knows it.

*

A lot can happen, it seems, in two months, but before more can be said between the two, loud screams and curses from the schoolyard interrupt them. They look up. More screams. They run.

'Yueyue,' a girl points when she sees them, 'She is being attacked by a drunkard!'

A large, burly man is indeed dragging Yueyue along by her

216

hair. At the sight of the two teachers, the girl cries out: 'Madame Wu, Madame Shen, save me!'

'Let go of her,' Wu Fang orders.

Ignoring her, the man twists Yueyue's hair tighter, pulling the girl closer to him, a strong, sickening smell of yellow plum wine reeling off him.

'I said, let go of her, now!'

The man sneers. 'If I want her to work, then she will.'

'Work? You are selling her to the brothel!' Jiali steps forward.

'Who are you?' Wu Fang demands.

'I am her father. Who are you?'

'The headmistress of this school.'

'So you are the head!' The man glares at Wu Fang. 'Call this a school? Want to know what the townspeople call it? The House of a Hundred Flowers! Are you any different from the House of a Hundred Pleasures? It's a surprise the yamen has not shut you down. Think we don't know what's going on here? Young girls mixing with grown men. Ocean men, too!' the man spits hard. 'Harlots, all ... Ouch!'

Yueyue has drawn blood. Cursing, the man withdraws his hand quickly and strikes the girl with the other, sending her flying. As the girl writhes with pain on the ground, he starts kicking her.

Wu Fang feels a tingling in her fists, as a cat must feel in her paws before striking. But someone else is there first. Wu Fang catches only the shadow of Jiali moving, and the next instant she sees the man recoiling from Yueyue, bending down on the ground, holding his belly.

'Roll away. Don't let me see your face again!' Jiali hisses.

*

Having settled the girls, the two women, shaken, retire to the staff room.

'You should not have done it, in your present condition,' Wu Fang says to Jiali.

Unable to speak, Jiali sits down, her breathing shallow and fast. The exertion was not without cost. She puts a hand to her bump. She has been so well until now.

'He's not a deserving opponent,' Wu Fang sighs.

'I wasn't thinking, but I couldn't stand by and watch,' she says between short gasps of breaths, 'I haven't had time to tell you, Wu Fang. This is not the first time he has come to the school to make trouble.'

'Sit and do nothing.' Wu Fang watches her with worried eyes. 'I will send for a carriage now.'

'I'm fine. But Yueyue ...'

'When the carriage comes, go home and lie down. I mean it. Make sure you lie flat and do not get up. At any rate, I think it wise that you keep away from the school for a while. Whatever happens with Yueyue, or any other girls, I will deal with it all. I'm back, I will be in charge.'

'Will you come to me then, tonight?'

'Of course, I will as soon as I finish at the hospital.'

'I have so much to tell you.'

'Me, too.'

*

The route from the hospital to the Yans' is familiar, and now Wu Fang wishes it longer: suddenly she lacks the courage she had gathered during the long journey back from Beijing. Only now, about to confess her love to Jiali, does Wu Fang realise how much of her strength has been drawn from Jiali's reaction in that dream; such a vivid dream that Wu Fang can still recall Jiali's scent, the folds of small wrinkles at the corner of her lips as the two kissed … But it was a dream. How will Jiali take it in reality? She risks losing her best friend. Wu Fang breathes long and hard outside Jiali's room: she has to say what she feels, for to carry on living a lie would be unbearable. Even so, her hands are tight with sweat.

'Jiali.'

But the other, more impatient, rises at the sight of her, and says: 'I'm in love.'

'So you are.' Even though her heart drops with a thud, Wu Fang keeps outwardly calm. She sinks onto the low bench by Jiali's bed, her eyes passing over the familiar objects in the room, how ordinary everything seems. Once again, though near, Jiali's voice seems to come from afar.

'I've been dying to tell you.'

Wu Fang forces herself to speak. 'I should have guessed from your letters. You have forgiven him.'

'There's nothing to forgive. He's done nothing wrong.'

'Nothing wrong?' cries Wu Fang in disbelief. This is too much to bear. 'He lied to you. Your whole marriage is a shambles.'

Then Jiali shakes her head and laughs, a cruel, clear laugh. 'Wu Fang, you've got it all wrong! I'm not talking about Yanbu.'

'I don't understand.' Wu Fang whispers.

219

'It's Charles! It's been so hard not to write to you about it, but I've been saving it up, so I can tell you in person.'

'Charles?!'

'We kissed, our very first, only two days ago; but oh, Wu Fang, I have been in love with him for a long time!'

She carries on, so absorbed in the telling of her secret, so long suppressed, that it takes her a while to notice Wu Fang looking pale and discomfited.

'What's the matter?' she stops, finally concerned.

'I'm not feeling well. It must have been something I ate on the journey,' whispers Wu Fang. Then, looking up with pitiful eyes, she begs, 'Can I come to you tomorrow, first thing? I ... I don't think I recovered properly from the trip. I came straight from the school to you today.'

'Of course, Wu Fang. Take all the time in the world to rest. I am not going anywhere, and you must be so, so tired,' soothes Jiali, noticing nothing odd.

22

Her second day of bedrest.

The encounter with Yueyue's father has triggered some light bleeding, but how hard it is to keep herself away from the school — the memory of that kiss is still fresh, as is the urge to see Charles again, and to hear his voice. Asking Lanlan for wool and knitting needles, Jiali busies herself making a scarf for her unborn child. Her fingers moving fast, she casts her mind back over the two months that Wu Fang has been away.

As soon as Wu Fang left for Beijing, Jiali felt the stir for freedom. It was almost torture to see Charles in her class every day; she had become familiar with his expressions: how the curl of his lips indicated appreciation, how a quick closing of his eyes showed understanding. Other people barely existed for her. She knew nothing could happen, but as the date of Wu Fang's return approached, she felt something must.

Then came the last day she was to be painted by the art teacher. And once again, in the middle of the session, to her secret delight, Charles slipped in with a stack of pencils and a large notebook, as he sometimes did. Usually, he sat afar, and hardly seemed to stir; but that day, he drew his chair near. A sudden ray of late afternoon winter sun streaked through the window, and shone on her face, a warm stroke, causing her to temporarily close her eyes, and she thought she heard a sigh coming from where he sat. Nervous, when she opened her eyes again, she kept them on the map of China on the wall opposite, though she was, more than ever, aware of Charles' eyes on her as he sketched her alongside Mr Lu. Something powerful seemed to radiate from where he was seated, close to her, and the glances she stole, when she dared, were at his hands, fast moving with intent; she thought she'd never seen anything as beautiful and elegant; the sounds of the pencil moving swiftly on the papers, too, were almost hypnotic. What luxury, to be bathed in his proximity and full attention. She knew then she was beautiful — felt herself blossoming in his gaze — and yet how hard it was to hold her nerve.

The art teacher left, though neither seemed to notice. To break the unbearable silence, she asked Charles timidly to see what he had been drawing. He leaned forward to show her, and she saw her own face staring back at her: truth was written all over it. Then it seemed time stood still, and something exploded inside her body. With no forewarning, she leaned forward and pressed her lips against his. There was a sense of inevitability: she had to obey the command of her too-long neglected soul. It mattered not to her that it was one-sided. She has simply been delighted he'd let her kiss him. Who cared about the future? The present was quite enough.

*

'You look very fine indeed.' Wu Fang's tender voice interrupts Jiali's thoughts.

She sets her knitting down. 'Do I?' She puts her hands to her burning cheeks. Then, looking up, she studies Wu Fang. 'You

222

still look tired. Did you sleep well last night?'

Wu Fang nods slowly, though her hair, Jiali notices, is uncombed — she must have left in a hurry. She has an air of weariness about her that Jiali attributes to the long journey. She realises suddenly how much she'd missed Wu Fang, even though she'd also been nervous of her return — unreasonably, she thinks now, for surely her best friend would be rooting for her, and rejoice with her now that she'd found true love.

'I missed you dreadfully,' she says with feeling.

'Really?'

'You don't know how hard it was, not being able to talk to anyone.'

'You don't know how hard it was, being away.'

Something in Wu Fang's voice makes Jiali say, 'You came home earlier than you said you would.'

'I rushed back because …'

'… because what?' suddenly Jiali grows excited. 'Oh, let me guess. Did you meet someone in Beijing?'

'As a matter of fact, I did.'

'Oh, tell tell!' Wouldn't it be wonderful, both she and Wu Fang in love?

'There's nothing to say, same old story, I met someone who liked me enough to propose, but I didn't feel the same way about him.'

'I see.' Jiali is silent for a breath or two, then: 'Wu Fang, has there been no one at all?'

Wu Fang leans to examine the scarf, her fingers smoothing the patterns already emerging. Then she straightens and smiles. 'Actually there is someone I have always loved.'

'How come I've never heard of him?' Jiali's eyes enlarge.

'It's … difficult for us to be together.'

'Why?'

'This person is married.'

'I see,' she nods, then, 'But that doesn't mean that …' She pauses, then sails on, 'If the love is true, then the marriage is not and must not be a barrier.'

Wu Fang smiles again, and it seems to Jiali that there are tears in her eyes.

'You should tell me though, who this man is.'

Wu Fang swallows. 'I will, one day. But for now, I've got something else to tell you.'

'Yes?' Looking a little apprehensive, Jiali whispers.

'I have decided to give up the revolutionary work. I told them that I wouldn't be involved anymore.'

'Wu Fang!'

'I lied about my trip to Beijing, Jiali. I told you it was for the hospital, but it wasn't, not really.' Wu Fang speaks in a low, subdued voice. 'The Society had called an emergency meeting — that was why I had to go so suddenly. And while I was there … Oh, things were bad, so bad!'

She tells Jiali about her brother's dismissal, the many meetings, and Du Wei's daring plan to assassinate high-ranking die-hard Manchu aristocrats and officials. Jiali listens attentively, her eyes hardly blinking.

'I felt so far from Fudi, from you, and Beijing was so cold and bleak. Then,' Wu Fang shudders, 'one day, my carriage was stopped at Caishikou, where the autumn execution was taking place. We were delayed for a long time. There was a huge crowd, and we were a long distance from where it happened; still, the silence before, then … I heard a woman scream.'

'I read about this year's list,' Jiali whispers.

'One of the executed was a good friend of my brother's, and it really hit home how utterly awful it would be for those close to me, if anything were to happen, and I cannot bear ...' Wu Fang's voice breaks.

'Oh!' Jiali pulls Wu Fang to her.

Burying her head in her friend's shoulder, Wu Fang sobs softly.

'Now you know what I truly am: a coward, a traitor. How can I face all those people who look up to me? I am nothing, nothing!'

'You a coward? You a traitor? You nothing?' Jiali pushes Wu Fang away. 'I forbid you to tell such lies. You are everything to the girls at the school, you are everything to the patients at the hospital, you are everything to all the women you have helped, and,' she clasps Wu Fang's hands, 'you are everything to me!'

Everything? Wu Fang searches Jiali's eyes and sees only concern and affection. There has never been anything else, and against hope, she now realises she has always searched for that something else. Thank the Buddha Jiali never knew, Wu Fang tells herself gratefully even as she cries in her friend's arms: at least, she gets to keep her friendship. After the devastating revelation from Jiali yesterday, Wu Fang had dashed home and gone straight to bed, crying herself to sleep. Then, totally awake, she spent the second half of the night debating with herself whether she should confess her feeling to Jiali. She hardly slept a wink, and by dawn she was still undecided.

Now she knows she will never tell. There is peace in that resolve for Wu Fang, though she grows nervous at what Jiali's reaction might be with what she will tell her next.

For now, though, her tear-soaked face is right next to Jiali's; the two clasp together with their eyes closed, luxuriating in their closeness. Jiali finally breaks the silence.

'Say you're pleased for me, that you've forgiven me for not writing, that you're fond of him.'

'Him?'

'Charles.'

Gently, Wu Fang pushes Jiali away, and the other, taken aback, whispers, 'Surely you approve?'

'It's not right, Jiali.'

'Because I'm married?'

'It's not that. Charles can't give you anything, this will only end in pain for both of you, especially you.'

'But I live in misery, my marriage is a sham!'

'No marriage is perfect. You have respect and security ... You have friends!'

You have me! she wants to scream, but the words do not come.

'What do I care for respect and security?'

'Think realistically, Jiali, you will be scorned and disgraced.'

'By who?'

'People that ... matter.' This is whispered in an uncharacteristically small voice.

'Really?' Jiali raised her voice . 'Don't you know me, Wu Fang? What's the matter with you?'

'It's ... for your own good that I ...' she stops. She is sincere and means well, so why do her words sound so false?

'I see what is happening here.' Suddenly enraged, Jiali springs apart and points a finger at her friend. 'You are jealous!'

'What?'

'You always protested that you didn't love Charles, but actually you do. You cannot bear that I am with him — that we are happy!'

'Ridiculous!' It is Wu Fang's turn to be enraged.

'Isn't it the truth?'

'The truth is I cannot bear for you to get hurt! Even Charles has more sense than you; he sees the stupidity of it all, even if you don't!'

'Charles? What do you mean?' Jiali's voice is hushed.

'I talked to him.'

'You what?'

'I talked to him, and he agreed that it was all a folly.'

'Wu Fang, how dare you!'

'He will be leaving Fudi soon, he is looking for a new post in the north.'

'You, you've driven him away!'

'It's his decision. If you don't believe me, here's his note.'

She places the note carefully in Jiali's hands, and watches as her friend quickly scans the paper.

She lied. In truth she sought Charles out, this very morning. Finding out that he'd not been at the school for quite a few days, she went all the way to the naval college, and waited outside the classroom for him to finish his lesson so she could talk to him. Charles did not seem at all surprised to see her there. A thief caught red-handed couldn't have been more compliant. He owned up to everything she accused him of.

And yet how unfair she had been, heaping all the blame on him, when Jiali was the one who sought to kiss him! Now Wu Fang feels sorry for him, for the look on his face, as he wrote the note, comes back to haunt her. They stood in a busy corridor,

227

students and teachers coming and going, some throwing curious looks at the two, and yet, seemingly oblivious to all, Charles wrote, half kneeling in front of her, carefully and diligently, the words she demanded he write there and then, so she could take it back and destroy his — their — happiness. But she had the moral high ground, and Charles did not need much convincing. It was the right thing to do, he had agreed, with a dry, raspy voice and a brief nod, before tearing himself away from her.

Slowly Jiali moves her eyes up, and it seems to Wu Fang that there is a fire dancing inside the black pupils she knows well. Wu Fang is frightened. *Please, Jiali, please. Do not look at me like that,* she pleads silently, and takes a step forward.

Ignoring her outreached hand, Jiali speaks coldly. 'Do you hate me that much?'

'Jiali!' Wu Fang begs.

'To rob me of my only chance at happiness.' Jiali's face seems frozen in hatred.

'Charles is not the man to give you happiness!' Wu Fang whispers, paralysed as if in a nightmare. 'Jiali, please, I want …'

'You seem to forget this is my life, how dare you decide for me who to love?'

Wu Fang swallows. 'The decision was not made by me. Charles has to leave, if not for this, then …' She looks away. 'A war is going to break out between our countries.'

'You are making all this all up, just to spite me?' Jiali's voice is that of disbelief.

'I first heard about it in Beijing and hadn't wanted to believe it, but it is true. Charles and all the ocean people are leaving Fudi as we speak. Once the bombing starts, we will be enemies.'

'I don't care if he is the devil himself. I love him and I want to be with him. No one can stop me, and you,' she glares at Wu Fang with contempt, 'you've said enough, Wu Fang. You should leave.'

Even in her despair, Wu Fang admires her friend. How passionately Jiali speaks, how beautiful she looks, standing there declaring her love, despising Wu Fang. She is sure she couldn't love Jiali more. She is telling the truth about the war, and yet how wrong it feels. How false and cruel the world, herself included, to the lovers!

'Go, Wu Fang. Leave.'

'I only want the best for you.' Wu Fang beseeches weakly. 'Please let's not argue, it's not good for you.'

'*It's not good for you,*' Jiali mocks. 'Who gives you the right to decide what's good for me, what's not?' Her voice quickens as she becomes more animated. 'You told the boat family to go to the ocean hospital, didn't you? You decided that was best for them, you want to know what they said to me after?'

'No, I don't.' Wu Fang pleads in a subdued, miserable voice. She is not used to this, being on the receiving end of Jiali's wrath.

Jiali ignores her. '"That rich lady thinks it's all about money, and she keeps boasting that the ocean stuff is superior to our own Chinese medicines. We don't trust her." See, that's what they thought of your interference. You said their ignorance killed the boy, but what about your own arrogance? If you had tried to gain their trust first, that little boy might still …'

'Stop!' Wu Fang cries in angst. 'That's cruel and unfair!' Her voice chokes. 'You don't know how often I blame myself for it …'

Her heartfelt plea seems to put Jiali in check, and at the softening of her eyes Wu Fang sighs.

'I know I am not perfect, Jiali, and I so often do things without thinking, but whatever I do, it is with the best of intentions.' She reaches out her hands again. 'You, Jiali, of all the people in the world, you know the true me!'

Jiali greets her words with lowered eyes and slower breaths. Wu Fang grows hopeful: hard though it is, this is not the first time they have faced a crisis together. Jiali is bound to be hurt and resentful with the news of Charles' departure, that is to be expected. But she will see reason. At this thought, falling back into her usual role in their relationship, Wu Fang the doctor speaks up.

'Charles is not the right man for you, Jiali. Please, do think, if not for yourself, then for the baby you carry. He or she deserves a chance.'

Jiali's eyes harden again. 'You want to turn my own child against me, too?'

'I …'

'You really must leave now, Wu Fang. I don't ever want to see you again.'

23

A terrible loneliness fills each corner of Jiali's bedroom after Wu Fang leaves. The very air she breathes drips with a heaviness that oppresses. She has lost something precious, Jiali knows. She feels so tired that even lifting an arm seems to take tremendous effort. By banishing Wu Fang, she is punishing herself, too, and yet pride forbids her to do otherwise. She hadn't expected any of this to happen. Even now it seems unreal. Has Wu Fang really gone?

She drifts into a deep sleep. When she wakes again it has grown dark. She sits up and resumes her knitting, just so she has something to occupy her mind. Sometime later, sudden footsteps make her glance up hopefully, but it is not Wu Fang.

'Why have you come?' she stiffens her back.

Pale, thin, nervous looking, Yanbu steals in like a shadow.

'I have been watching you for a while, you never look up. You were so absorbed.' He picks up the half-finished knitting. 'For the baby?'

She nods, glances away, and repeats: 'Why have you come?'

'Elder sister. Jiali,' his voice is low and strangely tender, 'I am on special leave, and I have something to tell you.'

How odd. She abandons her knitting and laughs bitterly to herself. *Everybody confessing!*

'I should have told you this a long time ago,' he says.

'I, too, have something to tell,' she says quietly, guessing what he is about to say.

They look at each other, then Jiali, with trembling lips, says: 'You first.'

Twice a maid knocks on their door, informing the master timidly that his mushroom soup is ready, twice he waves her impatiently away.

*

Rain falls. When? They both cease to notice. He talks non-stop, with a strange sort of fluency; it is obvious that he has rehearsed what he has to say. When he has finished, she sighs, and the look of softness on her face gives him hope. After a long silence she says simply, 'I know already. I've known for a while.'

'But how?' he gasps.

She disappears into the study, and returns with a thick pile of papers. His fingers tremble as they touch the sheets.

'Li Jian had been teaching Charles calligraphy using these couplets. I found them in a book he lent me.'

'I suppose Wu Fang knows?

'And Charles.'

'Charles, too? All of it?'

She nods.

Yanbu's face drains of colour. He hangs his head. After a long while, he tentatively glances up and seeks her eyes. Finding them not unkind, he ventures: 'It was Li Jian's idea at first, and since I was hopeless at couplets … I …'

'I would have understood, but why didn't you tell me after we were married?

232

'On our wedding night, you asked me to match your couplets, and I couldn't ... I nearly did tell you then.'

'But you didn't,' she sighs wearily.

'I did so often want to tell you, but I was too ashamed.'

'Why now?'

'We are going to war.'

'With the Japanese?'

'With Charles' country.'

'What?'

'Negotiations have collapsed; their battleships are sailing very close to our coast. Our fishermen report that the covers on their cannons and guns have been removed.' He speaks with sudden animation. Talking about such calamity is almost a relief after his confession.

So Wu Fang had been telling the truth. 'Does Charles know about this?'

'He will by now. All the Chinese staff at the college are preparing.'

'Have they all been called up?'

'Only a few have been chosen to go on the ships. Director Zuo gave me leave to come home, to say goodbye.' The country needs him, and Yanbu does not wish to be thought a coward, especially not by his wife, he tells her, as he fixes his eyes on her.

His last night.

'Will you forgive me, Jiali?'

What else can she say but yes? What else matters now? She sits down, picks up the wool, and resumes knitting. The action soothes them both.

In a little while, he remembers what she said earlier.

'You have something to tell me, too?' he asks timidly.

'It's nothing important,' she sighs.

He admires her bump: 'It has grown so much.' Then, reaching out a hand tentatively, he touches her belly and is grateful when she smiles gently and says, 'Wu Fang has checked him. Everything is perfect.'

Wu Fang had actually forgotten to check the foetus this one time, but the last thing Jiali wants is for Yanbu to be worried about his unborn child before the battle. She owes him that much.

*

While Yanbu goes to see his mother, Jiali lies in their big bed, still and unreal as a ghost. Poor Yanbu, poor her. They never loved each other, but they did once like each other and should at least be able to comfort one another in their loneliness; but that is not to be, since she can't confess her own sin. This misery is all of her own making: who knows now why she so insisted that couplets be the ultimate test of her suitors' suitability? And what does she care now for words? Charles, a foreigner, can never write couplets the way she could expect a fellow Chinese to, and even if he could, what would be the use? Anyway, he is leaving, Wu Fang has left, and all is lost.

Drifting out of sleep she hears Yanbu's soft footsteps by her bed and holds her breath. If she feigns sleep, then the decision will be in his hands. She won't refuse if he attempts intimacy — it is his right as a soldier departing for battle. A part of her desires this sacrifice. But when he tiptoes away to the study, she is also relieved: it would have been a reckless thing to do, both for herself and for the baby.

Yanbu wouldn't have tried, of course, for he is a gentleman.

*

Just before dawn, she wakes, panting from a nightmare. Only fragments of the dream remain: she is on a cliff, about to fall. When she is more awake, she knows what the dream is really about: loneliness. There is only one person in the world who she can tell all her secrets, and she has driven her away.

Jiali slumbers on in misery, and does not know that Yanbu has come again and stands in front of her. Though the subsequent dreams she has are still troubled, she smiles, and that he takes as a good omen. He steps out.

24

The cabin, though luxuriously decorated, is small and claustrophobic. A fragrant cup of tea is offered by a delicate hand he's already grown alarmingly familiar with in such a short time. Charles accepts it gratefully, though avoids her eyes. That way, she can still be a stranger with whom he has shared unexpected intimacy; he does not need to know her face.

Then, ungratefully, 'Please leave,' he says in a low voice. She handled the most private parts of him with delicacy and dedication. The encounter had been brief, the girl herself faultless. She had wiped him and herself clean and waited on him, and waited, patiently, as if the real thing, whatever it was, was still to come. He has no idea what she is waiting for. He knows only that his body has done what his mind and heart are slow to catch up with.

Finally alone, Charles groans softly. He's just had intercourse, if he can call it at that, for the first time since his marriage. It wasn't awful, but now he is full of regrets. He should not have come to Pierre's farewell party — what had he expected? The first part of the evening, at Pierre's mansion in town, had been mild enough: a Chinese banquet followed by ocean dances. Indeed, Director Zuo and the governor had both been there, casually attired, with their respective concubines. The prevalent atmosphere of benign indulgence beggared belief that the two countries would soon be at war, as Paul had announced at the club; Paul, who had urged Charles to leave, along with all the other ocean people in Fudi.

Somehow Charles had ended up on Pierre's boat: Pierre's famous pleasure boat, a little further up the harbour, full of young people, girls and boys, some boys prettier than girls. He was offered a drink and the next thing he knew he was in a cabin with a pretty girl who made sure he was comfortable, nauseously so.

He really shouldn't have come. But having been used to spending every spare moment at the school, he had nowhere else to go. He had not reckoned with the extent of the loneliness he felt at being banished from Jiali.

Banished, yes. Wu Fang has used a different word: 'Leave, Charles, for the good of both of you. You know that is the right thing to do.'

How merciless she could be, always with justice and fairness on her side. He had quite forgotten Wu Fang's judgemental nature during her two month's absence from Fudi, entranced by the heavenly company of Jiali. Until that kiss, he has been fooled into thinking he could have it both ways: to simply stay in that exalted place of being adored, enjoying Jiali's ravishing gaze, all without consequence — for she had no idea how quickly he had seen through her. Being Yanbu's friend was the reason, he claimed time after time to himself, for doing nothing; it was his armour against any dangerous emotional entanglement with Jiali.

But that kiss! How the sealing of their lips jostled him out of his own pretence! It was all he could do not to respond, to gently pull himself away, and leave her abruptly.

And live in hell ever since.

Someone is calling him, and he gets himself dressed with speed.

*

Holding his hurting head, he rises and opens the cabin door. He stares at the river. He had seen how much leftover food and wine from the boat had been poured down the side earlier. The river is still beautiful: broad, generous, trusting. The river is China, is all that is good about China, all that he believes in, still. But how much dirt it swallows! His own guilt reflects back at him from the smooth surface well oiled with grease. The night is young still; right at the other end of the boat, an opera is being staged on a raised platform. Glasses clink and cheers echo. Standing up to hail 'Bravo', the host Pierre catches sight of Charles and calls: 'Come, sit by me.'

'I'll just say bon voyage.' Charles remains where he is. After what just happened, he wants simply to melt away.

'But you must stay, really, this is based on that classical novel you said your Chinese colleague lent you. You know, kingdom falls and emperor dies. Just stay to the end of this act, and we shall say goodbye properly. I have something to ask you.'

Charles stays. He loves Chinese opera. He remembers the very first time he had heard one, the third afternoon he had arrived in Fudi. Paul had taken him; they'd watched it in the open air, up on the pagoda hill, beneath a large banyan tree whose spidery roots spread far and wide. A soft breeze blew. 'Caterwauling,' mouthed one ocean guest, before one by one, the rest of the foreigners made excuses and left. The singing was like nothing he'd heard before, the rhythm irregular, the vocals clashing terribly with the instruments, the whole ensemble hurtling menacingly at him like alien stars spilling out of orbit, and yet he'd stayed and endured, welcoming the assault because, still grieving for Anne, he had felt numb. But the crash came, and he wasn't destroyed. The sharp, needling voice clawed his soul and pummelled his wounded heart; then, extraordinarily, it soothed. The solid, unbreakable iceberg of grief was broken, then dissolved in the all-forgiving sea of this strange new world. He had shed feeling-good tears. How did she do it, that young girl of, what, no more than eighteen?

The story he hears now, as far as he can make out, consists of a woman being first promised to one man, then to another, with the fairly predictable outcome of the two fighting over her, and the young man killing the older. His reading of the book, meticulous because he wants to understand each sentence, has been painfully slow; he hasn't reached this particular chapter yet. No Chinese is here to explain the finer points of the language, and the ocean men, all drunk, show their appreciation by laughing raucously at the explicitly flirtatious scenes. Charles feels sick again. What a sordid thing he has done! He has become one of those ocean people he used to despise.

'Don't look so downbeat, old boy. Aren't you having fun? Wasn't my girl exquisite?'

'Your girl?' Charles nearly jumps out of his chair.

Pierre's eyes are on the stage as he talks: 'That's what I was going to speak to you about. Suiyi's been with me for nearly three years. Real good sort. Pretty, as you've seen, faithful, no trouble at all. I'll be honest, it breaks my heart to leave her.'

'Sounds like you should take her with you.' Charles speaks calmly, though his left leg starts shaking. *He talks as if the girl is a pet dog.*

'I would, but I can't. I'm becoming a customs officer and they won't have that sort of set-up, not good for my career, really frowned upon these days.'

Neither can he marry the girl. It's simply not done. Charles knows of only one ocean and Chinese marriage and that is between a missionary and a local Chinese Christian. Religion had played a big part in the union.

'She won't cost you much. I'd offer her to Paul, but he is in the government. You are all right, though. You work for the Chinese. They don't mind. Even Director Zuo has a concubine.'

'Thanks awfully but I can't.'

'Why not?'

'I'm leaving, too. I'm looking for a job elsewhere, somewhere up north. I've a friend in Tianjin ... '

'Ah, Paul said you weren't leaving, that's why I asked you.'

'Paul was wrong.'

'But what's to become of her? She's not used to her people after ...' Pierre jerks his head briefly, then continues, still not looking at Charles. 'Nobody will want her now that she's been with an ocean devil. Take her. She liked you, she told me. She chose you. Really. You lucky man.'

Cold sweat forms on Charles' forehead. Stepping away from Pierre, he leans over the side of the boat and throws up.

'Feeling better?' Pierce resumes when he returns. 'Think over it anyway. I am not leaving until tomorrow. To be honest I am glad to be leaving. Did you hear that Father Jacques was attacked the other day? Mrs Creswell and her little girl were spat on by coolies on their way to the church. This can't go on; the Chinese need to be taught a lesson.'

Charles rises and leaves him.

*

'Did you enjoy the play?' Paul asks, glancing back at the stage. They are in a quiet corner by themselves. 'It was adapted from the book I am translating. The play is called *General Lubu Flirts with the Beauty Diaochan*. A fascinating story. How did all those fierce war lords of the Middle Ages ever find time for dalliances with women between fighting vicious wars against each other, I wonder? Didn't end well, did it? A lesson or two for us all, no? Romance during war time might not be such a good idea.'

'Paul. Please, are we really going to attack?'

'Of course, why should I lie?'

'Do the Chinese know?'

'Didn't you see the chaos all over town?' Paul smiles. 'Everyone in Fudi, Chinese or ocean, seems to know, except you.'

'How can we do this to them? I'm here to do good, to educate and modernise the country, and yet you plot to destroy it. China is so weak, it would be like a hunt, seriously, firing cannons at people armed with arrows and spears. Aren't you ashamed? We should all be so ashamed! I don't understand. Is it all a game?'

'See it this way, we want the Chinese to be a little frightened, and they are very frightened.'

'Then why do it?'

'Because we can.'

'This is horrible.' He glances at the chattering crowds, incredulous. 'How calm you all are.'

'That's because there really is nothing to worry about, for us. We'll evacuate Fudi by tomorrow morning. Most, as you see, will head for Shanghai. The bombing will not be protracted, and we will be back soon.'

'Is it really necessary?'

'Not if the Chinese give in at the negotiations. So far they have stubbornly refused.'

'But can you blame them for not wanting to concede more land?'

'Sit down, Charles, what's the rush?'

'I'm going back to the college.'

'Or to the school perhaps? I would stay away, Charles.'

'What do you mean?'

'You might as well know that we suspect the two female teachers there of having associations with Han nationalist agitators. They plan assassinations.'

Charles' head, which has not stopped hurting since leaving the cabin, now spins too: Jiali and Wu Fang, assassins?

'Impossible!' he cries out. 'I know these women, and I can vouch for them. It is true that they are active in advancing the cause of women and girls, and are not your average dutiful Confucian wives, but they are well respected, and both come from good families.' But even as the words are adamant, quick flashes of doubts come to his mind: Wu Fang's frequent mysterious disappearances to far-off corners of the country; her many unusual looking visitors, coming at all hours and seemingly encompassing all classes — they can't all have been former patients as she claimed; even Li Jian's occasional ambiguous references to Wu Fang's 'uniqueness' now takes on new significance ... Can there be truth in what Paul claims?

'Good family is no guarantee of good behaviour. In fact, many of these troublemakers are from old Han families who swore to restore the Ming dynasty. Your friend Miss Wu has been radicalised in Japan, and her accomplice is an accomplished sword master. The school and hospital are but a front only. Charles. Flirt with any maids you fancy, but don't involve yourself in politics. Pierre might be callous, but at least he knows which side he is on.'

Paul pauses, and watches Charles with pitying eyes. 'It is best that you do not go to the school again.'

'I no longer go there anyway, for different reasons, but Wu Fang and Jiali are my friends and colleagues. Paul, whatever you've been told is not true.' Instinctively protective of the women, Charles keeps an indignant face, but inwardly he feels anxious and conflicted: in general sympathetic to the reform and republican cause, he nonetheless recoils intuitively at the idea of violence of any kind.

'Charles. I will be blunt. We are in a foreign country, and none of us monks. Take Pierre's girl. You work for the Chinese, there will be no fuss. Nobody on our side will blame you either. But steer away from those other two. I have heard from my sources that you have grown close with the sword-fighting poetess.'

'She's married to one of my colleagues and friend at the college! You're being absurd. I have nothing but admiration for her.'

'Whatever your feelings are, refrain, old boy. If I were you, I'd start packing now. The ship leaves Fudi for Shanghai tomorrow morning.'

*

Returning home, now nursing a splitting headache, Charles scribbles a note and calls Lao Lin.

'Take this to Mistress Shen.'

'Now?'

'Yes. It's urgent. If she is not in …'

'I will go to Mistress Wu.' Lao Lin nods. He knows both addresses well. 'Why don't you go and see the ladies yourself, Master?'

Charles shakes his head.

*

In the still of the night, he is wide awake, not from a nightmare, but a feeling of loss. Then he remembers what he did, and the pain propels him from the bed, pacing the room. Unable to settle, he tiptoes into the study. Now that winter is here, all the doors are shut, and he stands in the middle of the room longing intensely for summer, for the soft breeze blown in from the balcony, bringing in scents of those delicious blossoms. How far that seems; now he is quite a different person and the room a different place altogether.

He shivers before Jiali's scroll, hung so high up, so out of reach. The words are beautiful as ever, even more so, now that they have become distant and unapproachable, like her. Now, in the dead of the night, not a soul awake, he sees how utterly and hopelessly he has fallen for her; so what if she and Wu Fang are assassins — even if they are the devils he would love her! This rotten country needs a good shaking by brilliant, brave women like these. He is glad.

Then he recalls the moment when, with his eyes closed, he had pretended that the girl Suiyi was Jiali, and his stomach churns. He'd been set up by Pierre, but the guilt is no less. He is ugly, treacherous, and despicable, like his country.

And a liar: to Paul, to Yanbu, to Jiali, to Wu Fang, and above all, to himself.

Wu Fang is right: he must never go near Jiali again, to do so would be to contaminate her, for she is pure, she is peace. The message, warning her and Wu Fang of the imminent attack, will have to do. Still reeling from the shock, he's refrained from writing to them about Paul's claim of their involvement in Anti-Manchu Movement: it hasn't occurred to him that the information would be passed on to the yamen, even if it were true, so he believes the women to be safe.

25

The naval college is eerily quiet. Quite a few teachers are missing, Yanbu among them. Faces turn in the corridor as Charles races to the staffroom to gather his books for his lesson. A letter from Yanbu, left on his desk. Charles snatches it and reads breathlessly on his way to the classroom:

Dear respected friend,

I have been called upon to serve on one of our ships. It is a great honour. Only a few of the teaching staff have been asked. I waited to say goodbye, but I cannot wait any longer.

I stand by my statement when we were at the hills, Charles. You have been like one of my own limbs — qinru shouzu, do you remember the expression I taught you? How I should deserve such esteemed friendship with my limited ability and virtue I never will understand. I have many words to say but I do not know where to start. If for any reason I am delayed returning, please look kindly on my son as yours. Whatever happens in the future and to our respective countries, I shall never regret having found a true friend in you. I know you do not wish it mentioned but let me mention it one more time: you saved my life, and I have not had the chance to return the debt, but I want you to know that not only me, but all my family are eternally indebted to you ...

The letter was obviously written in a hurry and is unfinished. Anger and pity both rise in Charles. A son! How can he be so sure? Oh yes: an aunt, a wise woman, who had been able to correctly predict the genders of many babies in the family. *Called upon to serve on one of our ships.* Even now, nothing about the attack. Loyal to his country, loyal to his friend. The letter upsets Charles even as he is moved by it: the stiff words, the earnest tone; it is Yanbu all over.

An ordinary enough lesson. The usual stubborn reluctance of the pupils to speak up. Cloaked in reverence, they won't volunteer unless absolutely assured of a perfect answer. They outdo themselves today. The girls at Wu Fang's school are much more responsive. He deliberately drops questions so simple that a first-year pupil would have been able to answer them easily, but the boys — a senior group — suspecting the simple questions are bait, cling to silence as if about to drown. He gives up. To punish them, he doesn't linger after the lesson. Only then do they ask questions — he usually saves a good ten minutes or so for it.

The staffroom is empty when he drops off the books, and as he comes out, unnerved by the eerie silence, he is met by Shuisheng and three others, hovering with dog-like devotion. He relents and feels childish.

'Sir, we were bad in class today. We are sorry. We couldn't help it.'

'Was it the news of the attack?'

'You know already sir?' They exchange glances and Shuisheng speaks again, his eyes downcast. 'Director Zuo told us to study as usual, but it was hard to concentrate.'

'Director Zuo is right. Don't get distracted.'

'It is you we are worried about.'

'What an idea! I will be safe, as safe as you all are.'

'But what if our countries go to war with each other?'

'If they really are foolish enough to attack, I know China will teach them a lesson they will never forget.'

The boys laugh: 'You are on our side, sir, against your own country?'

'Of course, I'm on *our* side.'

'We will protect you, sir, if it comes to that. You are our teacher. We all owe so much to you.'

'Thank you. Now go and study.'

He watches them leave, four in a row, one holding on to the elbow of the other, their long black plaits swishing behind them. In a blink of the eye, they are all Yanbu: all that talk about 'owing' something, affection wrapped in formal words of gratitude. Charles wants to call them back. For a moment he has a bitter sense of time slipping through his fingers, and feels old himself, and strangely, on Yanbu's behalf.

His lonely steps echo in the empty corridor. The words of Yanbu's letter haunt his mind, each an arrow slung into his conscience. What has he done to this man who's pure and devoted to him? He does not deserve such devotion; he does not deserve any of this. He does not deserve Jiali either, but at least she is as guilty of betrayal as he, and the two have each other, in thoughts, if not in action.

Yanbu is innocent, and gets nothing.

*

The harbour resembles the club, filled with ocean people on their exodus. There is a very tangible solidarity that Charles alone does not share. Gentlemen are extra tender and courteous to their women, and children are picked up more frequently and kissed ever so fervently. Paul, spotting Charles, beams.

'Glad you saw sense, Charles!'

Charles shakes his head. 'I'm not leaving.'

Paul sees that he is empty-handed. 'Have you lost your mind? You do realise there will be repercussions? Any foreigner in Fudi will be a legitimate target.'

'I will take the risk.'

'But why? Now is not the time to play the hero. Your head might be on that bamboo stick, before you know it!'

'I will be safe at the college. I am their colleague; the Chinese will protect me.'

'If you are so certain, why are you here?' Paul barks the words.

'I …' He can't very well say he feels a little lonely and is missing his fellow countrymen. 'Isn't that Pierre?' He spots the future customs officer with his book boy and a girl whose back is turned to them.

'Yes. He will be travelling on the same boat as us, leaving a day earlier than planned.'

'I thought him gone already.'

'He waited so Suiyi could go with him. Yes, that's her. He has decided not to leave her behind after all.'

'He's done the right thing, though she deserves better.'

'Pierre's all right. He at least understands where each of them stand. Don't look so outraged. Pierre treated the girl far more sensibly than … some others.' Paul's words sting; he meant them to. 'There goes the whistle.' He holds a hand up for the attention of the ship's captain, then turns to Charles. 'For the last time, hop on. Never mind the luggage, we can fix something for you at the other end.'

'No.'

'It's that woman, isn't it?' Paul sighs, exasperated. 'I had hoped to spare you this, but arrest warrants have already been issued and the yamen is probably on their way to them right now.'

'What?' Charles grips Paul's arm, making the man wince. 'How do the yamen know?'

'We share security information with the Manchus.'

'You don't mean *we* told them Wu Fang and Jiali are revolutionaries?'

'What if we did? Charles, you must see, certain orders must be maintained.'

'Orders be damned!' Charles cries. Letting go of Paul's arm, he runs.

26

The deeply upsetting parting from her son has so wrung Mrs Yan out that when she emerges in the morning, she has dark shadows underneath her eyes and stray strands of greying hair escaping from her usually tightly held bun, but with grim determination and strict order she springs the whole household into action. Setbacks and misfortunes are a widow's lot and let no one forget that Mrs Yan thrives in adversity. Grave and imminent danger threatens her son, weighing heavy on her chest like the Mount Tai, but despite her grief, she knows what has to be done. The big gate is ordered shut in case of nosy neighbours. Mrs Yan supervises the locking up of her silks, her jades, and her jewels. After the attack there will be chaos and she must ensure that all of the Yan property is safely guarded.

But then ... an emptiness grips her, despite the richness of her possessions. Her tasks complete, she seeks refuge in the old master's study, sitting on the creaking armchair, hugging her knees and biting her nails.

Restless, she turns to Wang Ma.

'Has everything been locked up safely?'

'Yes, my mistress, all has been taken care of.'

'I feel sure I've forgotten something, something important.'

A faithful maid of many years, Wang Ma knows exactly what to say at such times; speaking in a low, soft voice, she soothes: 'Mistress must not be afraid. Mistress is devout and faithful, and the Buddha will be sure to return the Young Master safely home.'

'My poor child!' Mrs Yan sobs, gripped by a premonition. The curse of the second concubine, Yanbu's birth mother, echoes in her head: *'You owe me a life, you owe me my child!'* The air in the room seems to thin suddenly. Now she regrets coming here; this room once symbolised oppression, and she'd fought so hard to be her own mistress. A terrible atmosphere hangs here — it is inhabited by too many ghosts — but this is also her past, without which she is nothing. Yanbu is her future, and now, that future is mortally endangered.

*

It's not every day that her mother-in-law comes to her bedroom. It's even rarer that she wears an expression akin to kindness. True, as the day of birth approaches, Mrs Yan has given Jiali less trouble, but still, the sight of the tall, thin widow standing slightly bent, forlorn, makes Jiali sit up in bed.

'Are you quite all right, Mother?'

'I've come to see how you are.'

'Shall I ask Lanlan to make tea?'

'No, don't stir. I don't need anything.'

Mrs Yan lowers down to perch on the edge of the bed, her eyes resting on Jiali's hands holding the protruding bump over the quilt that covers it. When she speaks, it is as if she is addressing the bump.

'How do you feel?'

'Restless.'

'Is there pain?'

'No.'

'Shouldn't there be, at this stage?'

'No.'

'Are you sure?'

'Yes. Wu Fang said so.' It occurs to Jiali that her own mother-in-law is even less experienced than her — she's never given birth. 'My pregnancy progresses with textbook accuracy, and Wu Fang joked that ...' she stops, choked by a sudden pang of loss.

'Wu Fang hasn't been, these last few days, has she?'

'She's ... gone.'

'Gone where? Didn't she just come back from Beijing?'

'Yes.'

'So where is she?'

'I don't know.'

'What happened?'

'We ... we had an argument.'

'And she just went?'

Jiali glances away. 'I said things that ... I don't think she will ever come back.'

Mrs Yan settles to a more comfortable position on the bed, and reaches out a hand to smooth back the straying hairs she's only just noticed. Then she sighs, and, with a look almost of tenderness, leans closer to her daughter-in-law.

'Sooner or later, you realise the truth.'

'What truth?'

'You can't trust. It was the biggest mistake of my life.'

'Trusting?'

'Yes.'

'Who?' Jiali asks, though she instinctively knows.

'Concubine Number One.'

'But I thought that ...'

'When I first joined the Yans, we were friends, we were like shadows of each other; she was the best friend I ever had. How naïve I was.'

'But me and Wu Fang ... it isn't like that.'

'You always think you are special, don't you? I did, too. Oh, how I trusted that woman! I thought: just because we were both concubines, we didn't have to be at each other's throats like the others, we would be different.' She laughs bitterly. 'How wrong I was! She was two-faced and came for me wielding three knives and I didn't see it coming, not until too late.'

'No, no, no,' Jiali shakes her head emphatically. 'Wu Fang will never betray me ...' She stops — what Wu Fang has done, turning Charles away, wasn't that a betrayal?

Catching her eyes, Mrs Yan nods. 'Are you terribly sure? What was it that you fell out over?'

'We ... She...' Jiali stutters, however hurt she was, there is no way she would share what has happened between her and Wu Fang with her mother-in-law.

Mrs Yan grins. 'You don't have to tell me but how could she have left you alone when you most needed her? If that's not betrayal, I don't know what is!'

'It's not like that.' Jiali protests weakly. It pains her to be pitied by her mother-in-law, of all people.

'You don't know, until the time comes, who can be trusted. If it only takes a few cross words for her to run away from you, how can you count on her with things that matter? Don't trust anyone, my dear. Especially women, they are your worst enemy.'

'But you are a woman.'

'I'm not just any woman. I am your mother-in-law. You are carrying my grandchild.'

She reaches out a long slender finger for Jiali's bump. 'You have no idea, how much I prayed.'

A spasm of chill shoots through Jiali's body, and she recoils.

Taking no notice, Mrs Yan nods. 'And you know my prayers are always answered.'

Jiali flips the quilt back and sits up. 'No,' she says resolutely, 'don't pray for me.'

*

The flags of all the nations wave weakly on the roof of the hospital in the light wind. Watching, Wu Fang remembers the day they were first hoisted up. The hospital, funded by charity donations from both Chinese and foreign sources, had been operational long before Wu Fang returned to Fudi, but it was not until after that it opened formally. Dr Johnson, the thin, bearded Scot, had announced in broken Chinese the name — Fumin Yiyuan, Hospital that Benefits the People — then fireworks were set off and dignitaries clapped. Standing in the back row among the Chinese medical staff, Wu Fang had vowed to work her hardest to earn the right to operate on her own. Now, fate has presented her with the opportunity.

Glancing at the neatly arranged equipment in the operation room, Wu Fang remembers the look of sadness and resignation on the ocean surgeon's face, and his parting words: 'Perhaps they might spare the hospital?'

Dr Johnson was the last of the ocean staff to go, not being

certain, until the very last minute, that he would leave. Despite herself, Wu Fang was once again impressed with the calm and togetherness of the ocean staff as they arranged the handover of the hospital to the Chinese staff. Something the Japanese were good at, too, she'd often marvelled while in Japan. Education and modernisation, she tells herself again. Look how hopelessly panicky the townspeople are, how the beating of chests by the literates morphs into bunting and scrolls declaring their devotion to the emperor, instead of tangible help to arm the inadequately equipped soldiers or feed the desperate poor, who are the ones who will starve when war breaks out.

Wu Fang sighs and starts to methodically jot down the medical supplies they have. Other Chinese staff will join her soon, but for the moment she welcomes the peace and quiet, better to sort through her own thoughts. The smell of disinfectant prevails, and she closes her eyes and inhales. Suddenly she knows what she is going to do. When the bombing ends, she will return to Japan; for real, this time. Dr Yamadori will take her back, she is certain of that. *'Such a shame you interrupted your study right at this moment, Miss Wu.'* She seems to hear the kindly teacher's slow and steady voice. She had come clean about her true gender as she said goodbye, thinking she had nothing to lose. *'I am honoured to have helped to train China's first female surgeon. Will you return?'*

Yes, she would. Nothing in Fudi is worth staying for anymore. What Jiali said to her was unequivocal, and now, in a calmer, reflective state, Wu Fang sees the woman she has been infatuated with most of her life for who she truly is: though she is feted for her many talents, deep down, how shallow and selfish she can be! Jiali has no idea the sacrifices others have made for her ... Wu Fang moves to the window, and stares at her own reflection: how cold her eyes. She turns away, but the reflection follows her, like some internal mirror, forcing her to confront all the questions she's been asking herself: if Jiali is shallow and selfish, isn't Wu Fang herself the same? For all their so-called accomplishments, she laughs bitterly, aren't they just two privileged, spoilt women indulging in their own selfish pursuits? To love another woman is in no way inferior to loving a man, but neither is it any nobler, and it can be just as selfish.

*

Her Chinese colleagues start to drop in; all, like her, are at first in awe of the autonomy they now have over the hospital. The absence of the ocean staff does not, as she had feared, create chaos; on the contrary, each takes on a new responsibility and gets on quietly and efficiently with it, collaborating when needed. In a crisis, it seems, the Chinese might well cope better than she expected. Anticipating a sudden influx of patients once the bombing starts, they borrow extra beds and sheets, and make sure that there are enough candles. Sitting down for a moment, tired and yet satisfied, Wu Fang has a sudden vivid memory of her ten-year-old self watching Jiali's father dressing a gaping wound on a peasant's arm. When the strong-scented herbs had been applied and the peasant' pained face smoothed, it had seemed to Wu Fang that Father Shen was no less than a god.

She tells him so, and he laughs. 'I can help people, but not all the time. Sometimes I cannot help at all, and that's frustrating.'

'What can't you do?'

257

'For example, cutting people up to take the bad things out. To do that, you need to go out of the country, to learn from others.'

'Do they know better than you?' Voice of disbelief.

'We know different things. To really help people, you need both.'

'Then I will go abroad and learn, then come back.'

'I can teach you about herbs,' says Jiali, sitting beside her. 'I know a lot already.'

'You can both be doctors,' smiles Father Shen.

'Wu Fang can be a doctor, because she has sharper eyes and stronger arms,' declares Jiali, 'but I am lighter and faster. I shall be a sword woman. I can go about bashing baddies.'

'The pair of you!' laughs Mrs Shen, 'sorting out the world between the two of you. But Jiali, remember brute force cannot make people do what you want them to do. You have a brain, too. The right words do wonders.'

'I know, I know. Couplet time!' Jiali sighs.

Wu Fang looks up. Against the neat and ordered silence of polished tools, weighed-down papers, and well-folded white gowns, her sigh echoes; where is she, the girl who has been by Wu Fang's side since their hair was still tied tight behind their ears? Where is she, the girl who always wanted to be the best of everything? Where is she, the girl that everybody who set eyes on could not help but fall in love with? Where is she, the girl who knows Wu Fang best and yet chooses not to know that Wu Fang loves her? The world is a strange and wonderful place, and Wu Fang can no more help her love than she is able to stop herself blinking or sighing.

Wu Fang closes her eyes, feeling faint. A smell comes to her, the strong scent of the osmanthus hair oil Jiali wears.

Wu Fang stands. What am I doing here, away from her?

Now is the time she needs me most, for Charles has left her, driven away by me, the poor man!

*

Distracted, she nearly misses Jiali's carriage. The two pass each other in the street, and Wu Fang, seeing Jiali first, pulls her horse, and rides back. Jiali's face emerges from the carriage, pale, gaunt, and anxious. The appearance of Wu Fang in the street seems so unreal that she dismisses it at first as an illusion of her own traumatised mind.

'Jiali!' Wu Fang whispers urgently, riding alongside the carriage.

Still disbelieving, Jiali simply stares.

'It's me.'

Her voice breaks the spell. Jiali's eyes widen. She shouts at the driver: 'Stop!'

The carriage stops in the middle of the street. Jiali turns to Wu Fang, her voice trembling: 'I was on my way to you.'

'Me to you.'

Wu Fang gets off her horse and climbs onto the carriage. Flipping open the curtain, she reaches inside, picks up Jiali's hands, and holds them in both of hers.

'Don't ever send me away again,' she almost threatens.

'Come back home with me,' Jiali pulls Wu Fang to her, 'I've got something to show you.

*

Wu Fang puts the note down and meets Jiali's eyes. 'Good of him to warn us about the attack.'

'It wasn't dated and what with the chaos of Yanbu coming home and my ... upset, no one seemed to know when it was delivered. Lanlan saw it on the bench at the door man's room and brought it to me this morning.'

Wu Fang reads the note again. She is relieved that the note is brief, with no mention of anything else apart from the attack. But ...

'Are you disappointed?' she asks.

'About the note? Why should I be?' Jiali exclaims, 'As you say, it was good of him to warn us.'

At Wu Fang's silence, she lowers her head and admits, 'It is true, I had thought he might have changed his mind.'

'Poor child.' Wu Fang clasps Jiali to her chest.

'He should be in Shanghai now. I hear the boat carrying all the ocean people left earlier today.' Resting her head on Wu Fang's shoulders, Jiali breathes in. A storm is brewing, but she feels safe somehow.

'Do you hate me for driving him away?'

'You've not driven him away.' Jiali tries to make light of it, but the thought of never seeing Charles again suddenly chokes her. She shakes her head resolutely.

'You've saved me from a huge embarrassment.'

'Jiali?'

'If he truly cared for me, he'd have stayed, whatever happened.'

'Come,' Wu Fang takes Jiali's hand, 'let's go to the school. The girls must be terrified.'

But the laughter they hear when they arrive is the opposite

of terror. It comes from outside the school building and the two hurry their steps, curious. Then Jiali, ahead, stops, gasps, and turns to Wu Fang with a wild look of joy in her eyes. 'It's him!' she mouths.

The girls, seeing their teachers first, hush each other. Charles, the last one to notice them, turns, pauses briefly, and walks slowly to the women. Jiali's expression does not escape him, but though his heart beats wildly, he sounds ordinary enough.

'We were just doing some stretches and …'

Wu Fang interrupts with, 'Where is Mr Lu? I put him in charge.'

'Mr Lu had to go home to be with his family,' replies Yueyue.

'The coward!' curses Wu Fang.

'We don't mind,' says another girl, 'we have Mr Cha.'

'They were unable to focus, so I brought them outside,' Charles adds, then, finally unable to keep up the calm exterior, he speaks with an urgent tone of voice: 'Did you get my note?'

'Yes,' Wu Fang says quickly, her voice stiff and guarded.

'Then why are you still here?'

'The cannons won't reach this far,' Jiali says, her tone absurdly light-hearted. In truth she feels even lighter-hearted: she and Wu Fang have made up and Charles has come back! What matters now?

'Even so, you have to leave Fudi!'

'Why?' Wu Fang frowns.

He glances over quickly to the girls, then: 'You are all like family, so I will speak freely. I came from the harbour, where I learned from my consul that you are both on the yamen's arrest list for being part of the revolutionary movement! My despicable government, to my eternal shame, is collaborating with the Manchus, and they have you and Jiali down as assassins and gave your names to the yamen.'

The girls exchange looks of shock, then their eyes are on their teachers, though with awe, not fear.

'I dropped that note off last night but when I heard this latest news I knew I had to come to find you.' He turns to Jiali. 'I searched everywhere: your house, Wu Fang's house, the hospital … Finally I came to the school and thank God I was here, for the art teacher had gone, leaving the girls on their own.'

'Thank you, Charles, for letting us know of this.' Relenting, Wu Fang finally meets Charles' eyes, and speaks to him as of old. 'But they flatter me. Though I was proud to have joined the revolution, I was never an assassin. I couldn't bear to cause suffering, not even to the Manchus, whom I hate. I am a coward. I fully admit it.'

'I forbid you to say that. Wu Fang, you are the bravest person I know.' Charles, also, is quick to resume the old familiar tone between them, and pleads.

'You are kind to say so, Charles. But I can't even claim to be a revolutionary anymore. I quit while I was in Beijing, and Jiali has nothing to do with it!'

'It won't make a dog hair's difference whether you are part of it now or were in the past or never at all!' exclaims Charles, impatient. 'They are desperate, and they want to punish people. You know how brutal they can be.'

'The yamen will be too busy preparing for the attack. They won't be organised enough to act on the warrant,' murmurs Wu Fang, somewhat unconvincingly.

'Nonsense. Even if they don't now, they will act soon. You

can depend on it. They might not be efficient at fighting the ocean people, but they are very keen on ruling over the Chinese. Wu Fang, you know I am telling the truth.'

The girls start to whisper among themselves. Jiali turns to Wu Fang: 'Charles is right. You must leave.'

'Both of you. Neither of you are safe, the warrant is for both of you.'

'And abandon the girls?' Wu Fang's voice is equally firm. 'Never! This is my school and so long as I am alive, I remain here. We are their guardians, what will happen to them if we leave?'

Yueyue steps up to Wu Fang. 'Mistress Wu. We can look after ourselves. We are big girls now. We know what to do.'

'But how will you keep safe?' asks Jiali.

'It's best that we don't come to school during the attack, that is for sure,' says Yueyue in a calm voice, 'but we can gather at the nunnery down at the other side of the market. I already know the abbess. She likes me. In the past, when ... bad things happened at home, I used to go and stay with the nuns and the abbess said I would always be welcome.'

'Food, what about food?' asks Wu Fang. The school provided the girls lunch, one of the main reasons some attended.

'They will feed us. In turn we can clean and do other work for them. We can write couplets for the temple, all the words you've taught us.' Yueyue smiles.

'It will have to do for the moment,' says Charles decisively. 'Remember the expression: so long as the green hill remains, one won't have to worry about running out of fuel. Let's get away from Fudi for now. Please, Wu Fang!'

All eyes are on Wu Fang, stony-faced, standing upright as if a ten-horse carriage could not move her.

Then, at a look from Charles, Yueyue begs: 'We are actually looking forward to going to the nunnery, Mistress Wu, it will be fun. Don't let us down.'

'Oh, you kids!' Wu Fang bursts into tears.

*

While Wu Fang leads the girls back inside to sort out books to take to the nunnery, Jiali and Charles stay behind. The emotions of the day finally catching up with her, Jiali leans on the wooden railings by the front gate for support. Charles steps up and lends an arm, helps her to sit down slowly on the steps. Jiali closes her eyes. Faint laugher can be heard from the school building, and in the distance the bustling of the market; life carries on still, perhaps even more intensely, now that normality is soon to be disrupted.

It is the first time the two have been alone together since that kiss. When she finally gathers the courage to look him in the eyes Jiali rejoices in the direct gaze he gives her; he has turned his back on his own people and linked his fate with hers, has taken a huge step towards her — will he come all the way?

'We knew about the attack, Charles,' she starts. 'Yanbu came home on special leave, for one night only.'

The mention of Yanbu casts a shadow over Charles' face. 'He was ordered to fight at the front at such short notice. We didn't get to say goodbye,' he says in a low, dejected voice, 'but he left me a note.'

With trembling hands, he passes her the now worn-looking paper. She reads it quickly, then gives the note back to him.

'It is a most dangerous posting. You must be worried too, Jiali, as I have been.' He drops his eyes.

'Charles, look at me, please!' she beseeches. 'I never loved Yanbu, nor him me! I think he knows that too now. He came clean … about the couplets.'

'I am glad to hear of it.'

'But that doesn't change anything.'

'Jiali, we talked about this before. Can you not forgive him? I know the confession was late in coming but he did confess and is ultimately honest.'

'I do forgive him. I told him I did,' she says vehemently, 'but I don't love him, nor him me. We lived a lie right from the start. I had thought I could carry on, because I have my family, my friends, my couplets … until I met you.'

'But Jiali, Yanbu is my friend, a dear friend, and the father of your baby!' His voice breaks, 'It … it would be wrong, so wrong. I would despise myself if … if anything were to happen between us. I already do.'

He raises his eyes, with a look of pity that brings tears to hers. 'You would be upset, too, Jiali, though you are far braver than me.'

*

Wu Fang, returning to the school gate, is struck by the image of the two figures: Jiali sitting on the top steps with one hand over her bump and another behind her back to support herself, her eyes eagerly searching for his; Charles kneeling in front of her on one knee on a lower step, his head leaning forward. There is no mistaking the expression — Wu Fang knows, only too well, how Charles must feel. This is no fleeting crush, she says to herself; this time, Charles truly loves. The blow she felt when she first saw that Charles had stayed dissipates: the ocean man has turned against his own people, a sacrifice no less than her own to give up the republican cause. Wu Fang admires his courage even as she laments her own loss of Jiali.

But judging from the lovers' posture and looks, their future is not at all certain. What is to become of them? Indeed, what is to happen to all of them? The road ahead is going to be bumpy, but Wu Fang will do her damn best to steer them all to safety.

Approaching, she makes her presence known by saying loudly: 'Amazing girls.'

'Indeed.' Charles springs up, 'Now for us. Have you any thought on where to go?'

'Ding Village, our ancestorial home by the sea, I have hundreds of relatives there, and my parents own two houses. It will also be the perfect place for Jiali to rest after the birth.'

'Your parents should leave, too,' says Jiali to Wu Fang, 'the sooner the better, for who knows what the yamen will do if they fail to find us.'

'Yours too, Jiali.' Charles speaks fast, 'They will surely go after them.'

Jiali nods, 'My parents are away visiting relatives in the hills, but I will send a message asking them to stay put.'

'Then it's settled,' Charles determines. 'Wu Fang, go home now, your parents will need time to get ready. They should leave as soon as possible. In fact, they should go first. All of you leaving at the same time will attract attention.'

Wu Fang nods. Used to being in a position of command, she nonetheless likes being told what to do by him.

'Will there be enough carriages, to take both your parents and us?'

Wu Fang nods again, then quickly remembers, 'Actually, no. We are down to just one now, I sent the other two to the hospital; once the bombing starts, they will be very useful …'

'Then I shall go and engage one. Lao Lin can help me.'

They agree to meet at Jiali's at nightfall, and set off from there.

27

Wu Fang is the first to arrive.

'Have they left?' Jiali asks.

Wu Fang nods.

'How are they taking it?'

'Upset, but not surprised,' Wu Fang sighs wearily. 'Ma had guessed the truth while we were in Beijing.' She sits down. 'I am just sorry that both their children have got into trouble, it's not what they bargained for in their old age. We will be poor after this, though they assured me that's nothing as long as we are all safe.' She glances over Jiali's simple bundle. 'Is that all you're carrying with you?'

'Mostly baby stuff. What else do I need?'

'Are you nervous?'

'About the birth? Not at all. I trust you, and I trust my own body. It's never let me down.'

'Indeed, it's what it's built for,' Wu Fang says, and glances outside at the dark. 'Charles should be here, I wonder what's taking him so long.'

'Carriages are difficult to secure right now, give him time.'

'So did you talk? I took the girls inside earlier partly to give you some time together.'

'We did talk, but,' Jiali hesitates, 'he doesn't want to upset Yanbu.'

'A faithful friend.' Wu Fang admires with reluctance. She's gained a new rival, but cannot despise Charles even if she wants to.

'I kind of understand, but I also hate him for it.'

'He's a good man, Jiali,' says the noble headmistress, with mixed feelings.

'And you are a good woman.'

'Am I?'

'I know how much I owe you, Wu Fang. I wish I could repay all the debts I owe you, if not in this life, then the next …'

'You are talking nonsense now, Jiali,' Wu Fang says quickly. 'Now where is Charles?'

'One more thing …' Jiali becomes hesitant,

'What?'

'My mother-in-law.'

'What about her?'

'If they fail to find me, they will go for her, surely? We should make arrangements for her …'

Wu Fang shakes her head. 'No. I don't trust her. We can't tell her anything. She might turn us in, or at the very least, panic and make a fuss, she'll ruin everything.'

'Still, I won't sleep easy if she is caught up in this. She is, after all, my child's grandmother.'

'She's not either of our parents, and so the danger to her will be minimal. Besides, it will be so obvious that she knew nothing about what is going on. But if you are really worried, I've got an idea …'

She bends down, scribbles a few lines, and shows to Jiali. 'Will this do?'

Against the fast-fading light, Jiali reads quickly, and

marvels: 'Very clever! This surely absolves her of all knowledge of my whereabouts. But I am sure she will be indignant about your tone of voice. She will feel so insulted …'

'That's the idea.' Wu Fang smiles. 'We would have both protected her and taught her a lesson in good manners. Now you just have to put the date and your name stamp on it.'

Jiali has hardly taken the inked stamp off the paper before Lanlan rushes in.

'Is Charles here?' Jiali stands.

'No, Mistress. It's Mr Li.'

'Li Jian? What does he want?' Wu Fang's voice is sharp.

'The arrest! He is the governor's son. If anyone knows, he does,' says Jiali anxiously.

'Is he alone?' Wu Fang turns to Lanlan.

'Yes. And a little drunk.'

'He's been away in Hong Kong all this time …' Wu Fang frowns.

'I will see him,' Jiali determines. 'You wait in the courtyard and warn Charles not to come in.'

*

'I have something important to say, please send the maid away,' Li Jian announces impatiently.

After a little hesitation, Jiali makes a gesture for Lanlan to withdraw.

'This is something I should have done a long time ago, Jiali, I came to apologise.'

'What for?'

'I apologise most sincerely for my role in the couplets.'

270

She blushes, knowing instinctively that instead of an apology, this is an attempt to forge intimacy with her. 'It is my husband who deceived me, not you.'

'It was hard to say no, when my best friend asked for help.' His voice is immediately smug and entitled.

'Don't think much of it. The couplets mean nothing to me now, they were merely the foolish daydreams of a young girl. I am ashamed to read them, and I beg forgiveness that you should have been exposed to such unrefined writings from me.' Keeping to this formal tone, Jiali hopes to fend off further advances, but she might as well have said nothing.

'But I don't regret having had the honour of being in correspondence with such brilliance. Not a bit.' He gazes at her. 'I am sorry to have been part of Yanbu's deceit and caused you pain, though I cannot honestly say that it was not a pleasure, these last three years, to have written to you and to have heard back. In fact,' he reaches inside the long sleeve of his Chinese gown, chosen for this purpose, and brings out a thick wad of papers, 'there are more, that I have written since ...' he reaches out to her.

She ignores his hand. 'The couplets will have to wait, Li Jian. Now is not the time.'

He gives a light, indulgent laugh. 'They are only going to bomb the harbour, Jiali. The cannons won't reach this far. It is all to do with the negotiation, which will take too long to explain, but we do have time, plenty of time, to talk poetry. In fact, there is no better atmosphere than the present, when, as Du Fu has written ...' He launches into 'The Kingdom is Broke'.

'Li Jian.' She stops him with an impatient gesture. 'I am tired. I think you should leave.'

His face changes colour. 'The last thing I want is to tire you out, Jiali.'

'Then goodbye.'

He makes to leave, then pauses, as if suddenly remembering something: 'Before I leave, I wonder ... do you know where Wu Fang might be?'

'Why?' The room suddenly chills, and her voice coarse and low, a near whisper.

'There is an arrest warrant for her.'

'What? Why on earth should there be an arrest warrant for Wu Fang?' her outraged voice does not fool him, for her eyes betray her.

He nods slowly. 'I believe you know about this, too, Jiali.' He breathes hard. 'In fact, I saw two arrest warrants in my father's office.'

She bites her lips.

He lets the silence grow, then speaks softly. 'I was outraged to see the one for you. What an injustice! Total mistake. I will vouch for you, I told father so, but Wu Fang, not so easy.'

He pauses for good effect, then says, 'So where is she?'

Unable to be cool any longer, she bursts out, 'Wu Fang is innocent! Whatever she is accused of is not true!'

'You would say that.'

Now that the seal of secrecy is broken, she feels able to appeal: 'You will too, Li Jian. You like her, so you have often said to me!' Her voice is urgent, 'You must help her, Li Jian, you must!'

He stands spellbound, stirred by her passion. 'Don't lose heart,' he whispers when he finally finds his voice, 'there might be something I can do.'

'Will you, really?'

'I wouldn't say there is no risk, in fact, there is a great deal of risk to myself, but I will be willing to take that risk, for I am fond of Wu Fang ...'

'Oh I know you are! Thank you, thank you!' Overcome, she takes a step towards him.

'... and fonder of you. I would do anything for you.' He grasps her hand and pulls her to him.

She shudders, and tries to free herself from him, but he holds her tight.

'Jiali, my goddess. We are meant for each other. You must feel it, too.' He searches her eyes. 'Wu Fang banished me from the school, and business took me away to Shanghai, then to Hong Kong, but all this time, I never stopped thinking of you, of what could have been between us. I should have come to you much sooner. The couplets ... the couplets are the red threads that link us.' He launches into: *'The delight in me finding a rare echo of my sentiments in so deep a well ...'* It is one of the lines written by him in response to hers.

Though she turns her face away from him, he carries on. It is inconceivable to him that any woman could ever refuse an advance from such a man as he. When the couplet reaches its end he lowers his head, seeking her lips, his breaths reeking of yellow plum wine.

Revulsion gives her the strength to push him away.

'Can't you see how humiliating this is for me?' she cries indignantly when she is free of him. 'I implore you, please, do not speak of the couplets anymore. I never want to hear a word of it!'

Breathing heavily, he stares with furious eyes at the strips of soft, inked paper in his hand. With one abrupt, determined jerk

273

of his wrists he tears them to pieces; then, still furious, he stamps on the pile of papers on the floor, the thick black Manchu boot thumping brutally.

'I wanted to give you romance,' he hisses, 'and you … *humiliating*? How dare you? You do know, don't you, that I always get what I want?'

'Do you?' Her anger turning to contempt, she smiles at his arrogance.

'You temptress,' he grabs her arms. 'God knows how,' he sighs, his voice coarse, 'With your grotesque bump and vulgar Hakka feet, you put a spell on me, you witch!'

She meets his insults with calm, and their proximity and her calm inspires the strangest desire in him, the body hitherto despised becomes once again irresistible.

'Come, Jiali,' he begs. 'Be with me, you know you want to, we are made for each other.'

Her fists tighten. How she wishes she could deal him a crushing blow with her sword, within easy reach of her hand. Even in her present condition, she is sure she could teach him a lesson he will never forget. But … Wu Fang's life is at stake, and she must do all she can to save her friend.

She speaks in a lighter tone of voice. 'I really mean it, Li Jian. The couplets no longer interest me, please. Let's forget it. With regard to us …'

A glimmer of hopes stirs in his eyes. 'Yes?'

'You pay me a great compliment as a woman.' She blinks, then proceeds, 'I'm not made of stone, Li Jian, but you seem to have forgotten the little detail that I am married.'

'You know as well as I that you do not love Yanbu. I saw it the first time I visited your house.'

'We might have our difficulties, but he is still my husband.'

He sighs with relief. 'If that's all you are worried about ...'

'I don't understand ...

'It's the smallest detail, easily overcome. Leave it with me.'
What does he mean by this? she puzzles. He smiles. 'So come, come with me.' He reaches out a hand.

'Now?' she steps back.

'Why not?'

'Li Jian. Be reasonable. Such things cannot be rushed. I need time. Even if ...' She speaks slowly, choosing her words carefully, 'Even if I want to be with you, I remain Yanbu's wife. Even a governor's son cannot change that fact. In the meantime, Wu Fang ...'

'What about her?'

'The arrest warrant ...'

'I see.' He stares at her, as if thinking hard, and the long silence that ensues makes her nervous. Suddenly he bursts out laughing. 'Oh Jiali, you nearly fooled me.'

'What do you mean?'

'I don't know why I bothered with all this sweet talk.' He grins, 'It could all have been so easy. Never mind your husband, Wu Fang is the person you really care about. You would do anything for Wu Fang. I shouldn't have worried.'

Her drained, ashen face is a sight he is pleased to see.

'I will do whatever you want,' she says, losing her composure. 'But you must let Wu Fang go first.'

'Gladly. Perhaps she's packed already? I know she hasn't left Fudi though, my men have checked.'

'You've been very thorough.'

'Naturally. I am fond of Wu Fang, as I said. I want to help

275

her, the best I can,' he says almost sincerely and rises. 'So now, come with me ...'

She tries weakly, one last time: 'Isn't it a bit hasty, though, to make such an indecent proposal to me? My husband, as far as I know, is still alive. How will it look — for you, as well as me?'

He sighs, 'I told you not to worry about the details.'

'But what will Yanbu say when he comes back and ...'

'You think he'll come back?'

'Naturally.'

He smiles, and she shudders: he is a step ahead of her, after all.

'Didn't he tell you that he was sent to assist in the commanding ship, the exact place the enemy cannon will aim for first? No? Perhaps he wanted to spare you the worry. How do I know? Well, let's just say that I ... helped a little.'

'You? How?' She recoils from him. A suffocating horror fills the room, making her feel faint.

'Director Zuo wouldn't let him go: mad idea, soon to be a father, and so on. But Yanbu was keen to prove himself, I knew he was, so I helped by putting in a word for him through my father. One thing led to another, and the Chief Commanding Officer of the ship made a direct request old man Zuo could not refuse. So I suppose Yanbu has me to thank for being right where he wants to be.'

'You ... you know what a poor soldier he will make!' she cries.

'True, he is not so keen on water; still, for a humble astronomy teacher, he will gain glory for being a martyr.' He smiles.

But the wife's outrage is not equal to that of the mother. A howling pierces the still air, surprising the two. Mrs Yan, having received reports from Wang Ma about the suspicious goings on that evening in her daughter-in-law's quarters, has been listening outside, and has caught the latter part of the conversation. The hurricane force of the enraged widow sweeps in through the door, holding a broom, hailing a trail of curses: 'Your conscience eaten by dogs! May the heaven strike you blind! Viper, murderer …'

The attack, coming so unexpectedly, unsettles Li Jian so much that he flees, though not before leaving Jiali with the whispered words: 'I will be back! And you better be ready if you want your friend to make it out of Fudi.'

Jiali dashes out of the room, and nearly clashes with Wu Fang striding in from the garden. It's only been half an hour or so that they have been apart, but to Jiali it feels like a lifetime. The two clasp together wordlessly; then, pushing Wu Fang away, Jiali whispers urgently, 'We must leave. He's gone now, but it won't be long before he comes back. Where is Charles? I thought I heard horses. Did he get the carriage?'

'He did, but now he is running after Li Jian.'

'Whatever for?'

'I don't know! To try to do something, anything.' Wu Fang sighs: 'I don't think he was thinking straight!'

'Oh why didn't you stop him Wu Fang?' Jiali stamps her feet, exasperated. Having been worried sick about Wu Fang, now Jiali is fearful for Charles: as has just been shown to her so plainly, Li Jian can easily turn nasty.

28

Charles rides furiously. The street scene, glimpsed fleetingly, is riveting, perhaps even more than usual, in the light of the imminent attack. Candles light up faces busy with concentration: a grandmother kneels in front of a statue of Guanyin, her whole life told in the folds of her wrinkles, watched by her grandson chewing sunflower seeds with innocent contentment; a ruggedly dressed beggar saunters past, alert yet serene, a pouch with all his worldly possessions on his shoulders. Catching his own reflection in one of the shop windows, Charles stares. A face stares back at him, a face he doesn't at first see as his own. Then it strikes him that none of the people around him stare, something they always do when an ocean man is about town. He puts a hand to his face, still his; it is his manner, of course. But he no longer behaves as an ocean man does. He's blending in, becoming one of them. A feeling akin to fear emerges. He's no stranger to danger, but for all the mountains he's climbed, for all the rivers crossed, he has never before feared as he fears now.

Now he understands the severity of Paul's warning. By allying himself with the women, he has turned his back on his own people; by being intimate with Jiali, he risks losing his own identity. There is no compromise. But even if he can brave the scorn of his own people, can he bear for her to be disgraced in front of hers? Her culture, the one he's supposed to know well, puts a woman's chastity above all else. Courageous and unconventional as she is, will she be crushed by this?

But the pleasure of knowing her. The vertical silk shop-signs flap down both sides of the narrow streets, flags saluting him as if he is an inspecting general. *Ten thousand miles starts with your first step, Three generations of happiness and health, Hall of a hundred tastes*, shoes, herbs and spices, mundane merchandise summarised by crude attempts at refinement against her nuanced couplets. When he was copying the couplets, he'd allowed himself to indulge in the immediate sensual pleasures: the elegant curves of the characters, the gentle flow of the brush, the intoxicating fragrance of the ink, the cadence and rhythm; but now, knowing they are hers, he feels even more the special intimacy between them.

'*Knows, earth, tears, crossroads* ...' he whispers the words from the couplets, words he learnt from her, and suddenly her scents and voice are recalled, as is her dear, beloved image. A wave of almost nauseating suppressed desire takes possession of him, making him feel dizzy. Now his body is awakened, and he remembers the sensation of his lips against hers: that kiss! The locking of their eyes, the close proximity of their breaths, her beaming face raised up to him, fearless, ecstatic. How brave she is. He trembles, and fears, and through the fear he knows he loves. How terrible this love, and how selfish; already Yanbu is being discarded, if not forgotten; Wu Fang, too, is at the altar, though she puts herself there willingly. Her love for Jiali is so much greater than Charles' own, but Jiali prefers him.

She tramples over people in the name of love, and where Jiali leads, Charles follows. He can't help it.

*

He catches up with Li Jian in front of the Earth God Temple, at the end of the street leading to the governor's mansion, deserted except for an old man walking with a stick. Li Jian, astride his horse, leans over and shouts for the man to get out of the way, and when the latter hesitates, he raises the whip in his hand and curses.

'Don't!' Charles cries, and gallops close.

'Louse! Crawl away! Now!' Turning to Charles, Li Jian cracks the whip in his hand and barks in a sharp voice: 'You're still here? I thought your lot had all left Fudi?' He squints at the ocean man, as if sizing him up.

'I stayed because I know I have friends I can count on here.'

'Did the women send you?'

'Nobody sent me. I came because I wanted to talk some sense to you. Li Jian, I thought you were fond of Wu Fang. Why not help her?'

'I would like to. Indeed, I offered. It is up to Jiali now.'

'In what way?' Charles asks, though he suspects the answer.

'It is a delicate matter, between Jiali and me.' Li Jian sneers. 'Though, seeing as you are a sort of go-between, I might explain. It is all to do with the couplets.'

'The couplets that you wrote on Yanbu's behalf?'

'She told you about that, did she? Good, that simplifies things. So you see, theirs was a marriage in words only. She never loved him, and he lied to her. And so I asked her, very fairly, to reconsider her misplaced affection now that truth is out.'

'At a time when she is heavily pregnant, and her husband away at war?' Damn, he can accuse himself of the same!

'Yanbu has no one to blame but himself.'

'Li Jian, you could have almost any woman you wanted in Fudi, why Jiali?'

Li Jian swallows, his voice suddenly coarse. 'Never in my life have I felt … What is all this to you anyway, Charles?'

'She is the wife of your oldest friend.'

Something in Charles' voice pricks the son of the governor; a long dormant suspicion awakens, and his face twists into a snarl.

'Are you lecturing me, devil?'

'I beg your pardon?'

'Devil, devil, devil!' Li Jian roars. 'The devil you are, the devil you shall always be, however many couplets you steal from me to try to impress her. Don't you think I see through your tricks? When we were using chopsticks, you were still spitting out hairs from the buffalos you speared and ate raw. She is not for you, monkey. How dare you covet my woman?'

Charles charges. But his horse, not as brave, stops short of Li Jian, nearly sending its master over. Li Jian reins his own horse in masterfully and laughs.

'Go back to her, Charles, and be the good messenger that you are. Bid her to get ready for me. I won't be long. Then run, before I call the guards. Your country is attacking us, so don't expect mercy!'

Charles flies through empty lanes as if possessed; people curse and jump away, but he does not slow down. He will not do Li Jian's bidding, but he must get to the women fast; any moment now, Li Jian will catch up.

*

He rides only a few steps before a bright light suddenly pierces the darkening sky above the sea, then disappears. In the quiet that follows he has a flashback to when he was on board the ship with Yanbu during the training exercise. The signal given for the firing of the cannons — with his back turned, Yanbu had not seen it. Charles had leapt up and pushed Yanbu out of the way with all his might. Yanbu was still injured, and yet Charles' actions probably had made the difference between life and death. It was only a practice trip, and still Yanbu had managed to get hurt — how would he survive the real thing? What madness to put him on the ship! A good but timid man, he will make a terrible soldier. What a waste, Charles laments, then: *I do care for him, too, so very much.*

Not in the same way he cares for Jiali, no, definitely not that; nor in the 'dear brother, deep, deep friendship' sense either. Charles has no name for how he feels for Yanbu, but it is a sentiment most sincere and almost as profound as his feelings for Jiali. *'I've never felt this way about anyone,'* Yanbu's declaration at the temple, which Charles had dismissed as sentimental, now comes to mind. *How true it is,* Charles admits to himself now, *and yet how can this be?* Is it to do with his love for Yanbu's culture? Can it be at all because Yanbu's life is endangered? Is this closeness — it is a closeness, for want of a better word, though it is absurd even to think about it — is it because Charles is in love with his wife?

It is nothing physical, Charles is assured of that, indeed any thought of physical intimacy almost degrades it. It is above physical, it is something pure and lofty.

It's love.

Can he be in love with both husband and wife, even though

they are not with each other? Is loving one disloyal to the other? He is thrown into confusion. That he is loved, equally fiercely, by both, he understands; indeed, he should really be congratulating himself for accumulating such an abundance of intimacy, a luxury for the soul, surely? and yet, holding two hearts in his hand, Charles knows no peace.

Another flash pierces the sky. Then: *Boom!* The shell lands not far from him, sending his horse into a frenzy. His mind connects the explosion with the bright sparks: the bombing has started. From where he stands, he is afforded a panoramic view of Fudi. Like all at the college, he knows the position of his country's warships in the harbour only too well. This is where the cannons have been fired from, close to the river mouth, on the far side; their targets are the Chinese ships docked further inland, at the foot of the hill.

The explosions come faster and closer. It is clear the college is now the target. His mind focuses. Jiali's part of the town will be out of range, so she will be safe for the moment. Li Jian would have been prevented by the bombing from venturing out, surely; Charles recalls the playboy being alarmed by the mere sound of the smallest cannon when he was given a tour of the naval college. Yes, Charles is quite confident Li Jian is no threat to the women, at least for now. Charles decides he will be more useful at the college, only a short distance away from where he is. He rides furiously on towards it, though a part of him, despite what he sees and hears, still cannot believe it is happening. He did not expect ships from his own country to fire at the college it co-founded, just as he would not have believed his left arm would strike his right one. He calculates the number of the blasts and listens out for counter blasts. It won't take long for the Chinese to fire back. They are prepared. Yanbu and the others have been on the ships for two days. Charles feels excitement at the thought. There is no fear, not yet.

*

The roar of cannons seems to move nearer, though it is him riding towards them. He reaches the front porch of the college just as a shot lands with ferocity. Windows smash, walls collapse in front of his eyes. He curses freely, secures the horse, and runs into the fray to help, all the while wondering about the silence from the Chinese front. Some of his best pupils are out there on the harbour; Yanbu must right now be standing next to the commander-in-chief, assisting with the positioning of the cannons.

Running back and forth in the darkened corridor of the college, carrying the wounded and fetching sandbags for barricades, Charles stumbles on what he first takes as a sack of sand placed diagonally at the door of his own classroom. In the dim light, the shape informs him it is yet another body. Charles stretches out a hand underneath the man's nostrils. No breath. Dead, but still warm. A flash of light and he recognises Shuisheng, the bronze cross at the boy's chest. Nothing protected him, not Charles' religion, nor his own. For a moment, Charles stands there stunned, holding the body, feeling its weight. Then, his arms aching, he puts it with the others.

'*Sir, let me tell you a story.*' '*Sir, we will protect you.*' '*Sir, I saw you once at the pagoda. You run really fast.*'

Charles sobs. How old was the boy?

*

In the windowless basement, lit by only a few candles, he joins the other exhausted teachers. He ought to go to Wu Fang and Jiali, but he doesn't want to abandon his colleagues. His own country is attacking the college, and he needs to show solidarity. Besides, the women are well able to defend themselves, he tells himself, they are no timid maidens, he knows that much. The real threat will come after, when the full force of the Manchus falls on them. That's when Charles will stand with them, to do his damn best to help.

There is a catch in his throat, as he realises how much in awe of the women he is.

Director Zuo sits on the ground with his staff, a blanket wrapped around his shoulders. In an exasperated voice, he says, 'I just had a message from Commander Zhu on the ship. Our orders from above are to sit still and not to fire back! He has checked and double checked.'

'Even though they were the first to hit us?' says a teacher sitting opposite Charles.

'The ministers are negotiating with the ocean country,' replies Director Zuo.

'This is not negotiating, this is slaughter!' fumes another teacher, throwing Charles a quick, hostile glance.

'Unbelievable! We are being hit by our so-called friend,' shouts the teacher who spoke first, 'but it is not like the Opium War, we have a navy now. We demand to shed blood for our country!'

'I told you. The navy has to obey orders from the court …' The director sounds weak and helpless, losing his usual composure.

'So what if our navy does nothing? The college has a ship of

285

our own. It will be ready. Even if we are heavily outnumbered, we can still deal the enemies a blow! Director Zuo, please, give orders yourself!' A chorus of indignant voices all speak at once.

Charles has a sudden, burning desire for the Chinese to fight back, and to win. He wants his pupils to prove their worth, to avenge their dead. He feels sorry for the old man, sitting there, his face flushed. He walks towards him, wanting to offer help, in whatever form. Then words from behind him arrest his steps: 'Ocean dog.'

'What did you say?'

Charles recognises the man: the drunken teacher who had called Charles his 'dear brother', and claimed 'deep, deep friendship' at the temple. Everything goes quiet suddenly. Director Zuo raises his head, his voice sincere and fraught with emotion: 'No one speaks rudely to our valued ocean colleague, I demand that ...'

Boom!

Darkness interrupts.

*

Pain in his left leg, shooting up the thigh. Charles opens his eyes. Above him hangs the dark dome of the night sky pierced with sudden, random brightness. Someone up there is frantically tearing at the black screen, an angry god perhaps, offended by all the treachery down below. Charles feels the vibration of noise, though the sounds around him are strangely mute. As he stirs, something warm and sticky flows out of his left ear. He's on a stretcher, being carried by two coolies. Lao Lin, his servant, bends down to him. The heavy quilt covering him smells strongly of garlic, which he associates with the man. But how did Lao Lin get to him? Charles shuts his eyes tightly as another jet of pain stabs up from his thigh. Lao Lin says something, Charles points at his ears.

'We ... taking you ... ocean hospital!' shouts Lao Lin, close to his good ear.

'No.' He grips Lao Lin's leg tightly, forcing him to bend down. 'Not to the hospital. Nobody there, no use. Take me to Mistress Shen's.' Wu Fang will be there, Wu Fang the doctor will save him.

*

The terrified coolies drop the stretcher often, at any sound of explosions nearby. Charles is horribly thirsty, but, not having the energy to ask for a drink, he bites down instead. The bleeding from his left ear has inexplicably stopped, though he can hardly hear anything. The prospect of re-joining Jiali and Wu Fang cheers him briefly. He clings on to the thought.

It is strange to hear the screams and crying, muffled through his bad ear; to see the destruction around him so vividly, even though his vision is distorted by his position lying half-conscious on the stretcher. Ocean villas broken in pieces like crumbled cakes; Chinese tombs split open like half-eaten pomegranates. People scatter from collapsed houses as ants from underneath a giant's feet.

'Our home, our home!' Lao Lin mouths. Charles tries to raise his head, but the coolies do not stop running. He glimpses only smoke rising like waves out of the shell of his former home. He thinks of stuff he'd collected; mainly books, but there are other things too. Though he travels light, sometimes there are objects he simply cannot resist possessing: the ubiquitous scrolls (thank God he'd had the foresight to give Jiali's to Paul for safekeeping); numerous fans given by grateful students; that pair of binoculars he often used to look at the hills from his upstairs balcony; his camera, which had captured many moments of his first impressions of Fudi — such a long time ago it seems. He should perhaps have packed some of this earlier, when he'd had the chance, but believing he would return soon, he'd left it mostly untouched. And now it is ash.

He turns his mind resolutely away from his burnt home. What's gone is gone, the thing to do is to carry on living. And — he hardens his heart — it is fair that he has lost his home and possibly his leg and his hearing when his country has bombed China. If that is the price to pay, and someone has to pay it, then so be it.

At the bottom of the hill, realising they are probably by now out of the range of the cannons and the spreading fire, the coolies slow down.

'Nearly there!' Lao Lin tells him loudly. Water, water! Charles thinks he screams the word out, but to Lao Lin it is only a soft moan. He hurries the coolies afresh as Charles, smiling weakly, turns his face to the night sky. Swallowing and licking his cracked lips, he prays soon to quench that thirst, to be with her. With Peace.

*

He wakes to coolness. Finally, he gets the water, is soaked through. Rain, delicious back-home rain that makes the lushness of meadows and crispness of rivers. So much of it. He empties his full bladder, but instead of relief and abandonment, excruciating pain. He cries out and opens his eyes. A tough-looking man is kicking his legs and splashing water on his face. Seeing Charles regain consciousness, the man drops the gourd back in the giant fishbowl behind him, steps back and grins. Charles shivers. How familiar the fishbowl is, he recognises it from somewhere. Where is he?

Definitely not with her, not on the stretcher anymore and the coolies have disappeared. He's lying on the cold, dark ground in the courtyard of a well-to-do family, though he is sure the group of men surrounding him are not from the family.

The man who woke him says something. Charles cups his good ear, and leans forward.

'... ocean devil ... my words? ... like him.'

The man steps aside.

Charles recognises Lao Lin's red belt, worn because it represents his birth year, for luck. He's never meant to take it off, and Lao Lin, a clean and tidy bachelor, has endured no end of teasing for its ingrained dirt. Charles' servant's mutilated body is contorted at an impossible angle. He stares at it, dumbfounded, then at the man. He can't make sense of it.

'... look a sight? ... for he died ...'

The man leans close to Charles, so he hears him clearly now. 'You are really upset, aren't you? I bet that dog served you well, licking your ocean bottom just so ...'

With impeccable aim and not much thought, Charles spits into the man's face. He would have used his fists, but he can hardly lift his arms.

He curls his upper body from side to side when the rain of

kicks starts, covering his face with his hands. Then one of the men stamps on his wounded leg. Charles cries out and begs for mercy in Chinese.

'So you do know Chinese, you dog!'

'I am not a bad person.' He murmurs with what little strength remains in him. The words come to him instinctively — to protest his innocence — and yet to atone for the wrongs his country has done China, he must endure the pain.

'Dog.'

'I am not a bad person.'

'You are a dirty ocean dog, that's bad enough.'

'I'm not a bad person.'

'Neither were my father and my brother. Still, they were beheaded in Shandong to please the devils.'

'I don't understand.'

'You don't need to. Tu'er, come here!'

A tall teenage boy emerges.

'Guard him.' The man rises and leaves Charles.

*

When he next opens his eyes, the boy is near, staring down at him with curious but not unkind eyes.

'I am not a bad person,' Charles repeats his mantra weakly.

The boy keeps silent.

'I work at the naval college.'

Silence.

'I'm not a bad person.'

Silence.

'My name is Charles, what's yours?'

'You also teach at the girls' school,' the boy speaks unexpectedly, and his large black eyes, formerly showing only curiosity and timidness, now sparkle.

'How did you know?' Charles becomes alert, and tries to sit up, but fails. He lies back.

'My sister goes to the school. She often talks about you.'

'Does she?'

'You often praised her writing, she said.'

Charles licks his dry lips. 'Is she quite tall, your sister?'

'Yes.'

'And she can knit.'

'Yes. She knitted a shawl for one of her teachers …'

'Deyi! You are Yueyue's little brother! Deyi is your name, isn't it? I know all about you.' Charles grips the boy's hand and speaks fast. 'Where am I, Deyi, and who are these people?'

'This is the governor's mansion, but the governor ran away the moment the firing started. These men, they hate ocean people. After the bombing began, they went looking for foreigners to attack. That man who led them, he has family that were killed in Yuandong.' Deyi lowers his head.

'Deyi, do you think you can go and tell your sister where I am?'

The boy steps back, looking scared. 'That man will kill me if I do, same as he killed your servant.'

Charles closes his eyes. Suddenly there is no strength left in him at all.

'Can you get me something to drink then? There's a good boy.' He murmurs.

Deyi brings water in a gourd, puts it close to Charles' lips so he can drink from it. Then, at a tiny sound, the boy slips away, taking the gourd with him. Drifting in and out of consciousness, Charles is vaguely aware of a fire being lit on the other side of the courtyard. People coming and going, throwing stuff on the fire, laughing. He wants to get to the fire, to the delicious warmth, but he is unable to move his arms, let alone his legs, which do not seem to belong to him anymore. The smell of food and wine. He is alone. Lao Lin's body has been removed. His hearing seems to have got better, for he understands the jokes and the bantering by the fire. He knows they have no feelings for him. But God knows he does not hate them, not for his own sake. He feels only a tremendous sadness.

How familiar this night sky has become. Is that the Zodiac? Back home it would have been on the edge of the sky, but here it is bang in the middle, though the tail of the scorpion disappears. What is it in Chinese? Jiali's told him the story, two lovers changed into two stars ...

All right, now that he is dying, it is she he wants: a woman, a feminine body and soul. Her smooth round face, those long eyes, her tremendous and gorgeous bump, her great, soft, empathetic heart.

The stars, they are coming to meet him. Such a hard feeling of wanting. Cold.

The stars drift away, and his eyes finally shut. The slip into unconsciousness is swift but not unpleasant, a feeling of detachment, almost a relief.

29

Only moments ago, it seems to Wu Fang, she was standing on the far side of the operating table, putting the scalpel and scissors into the ocean surgeon's waiting hand as he issued monosyllabic commands. Now she holds the scalpel herself, is looking down into Charles' bloodied leg, and is about to slice open the flesh, to prise out whatever alien body is embedded in it; her very own operation, with only Lanlan to help her, for, despite all their preparations, once the bombing started, the hospital finds itself greatly short-staffed. Many are away treating the wounded in town, only a few remain here. She has banned Jiali from the room, thinking her too emotional and affected.

Wu Fang calms her nerves by focusing on the procedure, giving clear and simple instructions that Lanlan can understand and act upon quickly and correctly.

'Pull the sheet further down, just a little.'

'Pass me the bottle, no, the blue one.'

'Yes, press that as hard as you can. Don't worry, he won't feel any pain.'

She inhabits a strange, timeless world, seeing, hearing, and thinking nothing beyond what lies in front of her: the body waiting to be fixed. She will do it, she can do it, she must do it. As the surgery progresses, her mind remains crystal clear: cutting, probing, suturing ... She is not squeamish about the sight of blood or ragged wounds, but she wonders why no one told her before how physical the job is.

Finally, having sewed up and dressed the wound, she leans back, deflated, and lets Lanlan wipe her brow, wet with sweat.

*

'It is done,' Lanlan emerges from the small dark room, mopping her own brow. Yueyue nods, then turns abruptly, her gaunt, tall shadow casting ahead of where she walks, footsteps echoing in the otherwise empty and deserted hospital. Yueyue has dutifully made them a simple meal of rice, bamboo, and chicken soup, the pleasant smell of which greets them as they enter the small kitchen.

Lanlan sinks onto a small stool. 'Mistress Wu nearly fainted during the operation.'

'If only they'd let me in there to help,' Yueyue growls.

'You are not still upset? Come, Yueyue. Mistress Wu only asked me because I always helped out when Old Master treated his patients. But you should have heard what Mistress Wu was saying about you even as she was cutting Master Cha up: "Master Cha was delivered just in time, a minute longer he would have died from losing so much blood! He would have definitely lost his right leg but for that hero of a girl" — yes, she did use that word, and now you are blushing.'

Yueyue, blushing more, hands Lanlan the warmed-up soup, and manages to keep a straight face. 'What else did she say?'

'"Such strength for such a young girl" — those were the words. She is right. You and your little brother, how you two managed to carry Master Cha all by yourselves, for he is a big man …'

'There was an abandoned shoulder pole in the courtyard of that large mansion he was held in. We just made use of it. And the men were so drunk. Deyi is strong for his age,' Yueyue continues proudly, 'he is the one who deserves praise. I am so glad he dared to run to me. He is usually so timid. Father beats him often.'

'You are practically a mother to Deyi. So it is all credit to you. Now are you happy? I haven't made up any of the mistress' words, you know.'

Yueyue grins, her face softening: 'I should have so much liked to see how it's done.'

'The operation?' Lanlan shudders. 'Even Mistress Wu was nervous. She said she hadn't really been trained to do it all by herself, but since Master Cha's life was in danger, she had no choice. It was not at all nice. Look, my lip is still bleeding, for I bit it hard, and I shut my eyes most of the time.'

Mine would be wide open all the way through, says Yueyue to herself.

*

The operation complete, the gas lamp is turned off. Though they are almost certain the bombing won't reach them, they must keep the hospital dark, to avoid it being a target, just in case. A single candle is lit where Charles lies. The silence in the operating room gives Yueyue the impression at first that the room is empty. Lanlan's words ringing still in her ears, the girl runs greedy eyes over the unfamiliar objects. Gingerly, she picks up an oddly shaped pair of scissors and clasps them tightly to her chest. At a sound coming from a far corner of the room, she puts them down carefully and quickly. With the stealth of a fox — for that was how she had learned to live, and how she had been able to steal Charles away from the mob — she turns slowly, holding her breath. Only then does she see Jiali sitting on a chair next to Charles' bed, her body leaning over his torso, her cheeks against his arm, fast asleep. Yueyue backs out of the room noiselessly. Not until she is outside the gate does she let out a breath. Then her heart releases the tender scene she had just witnessed, and she allows herself the luxury of watching it play in her mind several times. Master Cha and Mistress Shen! The little girl in her indulges. Rubbing her hands and stamping her feet, she paces the cold, stiff ground outside the hospital, her eyes glancing up from time to time to the clear, crisp sky, picking out the stars that earlier had caught Charles' eyes. There is the Silver River, where the cowboy and the weaving fairy meet. Two lovers. Master Cha the cowboy and Mistress Shen the weaving fairy, the girl tells herself, admiring.

*

Unable to resist going back to the room again, the girl finds Charles, alone this time. Tiptoeing out, she hears her name: 'That you, Yueyue?'

She runs to Charles.

'Where am I?'

'In the hospital. Oh Master Cha, please stay still. You just had an operation. Mistress Wu did it. Let me go tell them that you are awake.'

But he clasps her hand tight before she can run away.

'Jiali … Mistress Shen. Where is she? I dreamt … I thought …'

'She was here. Just now.'

'Then it wasn't a dream.' He lets go of her hand, a faint smile on his face. Then, at her broader smile, he puzzles, remembering. 'How did I end up here?' he whispers, licking his dry lips.

'My brother Deyi came to me, in the middle of the night, to let me know what had happened. We went first to Mistress Wu's house, but there was no one there; we would have gone to look for her at Mistress Shen's house, but we were worried the men would do something bad to you while we were gone so we ran back to the Governor's mansion and carried you to the hospital, thinking this was the safest place to put you. Then I went to Mistress Shen's house and found both of them there, and they came straight away with us here, and Mistress Wu operated on you …'

She speaks breathlessly, and Charles can only stare and marvel at the tall, thin girl in front of him. The words are plain, but Charles is once again struck by the pride and courage of the girl. What is it with these Fudi women? Saving his life has surely become a habit of theirs!

'Master Cha?' The girls stops, looking at him nervously.

With great effort, he leans towards her. 'You and your brother, you saved my life,' he says humbly.

Yueyue blushes and jumps up. 'Mistress Shen must be resting in the kitchen. I will go fetch her now.' Along the corridor the girl skips, grinning to herself.

*

When he opens his eyes again, he finds Jiali's face next to his: furious, pained, and yet somewhat ecstatic.

'Kiss me,' she demands. 'It's your turn.'

He watches her, cautiously, almost curiously, and half in disbelief, until her scent convinces him that she is indeed real and present. Then, shutting his eyes and hardening his heart, he turns his face away. 'I am not Li Jian.'

With firm hands, she turns his face gently back to her again. 'He is dead. Yanbu is dead.'

'What?'

'Wu Fang has just been told.' She whispers, 'He was on the commanding ship, the first to be hit …'

'How can you be sure that he is dead?' Charles' voice is sharp. 'Even if the ship was fatally hit, it would take a while for it to sink. He might still be alive.'

'I don't think so.' She shakes her head. 'Someone saw Yanbu fall into the sea, and he was not seen again.' She pauses, then: 'You know about his fear of water — he never learnt to swim. He wouldn't have lasted …'

'Oh Yanbu!' the sudden catch in his voice compels her to lean towards him again. As he sobs, she strokes his head gently, as if comforting a child.

After a little while, Charles raises his head and meets Jiali's eyes. Expecting to see grief, he catches only concern and love for him. He is both moved and sobered. So fate has made the decision for them: neat, almost too neat. How terrible is this love of theirs, but he doesn't want to think too much of it, not now. He can be selfish, just this once. He's lucky to be alive.

'I'm so sorry,' he sighs.

'I nearly lost you, too.' It is her turn to lose her voice.

With almost superhuman strength, he pulls her to him, and, closing his eyes, kisses her weakly but fervently. The weight of her is on his chest, the sharp ridges of his thin ribs hurting, the roughness wanting, as much as the softness yielding.

She murmurs something.

'What is that?'

'Words, only words.'

*

'Mistress Shen and Master Cha!' Yueyue runs breathlessly into the small hospital kitchen, then stops, shocked to see tears streaming down Wu Fang's face. 'You are upset, Mistress Wu!'

'These are happy tears.'

The girl shakes her head. 'They are happy and sad tears, Mistress. I understand.'

Wu Fang sobs louder. Yueyue says: 'But you will always have Mistress Shen. Just because she loves Master Cha does not mean she loves you any less.'

'You speak like an ancient sage.'

'It's the truth, Mistress Wu. You and Mistress Shen have been through so much; no one can come between you. No one would dare.'

'Oh Yueyue.'

'Good to hear you laugh, Mistress.'

'We owe you so much. I wish there was something I could do for you.'

The girl shakes her head. 'It's the other way round, Mistress Wu. I owe you and Mistress Shen my life.' Then, looking shyly at the ground in front of her she speaks unexpectedly. 'But there is something I've always wanted to ask, Mistress Wu.'

'Do ask.' Wu Fang looks at the girl curiously.

'Please, Mistress Wu, make me a woman surgeon like you,' says the girl.

Wu Fang swears to do her very best.

30

How long have they been here? Jiali asks herself, as she slowly and carefully steps her way out to the stone boat in the middle of the lake. A day, three? A week? How time flies! She prays that Charles will recover soon, so that they can leave to join Wu Fang's parents in the Wu's ancestral village by the sea. It had been Wu Fang's decision that they should move to her house when, shortly after Charles's operation, he developed a dangerous infection that needed urgent treatment. Staying in the hospital was out of the question, and Charles could not have endured a long trip.

Was it a wise move to come here? Jiali is not sure. Though barely conscious, Charles had protested vigorously, worrying about the danger of being discovered by the yamen. But Wu Fang was adamant that they had hardly any choice: the Shen's house has been flattened — though Jiali's parents were safe, having heeded her words and stayed put with their relatives; the Yans' house was too close to the yamen, and there is Mrs Yan, not to be trusted. More reassuringly, a trusted servant reported that Li Jian had moved away with the rest of the Governor's household to the safety of their house on the other side of Pagoda Hill the moment the first cannon was fired. Wu Fang had reasoned that her house, though seemingly the worst choice, might actually be the last place the yamen would think to look for them, and with Li Jian gone, they would not be in action any time soon. Since her parents departed and the servants were sent away, the house had been empty — no one would suspect it of now being occupied if they were careful. And anyway, Wu Fang argued, they would only stay for as long as Charles needed to recover.

But still Jiali worries, as she ascends the steps to the stone boat, using the wooden railings, cold and hard to the touch, for support. Now that the pagoda has been flattened to the ground, she has an open view of the town below. The bombing has stopped, but the kingdom is surely broken; all is black, the foundations of some houses still smouldering, angry and brutal as open wounds. A bleak, desolate scene, and she seems to hear girls chanting: '*Mountain, river remains, though kingdom is broken …*'

The baby kicks and Jiali moves her hand to her belly and thinks of Yanbu; her heart aches. Though secure and joyful in her love for Charles, guilt still eats into her happiness like a worm. Largely, she is able to brush it away, but there are moments, like now, when Yanbu's sad face emerges suddenly, making her weak. She sits down on the stone bench.

She is glad of the distraction, as Lanlan runs to her, breathless.

'Mistress,' the girl comes near, 'I gave your letter to your parents to Lao Zhao the woodman, who will deliver it to them. I will go seek Lao Zhao again in the market tomorrow, for a message back. Lao Zhao asked where we were staying, and I didn't say. I know Mistress Wu wants us all to be careful.'

'You did right.' Jiali nods, then: 'Any news of my little sisters and my mother-in-law?'

'The two little mistresses have been taken in by Lao Jin, the porter, who was always so fond of them, as you know …'

'Why, why have they been taken away? What about my mother-in-law, what happened to her?'

'I am not sure I should tell you this, Mistress.'

'Lanlan! Come on.'

'The Old Mistress is dead. They found her in the Old Master's study.'

'My mother-in-law, dead?' Jiali holds her breath in shock.

'It wasn't a direct hit, but a bomb set fire to the town barn, which spread to the neighbourhood, and to the Yans' house. Nobody knew the Old Mistress was in the study: by the time they realised where she was, it was too late. Wang Ma said the door to the study was locked from inside. The rumour among the servants is that the ghosts of the Old Master's wife and first concubine dragged the Old Mistress to her death.'

'The poor woman!'

'Do not feel bad about it. You tried, both you and Mistress Wu, to get the Old Mistress to come to stay here, so many times.'

'She is stubborn. And now ...' Jiali shudders at the thought of her mother-in-law trapped inside the burning study. What a way to go!

Jiali's hands instinctively move to her belly. What is cradled inside is all that remains of the Yan family.

'Are you quite all right, Mistress?' asks Lanlan, concerned. 'Mistress Wu will scold me for telling you this bad news. Please do not worry ...'

'How terrible,' Jiali murmurs. 'The only comfort I draw from this is that neither she nor Yanbu knew of the death of the other.'

'Shall I help you back to the house? I am sure Mistress Wu wouldn't want you to be out in the cold for long. Besides, you might be spotted. Now the bombing has stopped, the yamen are back. I saw soldiers riding down in the harbour ...'

Jiali nods absent-mindedly, still too absorbed in the shocking news to really hear the maid's words, then she spots Lanlan's bulging basket. 'What is that?'

Lanlan flips the cloth cover off the basket, revealing the dozen or so eggs nestling inside.

'Lao Zhao gave me these.' She bursts into a childish grin. 'Yueyue will be so pleased. She's been asking for eggs to make soups.'

'We are lucky to have food at all, why would Yueyue make such a fuss over ...'

'Mistress Wu said that eggs are the best medicine for you and Master Cha.'

'I will come with you. Help me up.' Strength returns to Jiali at the mention of Charles' name. They head for Wu Fang's old study, where Charles sleeps. The heaviness in her, hearing of her mother-in-law's death, lifts at the sight of that giant of a man lying on Wu Fang's small couch. She makes a sign to Lanlan, who nods and turns away, leaving the two alone.

For fear of waking him, she refrains from touching him but instead traces the contour of the beloved body in front of her with greedy eyes. How extraordinary this feeling, knowing that this being, when awake, is completely entuned to hers, and loves each and every fibre in her, body and soul. Now she knows, even before the consummation, what the fuss is all about. Wu Fang was right: the ancients are not wrong. There is such pleasure, for she is already tasting it. For her soul is on fire, and her body already belongs to his.

Loving him is a selfish indulgence, she well knows; but the imminent birth empowers and frees her, giving entitlement to recklessness, so she chooses not to count the cost of this thing called love.

Not now.

31

'Finish the medicine, Master Cha, then you can have my soup,' urges Yueyue.

Once again, he is to drink a horrible herb concoction. Bitter as it is, Charles knows it is doing him good. And Yueyue's drop-egg soup is a powerful incentive: smelling deliciously of ginger, tomato, and topped with golden strips of eggs, it is to die for.

He gulps down the medicine. 'Now the soup please.'

Yueyue grins. 'Do you know how hard it is to get hold of eggs these days, Master Cha?'

'It is a miracle that I am alive at all. But you, Lanlan, Mistress Wu, and Mistress Shen are goddesses all, I am no longer surprised at what you can do.'

'There you go again, Master Cha, your lips are smeared with honey, as Mistress Wu said.'

'What else did she say?'

'Much more that I can't tell you.'

'Good things, I hope?'

The girl smiles.

'And Mistress Shen?'

'What of Mistress Shen?'

'Did she say anything about me?'

'Why, she came to see you just now.'

'Did she?'

'You were asleep, but,' the girl smiles again, mischievously, 'she stayed a little while by your side.'

He bids the girl fetch Wu Fang. He wants her to see how well he has recovered. This must be their third day at the Wus' — they delayed the departure to Ding Village for his sake — and he doesn't want them to stay longer than necessary. Any moment, surely, Li Jian or the yamen or both will get wind of where they are, and Charles fears the worst for the women. As an ocean man, he will get away lightly — foreigners usually do in China, as they are protected by the provisions in the treaties signed after the Opium Wars, whatever their misdemeanours; but the women will pay a heavy price. Wu Fang especially should expect no mercy. She will be tried for treason and if convicted — which seems very likely — punished severely. Charles has no doubt of it. A famous feminist, one of Wu Fang's few fellow female students in Japan, had indeed been wrongly convicted as an assassin and beheaded in public in the next province, back in the summer. It has caused a huge uproar, but the Manchus were unrepentant.

*

Waiting for Wu Fang, he admires the view of the lake through the window. It is dusk; how the light reminds him of the day Yanbu and he were on their practice trip out to sea. For Charles, Yanbu is not dead. That's probably why he doesn't mourn him yet. The news of his death seems unreal. Any minute now, he will emerge, alive as ever. A good man, a beautiful man, but alas, ultimately a man. So Charles chose her. So far, they've done nothing but kiss, though the sense of betrayal is still profound in

Charles. Once again, he is amazed by the boldness with which the two women take charge of their own fates.

What is it to be loved so completely and fearlessly by such brave souls!

What would Yanbu say if he saw Charles with Jiali? Charles closes his eyes and begs for forgiveness: *I do love you both*. As if that makes his crime somehow less serious.

Don't let us be like those youngsters: dropping tears onto the same handkerchief on the crossroads upon the moment of parting.

She had not liked him quoting this to her. Her couplet days are over, she had insisted, words without action are empty like vacant hearts.

Papers and a pen on the table: they must have been left by the ever-thoughtful Wu Fang, the extraordinary woman, his saviour. In the grand scheme of things, she is up there, a Buddha, all-seeing, all-forgiving. But she is flesh and blood, too. He sees it in her eyes, when she watches him and Jiali embrace.

How terrible love is.

What is it that Yueyue said to him earlier? She had seen ocean people about town? The bombing has stopped — does that mean the Chinese have lost the war?

Charles leans, with some effort, to get the paper and pen. Must write to Paul. Yueyue can deliver the note. Paul will want to know what has happened to his countryman.

32

Her home, this mansion that her father spent a lifetime building, has never been more beautiful. Memories flood Wu Fang wherever she looks; it is bare, but she loves the wide space now it's stripped off all the adornments: some her parents have taken with them, but most were given away. It's how it should be.

Moments ago, satisfied that Charles is better, Wu Fang told him and Jiali they were ready to leave. It won't be long before they are discovered, so the sooner they go, the better. Tomorrow morning, she reckons, no later.

Like Jiali, Wu Fang is drawn to the stone boat on the lake; as she ascends, scents and sounds swim back to her from the past:

'We swear to be eternal sisters. We shall never part, whatever happens …'

It feels like only yesterday. Where did time go?

*

There's Yueyue, running to her.

'Calm Yueyue,' Wu Fang soothes the breathless girl, but fears bad news.

'What are we to do, Mistress Wu?'

'What's that?'

'Mr Li and the yamen soldiers are outside the front gate! Mr

309

Li was most insistent that Mistress Shen be delivered to him.'

So they have found them; Wu Fang knew it would only be a matter of time.

'Here's the message from Mr Li,' the girl hands Wu Fang a note. 'He said he expects an answer straight away.'

Wu Fang quickly scans the note, then glances up.

The girl lowers her head. 'I'm afraid it must be my father who turned us in. Deyi told me that Father saw me bargaining at the market for rice and followed me back here. I saw him just now, at the back of the crowd of soldiers. It is just the sort of thing he would do, that cowardly man.'

'Don't lose heart, Yueyue. They haven't got us yet.'

'But they are right outside, and there are so many of them!' The girl, usually so calm, now speaks with a trembling voice.

'Do you think they have people at the back of the house, too?'

'I guess not, but it won't take them long to find out there is a back entrance.'

'Mr Li had sick designs on Mistress Shen, he said …' Yueyue hands Wu Fang a parcel that she had not noticed the girl holding before. Wu Fang pulls a wedding gown out of the cloth wrapping, the soft red silk seems to suddenly stain her hand. '… Mistress Shen is to wear this …' the girl finishes indignantly.

Wu Fang wraps the gown back up. 'Go and tell Mr Li she will come.'

'Mistress?'

'On one condition: I will need time to get Mistress Shen ready for the wedding. I will need until tomorrow morning.'

'But Mistress Wu, surely you are not going to …'

'Trust me, Yueyue. I have a plan, I will tell you later, but for now, we need to ensure that Li Jian thinks we will do his bidding.'

'So we can have time to get ready, to escape?' the girl speaks hopefully.

Wu Fangs nods. 'Go deliver the message, then come straight back and find Lanlan, you two must get Mistress Shen and Master Cha ready for the journey. They both knew we were leaving, but not so soon.'

Yueyue nods, and turns to run.

'Wait.' Wu Fang calls her back, 'Don't tell the Master and the Mistress about this,' she points at the note and the bundle in her hand, 'I don't want them alarmed.'

The girl makes to leave, then turns again: 'Mistress, Lanlan told me just now, about Mrs Yan.'

'Yes, I know.'

'She is not a nice person, but I feel sad that the baby will grow up without a father or a grandmother.'

'He or she will indeed grow up without a grandma, but as to the father, we cannot be sure yet.'

'But I thought …'

'The death of the young Master is not confirmed. We knew the ship he was on had sunk, and that he was tossed into the sea, but I suppose it possible that he might have survived.'

'But you told Mistress Shen …'

The girl stops, and they look at each other, then the girl nods emphatically. 'I understand.'

*

When Yueyue is out of sight, Wu Fang reads Li Jian's note again:

'Esteemed Miss Wu,' it starts, *'Good to see that all three of you have survived the bombing. I won't waste words but now that Yanbu has surely become a martyr, I consider it my duty to take care of his widow, whom I have long admired, as you well know. A suitably decorated wedding sedan awaits patiently at the porch just outside your front door, and your efficient pupil Yueyue has been given the bridal clothes, in case you are short; I ask that you dress my new bride suitably for the occasion.*

Should you find it inconvenient to hand over Jiali, my men, all eager for revenge, will be glad to seize the ocean man, with whom the townspeople have a lot of scores to settle.

Finally, I beg you to remember that your own fate also rests in my hands — if I, the governor's son, instruct the yamen that you are innocent, they will have to believe me. If not, well, you know what will happen.

I leave the decision entirely in your capable hands. Don't attempt anything funny, your house is watched. I remain, as ever, your most faithful admirer, Li Jian.'

Even as she finishes re-reading it, she hears the impatient tapping of the horses' hooves on the street outside. Moments later, Yueyue runs back to her.

'I delivered the message, Mistress Wu, and here is another note from him.'

'Very glad you saw sense, Wu Fang, wise as ever. For old time's sake, I will be patient and agree for you to get my bride ready for tomorrow morning. I will be back to marry her then. Li Jian.'

Wu Fang crumples the note in her fist and glances up at the darkening sky. The sun has already set. She is relieved: her gamble seems to have paid off. She hadn't at all been sure.

'There is no time to lose,' she says quickly. 'Go and check if there are any soldiers at the back gate. Do it carefully, make sure you are not spotted. Then come and find me in the front hall.'

The girl returns almost at the same time Wu Fang herself reaches the front hall.

'Mistress! They are at the back gate, too.' Wu Fang curses, so he doesn't trust her after all! But even as her heart sinks, she glances up at Yueyue with calm eyes.

'How many?' she asks the girl.

'Six soldiers.'

'How many at the front, when you saw them?

'I ... I think about twenty. Mistress, what are we to do?'

'Not so loud, Yueyue, come near and listen,' Wu Fang gestures, an idea forming in her, 'this is what we will do.'

*

The night is deep, and all are quiet. Next to Wu Fang, Jiali sleeps soundly, dressed in her own lovely bridal top, the one Wu Fang had stolen for her trip to Beijing. It had not been hard to persuade her to put it on, to convince her to marry Charles before they set off, to ensure her baby is not born fatherless.

Such a fun time they had, just like the old days, Jiali putting on her old wedding top. Wu Fang wore the gown Li Jian had sent. 'Where did it come from?' Jiali asked, curious; 'From a secret admirer,' Wu Fang told her. They laughed so much to see Jiali's bump protruding underneath the stretched top; Jiali was in such high spirits that when Wu Fang slipped the drug into her tea, she didn't suspect a thing. It was the mildest drought, totally safe; the same had been administered to Charles, by Yueyue. It was absolutely necessary to sedate the two as, conscious, they would fight tooth and nail not to go without Wu Fang, and Wu Fang could not run that risk.

Her back now turned to Wu Fang, Jiali sleeps the way women do in late pregnancy to be comfortable: one leg raised over a pile of cushions, to give room to her large belly. Leaning close, Wu Fang gives Jiali one long hug from behind, fitting the contour of her body to that beloved flesh, careful not to wake her. *My heart, my soul, love and live with the man of your dreams, and be blessed by me wherever I am. I might get out of this, who knows, but if I don't, at least you will be free.*

It is unbearable, the thought that she might never see Jiali again. Wu Fang feels lonely as she never has before.

But something, someone, nudges her from across Jiali's belly, the unborn baby, a holding of hands from another world. *Hello there*, Wu Fang pushes gently back, her mood changing. *I'm your other mother, the Black Snake. What? Say you I failed you? Say you I won't be there? Nonsense. I might not be at your birth, but I will do my damn hardest to be in your life. It will be you, me, and her against the world.*

*

She waits in the hall. Lanlan is already there with all the luggage. Soon they see three figures emerging from the far side of the mansion, beyond the stone boat. In the moonlight Wu Fang ascertains it is Deyi, Yueyue, and a man she had met before, a kind family friend of the two.

'The carriage is ready, by the back gate,' whispers Yueyue.

'And the soldiers there?'

'All drunk, and fast asleep, with the wine we gave them.'

Wu Fang smiles, the draught given to them is strong, and it will be a while before they are conscious again.

'So now let's hurry,' she orders.

*

When the five of them finally get Charles and Jiali in the carriage, the first bright ray of dawn is already breaking. Wu Fang turns to Yueyue: 'Go now. It's time.'

The girl hesitates, noticing the bridal gown Wu Fang wears. 'Mistress, surely you are not going on the journey in this?'

'The plan has changed. I will not be leaving with you,' Wu Fang turns to Lanlan, 'and I would like you to stay with me, Lanlan.'

'But Mistress, I don't understand. Why are you staying behind? And why with Lanlan, not me!' Yueyue's agitated voice becomes louder.

'Shh.' Wu Fang hushes her. 'Listen. I thought more of it in the night. If we all leave now, even if the drunken soldiers at the back cannot raise alarm, as soon as the soldiers open the front gate, they will find the house empty and realise immediately something is wrong. Li Jian can easily send messages to all the checkpoints, and it won't take long for them to catch up with us at all. So I think it best that I stay behind to gain you time. That's why I am wearing this and why Lanlan must be with me, so that Li Jian will be fooled into thinking that I am Mistress Shen. He won't suspect anything, not for a while anyway. I will be wearing a veil, of course. I will distract him for as long as I can.'

315

'But it's too dangerous,' Yueyue whispers earnestly, 'and I am sure Mistress Shen and Master Cha wouldn't want ...'

'Do not stop until you get to Ding Village. Remember, no stops. Either Master Cha or Mistress Shen might wake up if you do, and I don't want that to happen. Do you still have the letter I wrote to my uncle? You know what to do when you get to Ding Village?'

The girl nods. 'Yes, but ...' she sobs.

'It's an order.' Wu Fang speaks with a stern voice. 'It is Mistress Shen that Li Jian wants, not me. Once he realises the truth, he will let me go.'

'But Mr Li is a vain and most vindictive man. He will want to punish you!' cries Yueyue.

Wu Fang smiles. 'He might be angry at first, but have some faith in my power of persuasion; Yueyue, didn't you hear your mistress say often that Li Jian is rather fond of me? I do believe I have some hold over that playboy.'

'With my utmost respect, Mistress, you can't be certain!'

Wu Fang soothes, 'Come, Yueyue, be a good girl, and trust me. I have every intention of joining you soon. Before then, I am counting on you, don't let me down.'

'Mistress Wu, please!'

Becoming impatient, Wu Fang glares at the girl. 'You are wasting precious time. Go, now!'

*

In silence, Lanlan and Wu Fang walk back through the large empty grounds. Against the dawn light Wu Fang catches sight of her own reflection on the polished surface of a giant porcelain flowerpot. A most feminine appearance. She looks the part.

They hardly reach the gate when they hear the sounds of people outside. Then, a loud impatient knock.

'They are here already!' Lanlan whispers anxiously, her face pale.

'Go open the gate,' Wu Fang says in an ordinary voice. 'Do so slowly but steadily; then come and stand next to the sedan.'

Wu Fang steps into the sedan and is instantly surrounded by a rich, almost suffocating redness. Is this what Jiali saw on her wedding day? Wu Fang feels Jiali close, almost right next to her. Taking a long breath, she picks up the red veil on the cushioned chair beside her and drapes it over her head. She closes her eyes.

Suddenly, that stolen kiss on the river during their trip to Shanghai is restored to her, unwrapped from layers of past memories: vivid, warm, bewildering, and passionate, and Wu Fang's heart breaks into a thousand pieces. Feeling a little sick she leans on the side of the sedan for support. What to do? She feels weak as a kitten; she needs every ounce of courage left in her to resist the urge to drop everything and run, not because she is afraid to be caught and hung, but because she can't bear the thought of never being with Jiali again.

Lanlan's small, sudden, angst-ridden voice breaks the spell. 'Mistress Wu, I don't want to open the gate.'

Then Wu Fang becomes herself again: for the black snake's mission has only just begun.

'Open, Lanlan.' She says calmly, 'Don't worry. I know what to do.'

Acknowledgements

I owe a huge debt of gratitude to the following.

For putting me in the mood, these operas:
Hua Wei Mei (Flower as a Pledge of Our Love, Chinese Northern Opera)
Qin Xianglian (The Wronged Woman, Chinese Peking Opera)

I don't know Italian, but:
Aida
La bohème
La traviata
Madama Butterfly
Turandot

It would be impossible to list all that I have read in the past ten years, for I am a hopeless bookworm, but for inspiration for this book, these authors and their books, in particular:
Sarah Waters (*Fingersmith*)
William Somerset Maugham (*The Painted Veil*)
Paul Claudel (*Knowing the East*)
E. M. Forster (*A Passage to India, Maurice*)
Jean Rhys (*Wide Sargasso Sea*)
Isidore Cyril Cannon (*Public Success, Private Sorrow*)
Cao Xueqin (*A Dream of Red Mansions*)

For being my first readers, kind, thorough, and wise: Andrew Gist, Susie Jolly, Lucy Aitchison, Tom Santhouse, Martha Franks, and Kirsten Valentina.

For their faith in me, and for their insightful comments and editing: Jessica Woollard, Molly Slight, and Laura Ali.

For their generous grant: the Society of Authors.

And to my beloved Jonky, for everything.